STORM BLOOD

Montague And Strong Detective Agency Novel

ORLANDO A. SANCHEZ

BITTEN PEACHES
PUBLISHING

ABOUT THE STORY

How do you destroy a god? Power...overwhelming power.

With Mahnes defeated, Monty & Simon must now face the entity behind the attacks.

They must face one of the old gods...Chaos.

There's only one slight problem—they aren't strong enough.

When every strategy devised requires more power, Monty realizes he must make a potentially lethal choice: accelerate the shift to Archmage.

In order to do this, Monty and Simon must travel undetected to London, convincing York, an old and powerful mage who's currently missing, to help them. To find York, they will have to visit a reclusive member of the Ten—a witch who can prepare Monty for the cast they need. A witch with a reputation for obliterating friends and foes alike.

If successful, Monty will have access to enough power to imprison an ancient god. They're risking it all, but if they don't, Chaos will obliterate everything...starting with the Montague & Strong Detective Agency.

QUOTATION

Nothing vast enters the lives of mortals without a curse.
—Sophocles

ONE

"You want us to do *what?*" I asked, confused. "Seriously?"

"London is shut down to all teleportation and runic travel," Monty said after taking a sip from his cup. "May have something to do with our last visit there."

"You think?" I said, staring at him. "You practically leveled the city. I'm sure they're still touchy about the extensive renovations to London Tower."

"You mean the Tower of London?"

"That castle you blew apart where they keep the crown jewels," I said. "The real old one near the river."

"*That* was the Krampus," Monty said. "If I recall, aside from the bridges, there were major repairs to the Tate Museum in the wake of your creature 'cutting loose.'"

Peaches rumbled from under the table.

"Peaches doesn't 'cut loose.'"

"What do you call the wholesale destruction he unleashed?"

"I seem to recall they wanted to kill him," I said, glancing under the table where my hellhound sprawled. "I call it self-defense."

"Fair point," Monty said with a nod. "Still, he could have just plane-walked away, not toppling the building upon his exit."

"Okay, fine," I admitted. "That was all Peaches, but you have to admit the Tate deserves to be blasted from existence. A crater would look better than that monstrosity of a building. Don't even get me started on the supposed art they display."

"Be that as it may," Monty said, glancing to his left, "the Penumbra Consortium did not appreciate the destruction of the building while they were still *inside* it. Finally, my uncle is here."

I looked at the door at the end of the corridor. Its frame gave off a green glow before opening. to reveal Dex, who walked into the hallway which led to the kitchen where we were sitting.

Peaches rumbled again.

<*I'm so hungry. Can the old man make me some meat?*>

<*You just ate twenty minutes ago. How about you wait a bit?*>

<*You always say I should live in the moment.*>

<*Right. You should always be in the present.*>

<*In this present, I'm starving. Can you ask the old man for some meat?*>

<*I'll see what I can do.*>

<*I know what you can do, and it hurts my stomach. Please ask the old man.*>

My hellhound was now suddenly a Zen master of witty comebacks. I really needed to get him out more.

"Morning, lads," Dex said as he entered the kitchen. "I've made some calls."

Dex was dressed—which was a nice change—in a pastel-green Armani dress shirt, and a pair of dark 501s that looked like they were about a hundred years old. On his feet he wore a pair of dark brown Thursday Vanguard boots. His long, gray hair was pulled back in a braided ponytail, rounding out the bohemian mage look.

"Nice jeans," I said with a chuckle. "They look about a century old. Is this the vintage Dex look?"

Dex looked down and grinned at me.

"Like them? 1860 to be precise," Dex answered. "Got them from Levi, personally. Probably worth a small fortune today. This is Mo's effort to make me look respectable."

"What's that on your neck?" I asked. "That looks like a..."

"Don't ask questions you don't want answers to, boy," Dex said with a smile. "Unless you want the details?"

"Um, no, hard pass, thanks," I said quickly. "Some things are better in my imagination."

"I used to think the same thing," Dex answered. "Are you sure?"

"He's sure," Monty said, saving me. "Who did you call?"

"I have news," Dex said, his expression becoming serious. "But first, the dark elixir of the gods."

I held my breath in anticipation as Dex gestured. On the counter in front of us materialized two steaming mugs of the best Deathwish javambrosia on the planet. I grabbed my mug and brought it close to my face, inhaling the aroma.

"This smell should be illegal," I said before taking my first sip of the day and groaning with caffeinated delight. "If you're going to teach me anything, you need to teach me how to do this."

"Nothing like a proper cup to start the day," Dex said with a groan of is own after taking a long pull.

Monty rolled his eyes at us and sipped his tea.

"You were saying you had news," Monty repeated. "Who did you contact?"

"Yes, I have news," Dex said. "Not all of it is bad. Well, most of it is bad, but there is some that isn't entirely bad."

"Why does that sound like it's *all* bad?" I said. "Who did you call?"

"Some of my contacts in London," Dex said, materializing an enormous sausage the size of my arm and sliding it under the table to my ever-voracious vacuum of a hellhound. "That's a good boy."

"If you keep feeding him like that, he won't be able to move," I said, peeking under the table. "What did your contacts say?"

"Who exactly, Uncle Dex?" Monty pressed. "Which contacts?"

I wondered why Monty was so interested in knowing who, exactly.

"Does it matter?" I asked. "What's the news?"

"It matters, especially with a mage of my uncle's caliber and reputation," Monty replied. "I only know a few individuals who would risk providing him information." Monty turned to Dex. "Who was it?"

"Fine," Dex said, throwing a hand into the air. "It was Nana. Happy?"

"Yes, actually," Monty said with a smile. "It's good to know she's actually among the living again."

"Wait, what? Nana?" I said, confused. "How did you speak to Nana? I thought she was...?"

"Dead?" Dex said. "I'll believe that when I personally confirm the actual corpse."

"Is she in hiding?" Monty asked.

"Aye," Dex said with a nod. "The Penumbra Consortium is still irked over your last visit there. She's being held partially responsible for the destruction."

"That's foolish," Monty said after another sip. "Why would they risk angering her?"

"Because they're bureaucrats," Dex said. "London, as you

know by now, is locked down, but I managed a workaround to get you in. Here you go."

Dex reached into his shirt pocket and placed an envelope on the counter in front of me.

"What's this?" I asked. "Is it some secret teleportation rune that can get us in?"

"Two tickets to British Airways Flight 1220, departs from JFK at 10 PM tonight," Dex said. "Better for you to enter under the cover of darkness."

"Two tickets...? You're joking, right?"

"Then there's the matter of the pup," Dex continued. "I'll have to take him over myself. Smaller signature should make it easier. You two would be impossible without setting off failsafes all over the point of entry."

"You're serious?" I said. "I thought Monty was having a rare moment of hilarity when he told me your plan."

"I never have moments of hilarity," Monty said. "This is the best, safest, and only way to get over there without being detected."

"But Dex is a teleportation master," I said, turning to Dex. "Aren't you?"

"Teleportation master is a little much, but I'm good," Dex said. "If I tell you this is the best and only way, trust me, this is the best and only way."

"What about Peaches?"

"We'll pop over to Wales, which isn't locked down, and make our way to London by conventional means," Dex said. "With you in the air and my approach from Wales it'll be like burning the midnight oil at both ends. They'll be completely confused."

"Sort of how I am right now?"

"Exactly," Dex said with a nod. "This should work. I'll make sure to mask you two before you leave tonight. As long as my nephew doesn't cast on the plane, and you don't unleash one of your missiles, like you did last time, everything should go as planned."

"Like I did last time?"

"That's what I said, boy," Dex said. "Something the matter with your hearing?"

"I only created that orb because you instructed me to," I said.

"True," Dex said with an evil smile, "but you were the one who created it, weren't you?"

I opened my mouth and shut it again.

Dex laughed and clapped me on the shoulder.

"I can't believe you," I said, shaking my head. "I was set up."

"Sure you were," Dex said, waving my words away. "Now, a few things. First, Nephew, you will have to meet with Nana at some point. I told her it was a bad idea, but she insists and you know your Nana."

"I expected as much."

"Next is finding York," Dex said. "He is currently in hiding."

"In hiding?" I asked. "How are we going to find him if he is in hiding? How do we even know he is in London?"

"He can't leave London," Dex said. "As for finding him, I have that arranged for when you land. Leave that to me."

"Why does that sound like a disaster in the making?"

"Ach, boy, have some faith," Dex said. "Everything will be fine."

TWO

"This sounds like a perfectly horrible idea," I said when Dex left. "Do you think we'll find this Peppermint Pattie mage?"

"Excuse me?" Monty said, glancing my way. "The pepper-mint what?"

"Peppermint Pattie? You know, York Peppermint Patties?"

"Is this Patty an actual person or an imaginary friend?"

"It's a delicious mint-flavored dark-chocolate slice of goodness," I said. "You've never had a Peppermint Pattie?"

Monty pinched the bridge of his nose.

"No, and I don't intend to," he said. "I've been doing some research on this York person my uncle is having us visit. It doesn't look good."

"Doesn't look good as in he's dangerous, or doesn't look good as in he's going to be impossible to find?"

"Not good as in he's going to be impossible to find, and his mental state is uncertain, which makes him dangerous."

"You're going to need to be a bit clearer here," I said warily. "What do you mean, his mental state is uncertain?"

"According to my investigations, he's quite mad and

possesses phenomenal cosmic power," Monty said. "That makes him dangerous."

"Why would your uncle have us see him then?"

"The lost rune I used against Mahnes."

"About that," I began after taking another sip from my mug. "You never did mention where you discovered that rune. I mean, if it's a lost rune, how did you find it?"

Monty's expression darkened, and I knew I had touched upon a topic he'd rather not discuss.

"During my recent stay at Haven, I managed—"

"You managed to sneak past Pirn and his mage security to go find a lost rune?" I asked. "Where *exactly* was this rune lost?"

"During my recent stay at Haven I managed to discover the location of this lost rune," Monty said, avoiding the question. "Then I merely went there and recovered it."

"Where, exactly, is *there?*" I asked. "Why did Dex seem upset you knew it?"

"The actual location would be nearly impossible to describe. I'd have to physically take you there. Suffice it to say it's not on this plane. My uncle was upset because it's one of the blood runes."

"A lost blood rune? Why does that sound like the worst possible rune?"

"Also one of the most powerful," Monty added, his voice solemn. "It was the only thing that let us face off against a Chaos-controlled Mahnes."

"Why was Dex upset?"

"Blood runes are a shortcut to power," Monty said. "They use life force by utilizing blood to impart significant power to the caster."

"What's the cost? There's always a cost."

Monty nodded.

"They use life force," Monty said. "Repeated use of blood runes becomes addictive and deadly in a short time."

"The runes you have been using in the past, were those...?"

"No, those were runes powered by blood magic, but they were not blood runes," Monty assured me. "The lost runes were deliberately hidden to prevent power hungry mages and magic users from accessing these shortcuts."

"The same shortcut you used to fight Mahnes," I said. "You're saying the end justifies the means?"

"Absolutely not," Monty said. "It's the reason we're taking this trip to begin with. Blood runes are not a solution. The lost rune was a temporary stopgap at best."

"But you still used it," I pushed, concerned. "You plan on going there again?"

"Would you?" Monty asked, staring at me. "If *you* had access to god-stopping power, would you use it?"

"No," I said after a brief pause. "I had the offer and turned it down. There's always another way. Hopefully one that doesn't require sacrificing my, or anyone else's, life."

"That's what this trip is for," Monty said. "We're going to find another way to face Chaos."

"Which requires meeting an insane mage almost as powerful as Dex?"

"Whom I strongly suggest you refrain from calling Peppermint Patty, or any other kind of patty, no matter how tempting."

"Got it," I said, making a mental note not to call the insane mage a Peppermint Pattie no matter how tempting it was. "How are we going to find him?"

"Knowing my uncle, he'll reach out to the Ten," Monty said. "They have an extensive global network with the added benefit that they actually like him."

"Are you saying there are people out there who don't like

Dex? How can that be? What's not to like about a powerful mage wielding that nasty axe-mace of his?"

"Indeed, it boggles the imagination."

"I need to go finish packing," I said, getting up. "Who in the Ten is Dex planning on contacting? Fordey?"

"No. This is London," Monty said. "Chances are he will contact Josephine, which is in itself almost as dangerous as dealing with the mad mage."

"This Josephine is a mage?" I asked. "Is she as scary, I mean as *formidable*, as TK?"

"Josephine isn't a mage, but she is a magic user," Monty said after finishing his tea. "She is a member of the Ten; that should explain everything."

"Sorceress?" I asked. I could sense he was being evasive about answering me. "What's the big deal? It's not like she can hear us. Wait—can she?"

"Josephine wields an ancient, primal form of magic that is barely controlled and devastating when unleashed," he said. "There's a reason she lives apart from the other Ten, and most people for that matter. Even my uncle gives her a wide berth, and he fears very little."

"He fears her?"

"He holds a healthy respect for the power of the Ten," Monty said. "But I think on some level he has a small amount of fear for the power she wields."

"She's stronger than Dex?"

"Unlikely," Monty said. "But you're comparing apples to oranges. Dex is a mage."

"And Josephine?"

"Josephine is a witch they call Tempest."

THREE

"A witch," I repeated as I headed to my room. "Are you joking?"

"I don't possess a sense of humor," Monty said. "It should be apparent to you by now."

"It's not that you don't have a sense of humor."

"Really? What is it, then?"

"You're English," I said. "Humor is a"—I waved my hand around—"tricky concept for you."

"What you're trying to say is that my sense of humor is refined, whereas your sense of humor is puerile at best."

"Like I said, tricky concept," I said, shaking my head. "Since when do mages and witches form groups together?"

"They don't."

"Yet this Tempest person is one of the Ten?"

"So is Kristman Dos, and he is a weretiger," Monty said. "The Ten are not what I would call the norm by any stretch of the imagination."

"Do you know all of the Ten?" I asked, curious. "Is it always the same people? Or does the scary intimidating group rotate among its members? Are there always exactly ten scary people, or is that more of a suggestion?"

"They're not scary—" Monty began.

I gave him a look.

"Don't even," I said. "I have two words for you: Fordey Boutique."

He paused, then nodded.

"A valid point," he said. "There are several major sects in the mage world. At some point every member of the Ten was asked to leave their respective groups."

"Someone dared to throw out TK and LD from a sect?"

"Yes," Monty said. "From my understanding, it didn't go well for the sects that did so. This applies to all of the members of the Ten; each was respectively cast out, except for Tempest.

"What? Did she blow up her sect before leaving?"

"Witches don't form sects, they form covens," Monty corrected. "According to my uncle, no coven would accept her. She was too inherently powerful."

"You know, if you think about it, you could say that the Ten is a sect of sorts," I said. "A sect of outsiders. Powerful and intimidating outsiders."

"That's an astute observation," Monty said. "An observation you may not want to voice, but astute nonetheless."

"Remind me again why we're going to go see the scary witch?"

"Because she may be the only one who can locate the powerful mage that doesn't want to be found," Monty said, heading to his room. "We should go pack. Dex will be back soon enough."

"What *aren't* you saying, Monty?"

"Pardon?"

"This is me," I said, staring at him. "What are you 'leaving in the subtext' as you like to say? What aren't you telling me?"

"We are heading off to meet an unstable mage—one who is almost as powerful as my uncle, mind you—who is currently in hiding..."

"That doesn't seem so—"

"Who does not want to be found," Monty continued. "We will proceed to find said mage. Did I mention he will most likely try to kill us just for finding him?"

"No, I don't remember that part."

"Well there's a good chance he will try," Monty said. "How will we find this mage, you ask? We will, with great certainty, contact one of the most dangerous members of the Ten to do so. You'll forgive me if I seem to be preoccupied with our future prospects."

"You know what we need to do?" I asked. "We need to go get something delicious to eat. I heard Roselli is back in town with a new place. It's called The Bite. Hard to find, even harder to get a reservation. Used to be the site of Bohemian."

"And you propose we should just 'show up' to this establishment without a reservation?"

"It's us," I said. "I'm sure Piero will make an exception. Especially for us."

"Does this place really exist, or is this one of those myths of secret restaurants that are just stories and fantasy?"

"Real place. From what I hear, insane security, too."

"From what you hear. Have you been to this place? In reality, not in your mind?"

"Oh ha ha, humor," I said, shaking my head. "This is a real place. If Piero bought Bohemian, then I know exactly where it is."

"Fine, I could stand to eat. I do hope he has kept the salads on the menu."

"I'm sure he has. Let's go eat. We can have linner. I'm not really looking forward to this flight, and airplane food doesn't really qualify as edible, does it?"

"Agreed," Monty said. "I would like to catch up with Piero. *The Bite*, you say? A little on the nose, don't you think? How long has he been back?"

"A few weeks," I said. "You've been a bit distracted lately, or I would've told you sooner. This is a departure from Roselli's, I hear. Still great food, just not as upscale. Low key and out of the way."

"Low key and out of the way is just what we need right now," Monty said, "given your new status."

I heard a low growl and felt Peaches bump into my leg. My spine creaked in protest at the blow. I looked down and got a dose of enormous hellhound puppy dog eyes.

"Yes," I said, rubbing behind his ears. "Of course you can come."

He growled again and padded into my room ahead of me.

"I will be out shortly," Monty said, turning the corner and stepping out of sight. "Make sure you pack defensively for the trip, O Marked One."

"Pack defensively?" I muttered to myself, then called out, "What does that even mean? How do you pack defensively? Wait, are you suggesting...?"

"The mantle has been passed," he called out from his room. "Successors do not take holidays. I expect the next one will follow us to London somehow. Pack defensively."

"You've got to be kidding me," I said under my breath as Peaches sprawled on my bed. "I'm going to need to have a few strong words with Kali."

"Bad idea," Monty said from his room. "Unless you'd like her to test your immortality?"

"How are you even hearing me right now?"

"Magic," Monty said. "I'd suggest focusing on the successors. Kali will appear soon enough."

<Can we go to the place?>

<We're going to another place today. A new place.>

<Does the new place have meat? I need meat to grow.>

<If you keep growing we're going to need a warehouse to live in and a truck to carry you around in.>

<I'm a growing hellhound.>

<Tell me about it.>

<I just did. I need meat to grow. Will we be eating meat at the new place?>

<Yes. We're going to see Piero. Do you remember him?>

<I do. The old man with no smell. He has good meat. I like him.>

<Well if you behave, I'm sure he will give you plenty of good meat today.>

<I always behave. I behave like a hellhound.>

<That's what I'm afraid of.>

I sometimes wondered how Peaches classified those around him. It made sense he would call Piero odorless. Being part of the vampire community, Piero was undead. I guess that would make him the man with no smell.

I packed my bags as defensively as possible, though I made sure to exclude any weapons. I didn't think British Airways or JFK would appreciate me bringing my weapons with me. I would give Dex Grim Whisper and keep Ebonsoul hidden internally for the flight.

We were on the parking garage level below the Moscow twenty minutes later.

"Any idea on how to block the successors from tracking me?" I asked as I started the engine of the Dark Goat. "I'd really like not to engage in battle today, at least not on an empty stomach. Great—now I'm sounding like my hellhound."

"It's not as simple as a masking cast," Monty said. "This new designation Kali gave you is difficult to hide. It shifts and adapts. I'll have to do more research. Perhaps we can look into it further while we're abroad."

"Sure, as long as we aren't fighting or running for our

lives," I said. "That would be great. We can squeeze it in between meeting Tempest and finding York."

"Hmm," Monty replied. "That may be problematic."

"You think?" I said, letting the engine roar before settling into a low growl. "We really need to get this whole 'Mantle of Discord' thing under control."

"Agreed," Monty said with a nod while strapping in. "Maybe there is a way to pass on the mantle?"

"Anything that gets it off my shoulders would work," I said. "Let's go eat. I'm starving."

Peaches perked his ears at the sound of the word eat. We sped out of the garage and headed downtown.

FOUR

It took five minutes before she appeared. We were racing down the Westside Highway when something orange flickered in the rearview mirror.

It was the orange glow that gave her away, not that she was making an attempt to hide. We were halfway to Piero's new restaurant when I noticed the glow on one of the rooftops behind us.

"Monty, we have—"

"I know," Monty interrupted, gesturing. White symbols drifted out of the Dark Goat and rested on the cars next to us. "Keep driving."

"You knew and you didn't share?" I asked as I swerved around traffic. "You didn't think it was important to let me know a successor assassin was on our tail?"

"I didn't want you to panic," he said as he kept gesturing. "Do you think you could slow down somewhat? It will make this much easier."

"Didn't want me to panic? Now you want me to slow down? Why don't I just stop and let her end me while I'm at it?"

"Slowing down will suffice, thank you," Monty said. "Take the middle lane, and stay in it no matter what happens."

"Sure, I'll slow down and let her crush me, it's not like you're the one who assassins are after."

"Thirty miles an hour should do," Monty said, tracing one last symbol. "When I tell you, pull off the highway and park."

"So we can make for easier targets? Right, wouldn't want her to work too hard smushing me, thanks."

"Just wait for my signal," Monty said, glancing back. "Start slowing down...now."

I eased off the gas and suddenly realized we were surrounded by several Dark Goats, all going in different directions. A few of them accelerated and sped off ahead of us. A few more hung back, while even more started weaving in and out of traffic.

"What the...how did you do that?"

"Pull off at the next exit and park on the side," Monty said. "Do *not* exit the vehicle."

I veered to the right lane as the fleet of Dark Goats sped ahead of us. I saw the figure surrounded with orange energy take off after them.

"What was that?" I asked, craning my neck to look at the Dark Goats drive by. "How did you do that?"

"It's a powerful illusion," Monty said. "One imbued with traces of your energy signature. The situation is as I feared."

"As you feared?"

"The Mark of Kali is powered by your energy signature."

"Excellent. Then you know how to beat it, right?"

"Yes, I know how to beat it, but—"

"Perfect, make with the wiggle fingers and let's do this," I said, relieved. "No more successor stomping in my future."

"I'm afraid it's not that simple," Monty said. "There's a wrinkle."

"Wrinkle? Of course there's a wrinkle. Why would I even think it would be that easy? We're dealing with Kali. What is it?"

"I was able to shield you while we were in the vehicle because of the extensive runes Cecil applied to the exterior," Monty explained. "I was able to use them as a shield, while I created the illusion. Without the vehicle around you, due to your curse, you stand out like a beacon in the night."

"How powerful a beacon?" I asked. "Is there any chance of hiding my energy signature?"

"Doubtful," Monty said, tracing some symbols in the air. "It's your abundant life force. It gives you an incredibly strong energy signature, which is a double-edged sword. On the one hand, it is beneficial to casting your missile. On the other hand—"

"It makes it impossible to hide unless I'm in some kind of runed space?"

"I'm afraid so," Monty said. "We are dealing with the abilities of a goddess. It's really quite impressive. The curse that makes you immortal also makes you a target. It's very efficient."

"Glad you could admire the efficiency of my mobile death threat," I said, looking out of the Dark Goat. "How long before the illusion wears off?"

"Another ten minutes or so, and then she will be able to track you again," Monty said. "Unless we can find somewhere to mask you."

"Piero's will be masked, I'm sure, and it's underground," I said. "Will that work?"

"It should," Monty said. "I'd make haste before the glamour on this vehicle drops."

"Glamour?" I asked, looking around. "What glamour? We're in the Dark Goat."

"Not from the outside," Monty said. "I suppose the successor is far enough away for you to step out briefly. Make it quick."

I stepped out of the Dark Goat and nearly stumbled in surprise.

"That's not even remotely funny," I said, looking at the Dark Goat, which was currently disguised as a 1966 orange-and-white Volkswagen bus. "What the hell, Monty?"

"It was the most innocuous vehicle that came to mind," Monty said suppressing a smile. "Besides, I know the high esteem you hold for our fellow paranormal investigators of the arcane."

"A yellow cab," I said, getting back into the Dark Goat. "Now, that is innocuous. Not this...this pumpkin of a bus. Are those two even still alive?"

"As far as I know, yes," Monty said. "Do you think you can get us to Piero's new place in eight minutes?"

"Five, if it means getting out of this pumpkinmobile," I groused, stepping on the gas. "You never did say how much of a beacon Kali made me."

"Imagine it's a pitch-black evening."

"Right, pitch-black evening."

"Two of your baseball teams are playing—mind you, baseball is a peculiar sport. Does it want to be cricket, but has lost its way?"

"The point?"

"In any case, pitch-black evening. One of your teams is playing and all of the stadium lights are on at ten times their maximum power," Monty said. "Can you see it?"

"Yes, the entire city could see something like that."

"In this scenario, you would be the stadium lights."

"That sounds bright."

"Bright and bad," Monty said. "The successor will have no

issues finding you. The good news is that it appears to be only one successor at a time."

"The good news sucks," I said as we approached Piero's new place. "We're here."

FIVE

I parked the Dark Goat Pumpkinmobile in front of Japan Premium Beef.

"This is the place," I said, getting out of the Dark Goat. "When Piero goes low key, he really goes low key."

"This doesn't look like a new restaurant," Monty said, looking around. "As a matter of fact, I'm not seeing any kind of eating establishment here of any sort, just a butcher shop."

He was right.

Bohemian—and now—The Bite—really was a secret. The first part of the process was even locating the place. We had parked in front of 57 Great Jones Street, between Bowery and Lafayette Streets.

A plaque on the wall informed me that Andy Warhol and Jean-Michel Basquiat had both used the space to live and create art.

The only way to get the restaurant's phone number to request a reservation was by referral. The other way to make a reservation was to submit a request through their website, but I heard it was easier to hack into the NSA than to find that website.

The place was exclusive to the extreme.

The area looked like a typical NOHO block. An assortment of buildings, townhouses, and storefronts all jockeyed for position in a cramped mishmash of glass and brick.

We stood in front of a butcher shop whose graffiti-covered facade looked more like some throwback to a club from the 80s than a new, exciting place to eat.

"It's right here."

"Right here?" Monty asked, narrowing his eyes and peering at the facade. "Right where?"

"There," I said, pointing ahead of me. "In there."

"That is a butcher shop," Monty scoffed. "While I'm certain that it will appeal to your creature immensely, I'd prefer to eat something with a little less meat."

"My zenmaster hellhound proclaims that meat is life," I said, heading to the nondescript door. "That's some deep wisdom right there."

"That is the biased opinion of your creature, who effortlessly devours staggering amounts of meat," Monty countered. "I find there to be little wisdom in those words."

"I disagree," I said, touching certain parts of the door in sequence. "It's very wise to keep a hellhound well fed."

The door clicked open.

"You knew the sequence?" Monty asked, raising an eyebrow. "How?"

"Like I said, secret and exclusive."

"Am I to understand that you're part of this secret and exclusive clientele?"

"For Bohemian? Yes," I said, opening the door and entering the narrow corridor. "I heard Piero kept the same combination, so that was the easy part. The next part will be a little harder. Piero added some new security deterrents."

"Security deterrents?" Monty asked warily as he examined the walls. "What kind of deterrents?"

"That kind," I said, motioning to the young woman standing at the end of the corridor. Peaches growled next to me, but kept calm. I looked at the woman and stopped behind a red line about three feet away. She wore a pair of dark Chanel sunglasses, a black Ferragamo suit, with a pastel violet Valentino shirt. "Party of three. Piero is expecting us."

"He is?" Monty asked. "Since when?"

"Since I called him a few days ago to let him know we would be dropping by some time."

The woman was holding a small tablet and brought up a screen before looking at me again.

"Do you have a reservation?" the woman said. "Names, please?"

Monty stepped back and raised a hand, gesturing. He stopped himself halfway through the motion.

"Monty?" I asked, his reaction making me nervous. "What are you doing?"

"Her voice. This woman possesses an inordinate amount of power in relation to her nearly non-existent energy signature," Monty explained to me, before turning to the woman. "I've felt this power once before, but I never thought I would encounter it again—especially hidden here, in this city. My apologies for my initial reaction."

"Can we not antagonize the security?" I said, staring at Monty, before turning to her. "He's had a few rough decades. I apologize. "

The woman gave me a warm smile.

"None needed," the woman said with a short bow. "I get that reaction often from mages. Names please?"

"Simon, Tristan, and Peaches," I said. "Is Piero in?"

"Piero is always in," she said. "One moment, please."

She looked down at her tablet, located our names and smiled.

"Permanent VIP status," she said, touching the tablet screen. "Welcome to The Bite. Please proceed downstairs."

"Please take no offense at my question," Monty said as we stepped forward. "Which one are you?"

"These days I go by Eury," the woman said, then looked at me. "We have taken...steps, to ensure you have a pleasant dining experience, Marked One. The Bite is designated as a neutral zone and null area. No successors will make an attempt on your life while you are on the premises. Violence of any kind will not be tolerated."

"How...how did you?" I stammered, taken off guard. " Marked One? You can see it?"

"There's not much hidden from my vision," Eury said. "Enjoy your evening. Piero will be greeting you shortly after you are seated."

We headed down several flights of stairs to arrive at the restaurant proper. The recessed lighting was subdued, as was the music. I looked around and saw that Piero had kept the lounge feel, but had added an actual dining area off to one side of the expansive floor space.

Everything was warm browns, beiges, and stonework. The floor was made of large slabs of stone with extensive runes etched into its surface. A small, shrine-like area sat to one side with running water and grass, creating a small Japanese zen garden, complete with large stones and sand.

A sizable skylight let in the dying light over some low-lying plush furniture. Some of the walls were decorated with acoustic guitars, while others held beautiful arrangements of katanas in stands.

The Bite felt calm and inviting, feeling more like an upscale spa than an exclusive restaurant.

We were escorted to an empty private room with a large dining table that could easily fit six people comfortably. We had crossed the floor without any of the patrons even glancing our way, at least not overtly.

No one even looked twice at Peaches, which surprised me. He didn't exactly blend into these, or any other surroundings actually. It meant the clientele wasn't what I considered normals.

"Seemon," a familiar voice said with genuine warmth. "Tristan. It is a pleasure to see you both—and you brought the puppy. Very good." Piero patted Peaches on the head and gave him a stern look. "You will behave tonight, yes?"

Peaches rumbled and chuffed in agreement.

"Hello, Piero," I said. "He'll behave, if he wants to get fed."

"He will be fed regardless," Piero declared. "But if he behaves, I will give him extra meat."

Piero was dressed in a simple black Armani two-piece suit, and a bone-white shirt. As usual, his ensemble lacked any kind of neckwear. Peaches' ears perked at the sound of "extra meat" and he lay flat on the floor, looking up at Piero with the most extreme puppy-dog eyes I've ever seen.

"Stop being such a ham," I said under my breath. "Piero said he's going to feed you. No need to lay it on so thick."

Peaches rumbled and lay on his side as I shook my head.

"I have just the meals for you tonight, in honor of my return to this great city," Piero said. "Eat first; we talk after."

He silently left our room to visit with some of the other patrons.

"What was that about with the security?" I asked. "For a second I thought you were going to blast her."

"For a second, so did I," Monty said. "Then I realized the futility of the act. It was mere reflex. Apologies."

"How do you know her?"

"I don't," he said. "I know of her and her sisters."

"Sisters?"

"Yes," Monty said. "Eury is probably short for Euryale. She and her sister Stheno are not well known. I'm certain you've heard of her other sister, though."

"Who is?"

"Medusa," Monty said. "Eury is a Gorgon."

SIX

"Did you say Gorgon? As in, the 'turn people to stone' type of Gorgon?"

"Is there another type of Gorgon I'm not aware of?"

"Good point," I said. "Why would a Gorgon be working the door at The Bite? Wouldn't that be kind of like slumming for someone like her?"

"I can't pretend to know her motivations," Monty said. "According to the myth, she is immortal, along with Stheno. Perhaps she's bored?"

"How powerful is she, exactly?"

"You mean aside from the whole turning anyone she gazes at to stone thing?" Monty asked. "Did I mention she was immortal?"

"Yes, I caught that part," I said. "Why did you nearly freak out?"

"I did no such thing," Monty huffed. "I have never and will never 'freak out.' I was merely taken aback at her presence in such a place. The last time I was in her proximity, I was on a battlefield."

"She was in the war?"

"More like adjacent to the war, thankfully," Monty said. "She had crossed paths with some dark mages intent on wreaking havoc. It didn't go well for them."

"That bad?"

"They went from dark mages to dark-mage statuary in the span of a few seconds," he said. "I don't know if it was her, or her sister. Either way, the power she possesses is immense."

"How did Piero convince her to work the door here?"

"Why don't you ask him when he returns?" Monty said. "I'm sure he'll be delighted to share the story with you."

A few minutes later, Piero returned with a team of servers to bring our food. He oversaw the placing of plates, directing the team the way a general directs his troops. They moved in unison, seamlessly setting the table.

One server carried a large bowl, full of pieces of oversized wagyu beef, and warily approached Peaches.

"It's okay," I said. "He doesn't bite when it comes to getting meat."

<Do not scare the man. He's giving you meat.>

<I would never scare the person bringing me meat. Unless he wants to take it away. Can I bite him if he tries to take it away?>

<No biting. He's not going to take it away.>

<Good, because I'm starving. It's been so long since I ate.>

<Dex fed you a little while ago.>

<I know. It was so long ago.>

I sighed in surrender.

<Don't mangle the bowl, and don't forget to say thank you.>

The server nodded nervously, placing the bowl in front of my ravenous hellhound, hands slightly trembling, before backing away.

Peaches gave the server a low rumble followed by a growl, and the server picked up the pace, exiting the room. Peaches dove into the beef and began his usual process of inhaling of the meat.

The servers bustled around us for close to ten minutes, with Piero giving instructions and corrections.

When it was over, I was looking down at a huge steak, large enough to satisfy my hellhound for at least a good five minutes. Monty had a delicious-looking salad in front of him, and my mouth began watering from the smell of the food alone.

Piero grabbed a chair and sat at the other end of the table, looking at us expectantly.

"What do you wait for?" he asked, motioning with his hands. "Eat, eat."

"Where did you go?" I asked as I started in on my steak. "The last time we spoke, you were leaving town for an extended vacation away from the Blood Hunters."

Piero nodded.

"Yes, the *cacciatori di sangue*," Piero said. "I went to my people. Where it is safe. Now, I am here. It is also safe."

"I haven't seen them in a while, but I don't know about it being safe," I said after chewing on a piece of steak that melted in my mouth. "They are still out there, somewhere."

"I have better security now," Piero said, waving an arm around the room. "Tristano, you met my security? Yes?"

"Yes," Monty said with a nod. "Impressive. How did you manage it?"

"I am very old," Piero said. "Like these clothes you wear. I am gone for a short time and you forget how to dress? What is this?"

I looked down at my clothes and immediately felt self conscious. Piero had a way of making you feel that whatever you wore was beneath his standard of dress. I could be wearing royal attire, but if it wasn't Piero approved, I may as well have been wearing a potato sack.

"We've had a few rough days, weeks, months since we saw

you last," I said, trying to make amends. "Things have been a bit hectic."

"This is no excuse," Piero said and clapped his hands. "You must dress properly no matter the occasion. This is not proper."

He glanced at Monty and gave him a sniff and nod of minimum approval. He gave me the once over and shook his head in disapproval.

"I have clothes for you," he said finally as the door opened again. Two men came in, each holding a black garment bag. "You will wear this." He turned to the men. "*Grazie*."

"This is too kind," Monty said, before continuing his salad. "Thank you."

"No, thank you," Piero said. "You thank me by wearing better clothes. I will have these delivered to your home."

He unleashed a few words under his breath I didn't quite catch, but I was certain Monty understood as he gave Piero a serious look—well, more serious than usual—and nodded.

"Thank you again," Monty said. "We will make sure to uphold the Roselli standard of dress."

Piero seemed placated by Monty's words, and sat back in his chair while staring at me. He leaned forward slightly and pointed at me.

"How long have you had this mark, Seemon?"

"You can see it?" I asked. "Of course you can see it. Apparently everyone can see it except me."

"This is very powerful sign," Piero said, shaking his head. "Who gave this to you, which enemy?"

"Not an enemy, although I'm beginning to wonder about that lately," I said. "It was Kali. The goddess, Kali."

"Ahh," Piero said with a knowing nod. "Aspis. This mark is very dangerous. Did you ask for this mark?"

"Not exactly," I said. "Didn't have much choice. She didn't ask first."

Piero shook his head.

"Has it started? *Il Manto di Discordia?*"

"The Mantle of Discord? Yes, Kali neglected to mention that little part of the whole Aspis promotion."

"Have you ever seen it successfully masked?" Monty asked. "Is it possible to hide Simon?"

"Of course. You must kill the Aspis. There, it is easy."

"Not quite the solution I had in mind," I said. "Something a little less lethal?"

"The Aspis must fight," Piero said. "You have power through this mark. You must use it. Or you will die."

"Thank you for the advice," I said. "I'm going to try another strategy. Like leaving the country."

Piero shook his head.

"Not possible," he said. "This mark"—he threw his hands up, extending his fingers in the strangest jazz hands I had ever seen—"is like big light. You cannot hide. Better to fight."

"We have some other things to attend to first," I said. "We need to leave the country for a bit."

Piero nodded.

"You eat, we talk, then say goodbye," he said, standing. "I have something to help."

"Thanks. I would appreciate anything you can offer," I said.

"It will help, but you will not like it," Piero said. "Much pain for you."

"That sounds about par for the course."

"Thank you," Monty said. "We will make sure to see you before we leave."

Piero nodded and left us alone.

SEVEN

We had finished our meals when Eury stepped into our dining area. Judging from her body language, she was not pleased—that, and the large flaming blade she was holding in one hand.

"Let her speak first," Monty said as she drew closer. "She is clearly upset."

"Wonder what makes you say that?" I said, keeping my voice low and my eyes on the sword, just in case Eury felt like we needed emergency haircuts, heads included. "What's with the sword?"

"It's part of the security protocol," Monty replied, looking at Eury. "It's impressive to see it ablaze in such a manner, considering this is a null area."

"Right, the immortal Gorgon is wielding a flaming sword and you're impressed it's on fire?" I said, shaking my head. "Can you elaborate on the protocol that would trigger this response?"

"In a neutral area such as this," Monty said, rubbing his chin, "I would say casting, although that would be unlikely considering the potency of the runes covering this place.

Other than that, overt violence would certainly warrant this response."

"Did we somehow violate this protocol?" I asked, looking from Eury to Monty. "Something we missed?"

"Not to my knowledge," Monty assured me. "This seems like something else."

"Did you complain about the food?" I asked, keeping my eyes on the flaming sword. "Your salad looked delicious. Maybe she's the unofficial complaint department. None of this sending the food back to the chef. Here, Piero sends Eury to your table?"

"My salad was exemplary. Besides who could I have complained to?" Monty huffed as he relocated his napkin. "We've been alone this entire time. It's not like I would cast, if I could, to send a complaint."

"Can you?"

"Can I what?"

"Cast, in here?" I asked, keeping my voice low. "You know, in case of an emergency?"

"What kind of emergency are we going to encounter here?"

"The angry Gorgon carrying a flaming sword kind," I said. "Can you cast if you had to?"

"If I had to, yes," he said, closing his eyes for a few seconds. "The runes are formidable, but I could work around them if I needed to."

I nodded, partially comforted by the thought that Monty was slowly becoming unstoppable. The other part of me—the small, rational, and diminishing part of my brain—grabbed me by the shoulders and shook me hard, reiterating slowly: *Monty is becoming unstoppable.*

I shuddered and pushed the thought away.

"Have I mentioned how scary you're becoming?"

"Rubbish," Monty said, waving my words away. "In any

case, we did not cause this."

"Just checking," I said. "I figured you may have some kind of mage culinary displeasure spell or something."

"That's preposterous," Monty said. "Even I would not dare slight Piero or his chef in such a manner. For the record, no such spell exists."

"Pity. Think of all the time you could save at eating establishments."

"If a mage is displeased," Monty said, "there are easier ways to express such displeasure."

"Well, I doubt Eury is here to offer us the dessert menu," I said. "Unless whatever we order comes with a complimentary sword flambé."

"Gentlemen," Eury said when she had reached our table. "You have a guest."

"A guest?" I asked, confused. "This is our first time here. How can we have a guest?"

"I will reiterate," Eury answered, ignoring my question. "Violence of any kind will not be tolerated on the premises. Is this understood?"

"Absolutely," I said. "I'm practically a practicing Buddhist when it comes to my stance on violence in neutral zones."

Eury gave me a pointed look.

"The repeated renovations to The Randy Rump neutral zone speak otherwise," Eury said, as the flames on her sword increased gradually for a few seconds before dying down to regular searing length again. "This guest is here for you, Marked One."

"Oh," I said, somewhat speechless. "Can you tell whoever it is that I'm not interested? Kind of busy with dinner here."

"Simon," Monty hissed. "She is a Gorgon and an immortal, not your errand girl."

"What? I'm just trying to avoid a confrontation in Piero's place," I said. "I don't want a repeat of The Randy Rump.

Somehow I don't think Piero would be as understanding as Jimmy if we shred this place to pieces."

"There. Will. Be. No. Shredding," Eury said as the temperature dropped a few degrees. "Violence will be met with an overwhelming and fatal response for all parties involved."

"Understood," I said, my voice serious, as Eury released some of her energy into the room. It was an impressive flex, considering we were in a null area. "You will have no violence starting with me."

Eury nodded.

"However," I continued as Monty looked off to the side, "if this guest brings violence to me, I will answer in kind. In other words, don't start none, won't be none."

Monty sighed and shook his head.

Eury stepped closer to my side of the table and smiled. That creeped me out because the smile actually looked warm and inviting, right up until the moment that I remembered she was holding a flaming sword that was threatening to barbecue one side of my face.

"I understand," Eury said, still smiling. "If there is violence, I will, how do you say, answer in kind. If you or your guest start a single incident of violence, I will blast you both until there is nothing left of you except dust, which I will watch blow away. Don't start none, won't be none. Clear?"

"That's not exactly how the expression..." I started before Monty gave me a *do you want us all to die* glare. "Nevermind, let's see who this guest of mine is."

Eury nodded to the doorway.

A young woman walked in.

She was dressed in what appeared to be combat armor, but it was unlike any I had seen. Usually combat armor was made of thick leather and metal, designed to deflect or mitigate any incoming damage.

This woman was dressed in combat armor that seemed to be made of dark red silk. Every square inch of her clothing was covered in runes that slowly and rhythmically pulsed and shifted, except for an area on her left side where I saw the outline of a rose.

Over the clothing, I noticed the soft orange glow that covered her entire body. Even though she was unfamiliar, the glow wasn't. It was the same orange glow that had covered the glowgre that was focused on cutting my time on the planet short.

She was the next successor.

She grabbed a chair and sat opposite me, staring intently into my eyes.

"Just an FYI," I said. "I'm kind of involved with someone who wouldn't appreciate you making these googly-eyes at me. She's kind of touchy about that sort of thing."

"*You* are the Marked of Kali?" she said with obvious contempt. "How? Surely Kali must have been mistaken to choose one such as you."

"I keep thinking the same thing," I said. "Mrs.?"

"Dira," she said. "How did you create the illusion with the vehicles?"

"Smoke and mirrors," I said. "It's really a complicated cast."

She stared at me in silence for a few seconds. I get that response often. My brilliance usually drives people speechless, right before they want to attack me. Not everyone can appreciate my charisma.

"How did Kali pick someone so vacuous?" Dira said. "You must have angered her and this is your penance, to die as the Marked of Kali. What did you do?"

"I may or may not have interrupted a 5000-year-old plan she was about to complete," I said. "In my defense, there were children involved and I had no idea she was part of the entire thing. Shiva played me." I glanced at Monty. "Played us."

"How are you still alive?" Dira asked. "I cannot believe Kali didn't curse you immediately."

"Funny story about that—"

"Enough," Dira interrupted, raising a hand. "Just hearing you speak irritates me. Your words do not matter. I will relieve you of the burden of this life"—she glanced at Eury, who stood near the entrance with her flaming sword—"once you have left this neutral area."

Eury nodded.

"I was not aware the Black Rose served Kali," Monty said, looking at Dira. "I thought your sect rejected service to the old gods?"

"You are well informed, mage," Dira said, glancing at Monty. "The Black Rose does not serve Kali. I do. She brings death, as I will to the Marked One."

"You're not even going to interject?" I asked, looking at Eury. "Nothing about bringing violence to my life?"

"The violence in your life is no concern of mine as long as it occurs outside of these walls," Eury answered. "I'm certain you are accustomed to this as the Marked of Kali, yes?"

"Not so much, no," I said. "I don't make a habit of going around with people"—I glanced at Dira—"successors hunting me down."

"I see," Eury said. "I'd suggest acclimating to your situation with haste, then."

I turned to Dira.

"Why were you chosen for the Mantle of Discord?" I asked. "Did you have to take a test? Audition? Why did Kali pick you? Your pleasant attitude?"

"Do you even know who Kali is? What she is the goddess of? Do you worship her? Or do you bear this mark like a fool wearing an anchor around his neck and stepping into the sea, who then wonders why he is drowning?"

"The black goddess is the goddess of time, change, and death," I said. "As Shakti, she is also the mother of all living things. She is the end and the beginning. I know her pretty well, actually. Why did she pick you?"

Monty raised an eyebrow in my direction.

I had been studying.

After my last run in with her, and especially since whole this Marked of Kali business, I did my best to learn all I could about the black goddess of death who had cursed me.

"You are not as foolish as you seem," Dira replied. "She is all that and more. The Mark is offered to those who have gained her favor. Those who have excelled in what she is."

"Excelled in what she is," I repeated slowly. "I'm going to guess we're not speaking about her creative and protective side?"

"No," Dira said with a smile that chilled me to my core. "I have become death for my goddess many times, and I *will* wear her Mark."

"There's only one slight wrinkle in that," I said, raising a finger. "You have to kill me first."

"This is not a wrinkle, merely a formality," Dira replied, and slowly stood. "I will not be fooled by your illusions again. I am not the ogre who struck blindly without thought. I will wait. The Mark is my birthright."

"Trust me, if I could give it to you, I would," I said. "I don't—"

"You would insult Kali?" Dira hissed. "To wear her Mark is the greatest privilege, and you dishonor her? You would give it away?"

"No dishonor meant," I said. "Just pointing out that being the Marked One isn't exactly rainbows and roses."

"You mock the goddess," Dira said as she seethed. "If you

were not in this place, I would end your miserable life this instant."

"You would try," I said, letting some of my anger seep into my words. "Things are never that easy."

"You pose no threat to me, Marked One."

"Right, seems we are going to have to agree to disagree," I said. "There's no way I can get you to change your mind?"

"Of course there is," Dira said with a small smile that held an edge of death. "Slit your throat and end your life. Then maybe the goddess will forgive you for your impudence. As the current successor, the Mark will be mine regardless; all that is required is your death. At your hands or mine, it doesn't matter."

"That's going to be a hard no on the slitting of throats, especially mine," I said. "Anything else you need to share?"

"There is nowhere you can go that I will not find you," Dira said, stepping to the entrance. "Every breath you take, and every step you make—"

"You'll be watching me?" I asked. "I'm pretty sure that's taken."

"I will be there when you make your mistake, and I will snuff out your blasphemous life," Dira said, turning to face me. "I will take great pleasure in seeing your last breath."

"We'll see," I said as she turned back to leave the dining room with Eury behind her. "See you soon."

"Well, that could have been worse," Monty said, after taking a sip from his tea. "All in all, that went quite well. You seem to have gotten a handle on your tact."

"Were you not paying attention?" I nearly yelled. "She is a religious zealot who wants me dead. In what shape or form did that go well?"

"You're still alive aren't you?" he said. "The Black Rose is a group of mage assassins. Opposite of Quan's sect of White Phoenix healers."

"Mage assassins?" I asked. "They kill with casts?"

"They kill mages," Monty corrected. "They use specialized blades that neutralize magic, similar to a kamikira, but designed to deal with mages, not gods."

I stared at him.

"We need to get back, and you need to find a way to mask this insane Mark," I said. "You heard her; she's going to find me anywhere I go, eventually."

"Perhaps the solution is to stop running?"

"What are you talking about?"

"Clearly she is operating under the premise that she can kill you, correct?"

"That seemed to come across, yes. Several times."

"Well how exactly is she going to accomplish this?"

"I'm going to assume with as much pain as possible."

"That is her intent," Monty said, glancing at the entrance. "She clearly doesn't appreciate you bearing Kali's Mark, but that's not what I was getting at. I was speaking literally. How is she going to kill you?"

"Angrily?" I asked, not seeing the direction he was going. "I don't know. You just said she has a special blade."

"To deal with mages, which you are not."

"Then I don't know how she plans to end me."

"Exactly," he said. "You are death-challenged, and she isn't wielding a kamikira, at least not one I could sense. From my studies, the Mantle of Discord makes her more dangerous, yes, but it doesn't make her superhuman. How is she going to kill you, then?"

It was beginning to come together.

"You think Kali failed to tell her about the curse?"

"Does sound like Kali, doesn't it?"

"Ugh, yes," I said, after giving it a moment of thought. "She's all about making those who worship her prove themselves. How better to express your devotion than to try to kill someone who can't die?"

"*That* sounds very much like Kali," Monty said. "I have to say, I get the impression she really dislikes you."

"Have I mentioned how much I hate dealing with gods?"

"Once or twice, yes," Monty said, after taking another sip from his cup. "Let's go smooth things over with Piero and head back. My uncle will, most likely, be waiting."

"I really need to have a conversation with Kali."

"Your funeral," Monty said. "Figuratively speaking, that is, unless she changes her mind."

"Your humor is lacking in all sorts of tact."

"I never claimed to possess humor," Monty said, straightening out his sleeves. "Piero and my uncle await." He gave me a short bow. "After you."

We left the dining area.

In the pit of my stomach, the sense of stepping into a deeper and more dangerous situation clamped itself tightly around my midsection.

Peaches whined as he padded next to me.

"I totally understand how you feel, boy. Totally."

EIGHT

We made our way to the main floor of the restaurant.

Piero was sitting in a corner of the space with Eury standing next to him, sans flaming sword. He waved us over when he saw us.

Eury pulled out two chairs for us and glanced down at Peaches with a smile. Peaches rumbled back and settled on the floor near me.

Eury went back to standing behind Piero.

"Eury tells me you had a guest," Piero said, tapping his forehead. "Because of this mark."

I nodded.

"Apparently, Kali felt I wasn't unpopular enough," I said. "She decided to take matters into her own hands. Now I have fansassins wanting to end me."

"This is the price of power," Piero said. "Those you can trust grow smaller, those who want to see you fall grow larger. It has always been this way."

"Except I don't want and have never asked for this power," I said. "I didn't ask for an upgrade. She just decided it was time to make my very insane life, even more insane."

"This is why," he said. "Because you did not ask. You must be careful, Seemon. Power is a trap that corrupts"—he held out an open hand palm up—"before you understand what is happening, it corrupts."

He closed his hand into a fist and slammed it into the table with enough force that I expected it to shatter into splinters.

"Then it kills."

"I understand," I said, somewhat startled he hadn't obliterated the table. "I apologize. I didn't expect her to come here, but I guess she really can locate me wherever I am."

"Apology accepted," he said with a nod. "What will you do now? You cannot run."

"We have to go overseas for a bit," I said. "I just need a way to camouflage this thing so she will leave me alone."

"There is a way to hide this mark, for a short time," Piero said, his face grim. "But it is not easy or painless."

"Let me guess," I said with a small chuckle. "I have to die?"

Piero stared at me, eyes unwavering.

"Yes."

"Seriously?" I asked. "Because that's going to be beyond difficult. I have this condition."

"There is a method known to my kind," Piero said. "The living death. Tristano, do you know of this?"

"I do," Monty said. "But I thought that only applied to vamp—your kind? In order for that process to work on Simon I would need blood."

"Blood magic?" I said. "No. Hard pass."

"Not magic," Piero said. "This is deeper, older than magic." He raised a hand. "Eury."

Eury reached into her jacket pocket, pulled out a small vial, and handed it to Piero. He took the vial and placed it on the table between us.

"Piero...what exactly is—?"

"Blood," Monty finished. "Whose blood is that, Piero?"

"Mine," Piero said. "After tonight, you are persona non grata here. Take this as a token of my deepest apology. Until you resolve your situation, I cannot let you return."

I was speechless.

"We understand," Monty said, taking the vial. "Thank you, Piero."

Monty glared at me.

"I don't under—" I started. Monty gave me a look that said, *Do not insult Piero.* "I mean, thank you, Piero. I don't know what to say."

"When that's the case, silence is usually the best recourse," Monty interjected quickly before I could finish. "We'll take our leave and hope to see you soon."

Piero nodded.

"Please do," Piero said as Eury stepped out from behind him. She turned to us and waited. "Eury will show you out."

"This way," she said, extending an arm and leading us to the main entrance, "if you please."

"You don't need to go through all this trouble, really," I said. "We can see ourselves out."

"He must really like you," she said when we were some distance from Piero's table. "I've never seen him give anyone his blood. I don't know what you've done to earn that, but make sure you honor his gift."

"We will," Monty said. "Thank you for your restraint in dealing with this delicate matter. You were within your rights to remove us forcefully from the premises."

"Under the rules of neutrality, I had every right to execute both of you where you sat, because of the successor," Eury said matter-of-factly. "Piero forbade it. Like I said, he must really like you."

"Thank you for not executing the execution," I said. "Just

curious, why would you be in your rights to end us? We didn't violate the neutral zone."

"Did you know you were being followed?"

"Yes."

"Then you came here, to a neutral zone, bringing the potential of violence with you."

"Yes, but I didn't violate the neutral zone."

"You didn't," Eury said, unlocking and slightly opening the door. She glanced outside for a few seconds before opening it fully. "She did. Since you were the catalyst for her violation—"

"It was Simon's fault," Monty said. "He is responsible."

"Correct," Eury said, patting Peaches on the head. "I do wish you the best. You must have some redeeming qualities, I'm sure. Even though they were not in evidence this evening."

"Thank you, I think?" I said, slightly offended. "What makes you say that?"

"Hellhounds are excellent judges of character," Eury said, looking at Peaches. "This is a scion of Cerberus. If he is bonded to you, it was not by accident. I will trust his choice and wish you luck."

Peaches rumbled at Eury as she turned and closed the door.

NINE

We arrived at the Moscow without incident.

"What's with the blood in the vial?" I asked before getting out of the Dark Goat. "Piero mentioned the living death."

Monty retrieved the vial from his jacket.

"Once you drink this vial it will simulate your dying."

"Simulate, right? Not actual death?"

"I doubt Piero's blood could truly kill you," Monty said, examining the vial. "Even as powerful as he is, your curse is impressive."

"So I take this and drop dead?"

"It needs time to take effect," Monty said. "It should keep you hidden from your successor for a prolonged time."

"How prolonged?"

"From my studies, the average time from ingestion to collapse is usually five minutes," he said. " It then has an aftereffect that lasts close to six hours. That's an estimate."

"I'm going to be knocked out for six hours?"

"No," Monty said. "Your body will appear to cease to function for six hours. You will still be able to move around and act, but your energy signature will be hidden. Hence the name *living death*."

"Is there anything you haven't studied?"

"There are a myriad of things I still need to study."

"So, five minutes until it looks like I'm dead?" I asked. "Then I'm dead for six hours, not longer?"

"Good question. I would imagine it may be less than six hours, due to your curse actively fighting the effects of the blood. Probably long enough to convince a successor of your demise if the conditions are right."

"Can't really use this blood more than once, then."

"One-time use if I'm not mistaken," he said. "I'm not in the practice of drinking vampire blood. So I can't speak to the time frame with certainty."

"Fair enough," I said. "Does it need any special mage activation?"

"No," Monty said, handing me the vial. "You drink it and appear to die. Your body shuts down and, for all intents and purposes, you are deceased."

"I seem to remember a part about it not being easy or painless."

"It may have some unpleasant side effects," Monty said. "Nothing that should threaten you."

"Last thing I need is to turn into some kind of vampire," I said. "I think I'm going to save this until I really need it."

Monty nodded.

I put the vial in my jacket and examined the quiet garage. I doubted we would be attacked in the Moscow, but it never hurt to be aware. For the moment, I would appreciate the silence.

That lasted all of five minutes as I parked the Dark Goat in our spot. I turned off the engine and stepped out of the vehicle into the glacial stare of Olga, our landlord.

I realized in that moment that my life had become so

bizarre, so far from what I may have considered normal, that I didn't have an immediate heart attack. I just stared up into the freezing stare of the ice queen who posed as a building owner.

The first thing that caught my attention were the diamond earrings that reflected the light and nearly blinded me. The matching necklace that hung around her neck held a piercing blue diamond that easily distracted me from the earrings.

She wore a form-fitting, strapless, sky-blue embroidered silk Oscar de la Renta dress that came to her knees. The ensemble was finished off by a pair of white Bottega Veneta knee-high boots that glistened with what appeared to be real diamonds.

Knowing her, they were.

I didn't know where she was going. What I did know was that everyone else was going to be seriously underdressed. Behind her, and parked some distance away, idling with a low predatory rumble, sat a dark blue Rolls Royce Phantom. Its windows were tinted black, preventing me from seeing the driver or anyone else who was inside.

"Good evening, Stronk," she said, demonstrating her usual care around the mangling of my name, and looking down at me like an errant particle of dust. "We need talk...now."

It wasn't like I had much of a choice. If she took another few steps she'd stomp on me. I didn't tell her to back up and respect my personal space, because I wasn't looking for the Solo carbonite experience.

I got the impression that in the Moscow, and probably outside of it too, the concept of personal space was lost on her. Monty stepped around the Dark Goat and came over to the driver's side.

"Good evening, Olga," he said with a short nod. "You look stunning."

She narrowed her eyes at Monty, her mouth drawn in a tight line. The energy coming off of her in not-so-subtle waves was considerable. The thought of going toe-to-toe with her flashed through my mind for a split-second.

I slapped the thought away with zero hesitation. It was not a pretty thought.

"You say pretty words, but I see past the pretty," Olga warned and turned to me, snapping me out of my thoughts. "You have dangerous visitor here yesterday."

"I had a dangerous visitor?"

"This is what I said," Olga said, staring at me. "Do you not hear?"

"I hear, I hear," I said. "This visitor, was she glowing orange?"

Olga narrowed her eyes at me this time, slowly nodding her head.

"Yes," she said, stepping closer as the temperature around us dropped, causing ice crystals to form on the exterior of the Dark Goat. "I do not like this visitor. She scare Andrei. She scare other people in building. Looking for you. Why is she looking for you?"

"That's—wow, that is complicated."

"Make it simple. Explain."

No point in lying to Olga. Besides, the truth, as crazy as it sounds, is usually the best strategy when dealing with beings who manipulate large amounts of power.

"I've been cursed," I said, wincing. "Because of the curse, she wants to kill me."

"This curse, does it bring damage to building?"

"No, no damage to building," I assured her. "The visitor may try something, though."

"You make sure your visitor brings no damage to building, clear?"

What was clear was that in the hierarchy of things that

were important to Olga, I came in second to the Moscow. Maybe third or fourth.

"Totally clear," I said, taking a small step back, surprised at how well she was taking my situation. "I'll make sure to keep all damage away from the building. You're not worried she may hurt me?"

She gave me a glacial glance.

"No," she said. "Building is difficult to fix. You difficult to break. This makes building more important."

"That's some interesting logic, but I think I get it."

"Good," she said, somewhat mollified. She turned at the sound of giggling. Cece had bounded out from the Phantom before running over to us. "I say stay inside, Cecelia."

Cece was dressed in a mini version of the clothing Olga wore, minus the Harry Winston collection of jewels.

"I just wanted to say hello, Aunt Olga," Cece answered, and smiled at us. She gave me a huge hug and embraced Monty, who had no idea how to handle that much physical contact all at once. "Hello, Simon. Hello, Mr. Montague."

Rags bounded out of the car next. Olga threw up a hand, rolled her eyes, and stepped to the side, muttering something in a language I didn't exactly understand. I looked around, but didn't see Viana.

"Where's Viana?" I asked. "Is she in the car?"

"She had to go home for a few days," Cece said. "She has a big exam and needed to study there. I think she's moving up in rank, or something like that."

"She must be preparing for a shift," Monty said pensively. "I will have to make accommodations."

"Does that mean I get to stay with you and Simon?" Cece asked, her voice full of hope. "That would be great."

"In the interim, until Viana returns, yes," Monty said. "We will address your living situation when we return."

"Return?" Olga asked. "Where are you going?"

"London," Monty said. "I have a delicate family situation to attend to. You know how family can be."

"I know," Olga said, looking down at Cece with a knowing nod. "Do not be long. Cecelia needs her teacher."

"Understood. We will be back as soon as possible."

Peaches stood a little straighter when he saw Rags and I shook my head. What a ham.

<The beautiful guardian is here. She is looking more beautiful than ever.>

<Why don't you go say hello?>

<Without meat to offer her? That would be rude. I will stand here and then do some dashes. Frank told me that if I want to impress the beautiful guardian I need to do dashes. How do I dashes?>

<I think he meant look dashing, not dashes. I don't think she impresses easily, boy. Just go over there and say hello. That should work.>

He remained where he stood. My hellhound, who had faced all sorts of monsters and creatures out to kill us, was rooted to the spot by his crush. Amazing.

Rags, for her part, didn't even look in Peaches' direction. I felt bad for him, but I wasn't well-versed in canine courtship rituals enough to offer advice. Besides, these two barely qualified as canine. More like canine adjacent.

One was my hellhound bondmate, complete with scary abilities, and the other was the guardian of a very powerful ice-mage child. Giving them pointers on how to get together was beyond me.

"Have you kept up with your practice?" Monty asked Cece, patting her head lightly once he had gently extricated himself from her bear-hug. "Every day?"

I don't know what surprised me more: that she had been able to pull off the bear-hug, or the light pat of her head, demonstrating affection in a clear violation of his mage Spockness.

"Every day, yes," she said. "Aunt Olga said I could practice as long as I don't freeze everything. Right, Aunt Olga?"

Olga nodded and pointed to the Phantom.

"We must go before we are late," Olga said. "Say goodbye. You see your teacher *soon*."

The emphasis on the last word was unmistakable. Cece waved goodbye and bounded back into the Phantom, followed by Rags. Peaches stared after her, still riveted in place.

Olga came close to me and glanced back at the Phantom, making sure Cece was safely inside.

"This visitor is dangerous, Stronk," she said, keeping her voice low. "Fix this curse. If you must, you kill visitor first. This is not person to speak to. You must act."

I nodded.

"I will, thank you for the advice."

"That is not advice," she said. "That is truth. This is advice: Do not break building or I will break you. This"—she pointed a finger at my chest—"this is good advice."

She gave me a small smile and turned on her heels, disappearing into the Phantom, which glided out of the garage with a low rumble.

"Nice ride," I said as we headed for the stairs. "Did Cecil give her a Phantom?"

"Most likely. I did recognize the runework," Monty said, glancing behind us. "Although that vehicle isn't graced with the same amount of security runes as the Dark Goat."

"You mean Cecil's deathrunes?"

"Yes, those," Monty said, climbing the stairs. "The runes on the Phantom appeared to be the standard protection runes."

"How does she do that?" I asked. "Every time I enter the building. It never fails."

"Do what exactly?" Monty asked as he matched my pace.

"There are quite a few choices. Are you asking how she manages to mangle your name so eloquently? Or are you wondering how she manages to appear when you least expect her?"

"The latter, Your Drollishness."

"I don't believe that's actually a word."

"It is now," I said with a grin and a mock bow, letting him pass me as we reached our floor. "After you, Your Drolljesty. I can do this all day."

"Please don't," Monty said, shaking his head and walking past me. "To answer your question, I don't know how she senses you. It could be tied to the Moscow. She doesn't seem to appear anywhere else."

"Tied to the Moscow?"

"Like proximity sensors," Monty explained. "She may have a sequence of runes that alert her whenever you are on the premises."

"Wouldn't that be an invasion of privacy?"

"Is she appearing to you when you're in the bathroom?"

"What? No."

"Does she happen to pop up when you are sleeping?"

"Of course not," I said. "You'd hear about it if she did, trust me."

"Then she's appearing to you in the public spaces of a building she happens to own. Not an invasion of privacy. Disturbing perhaps, but not an invasion."

"She's as bad as the successors."

"Except she doesn't want to kill you," Monty said, pressing the door in a sequence. "I would call that a good thing."

"True," I agreed with a shudder. "I would hate to face an angry Olga."

"You and me both," Monty said with a grumble. "Would it have killed my uncle to make this sequence shorter?"

We'd had to increase our security measures ever since our door kept getting blown off its hinges. Dex had placed some nasty countermeasures on the door and the space around the entrance, in case anyone tried to force their way in.

I insisted they be non-lethal, so they consisted mostly of teleportation runes that would transport whoever it was to different parts of the planet in sequence. The fact that it was non-lethal also made the sequence longer than usual.

"Maybe you can ask him when he gets here?"

"He's already here, probably giggling his head off as I struggle with this sequence of his," Monty said. "Can't you sense him?"

I closed my eyes and let my senses expand around me. Monty was right. Dex was inside, sitting in the reception area...which faced the front door.

"Do you think he knows you're trying to get in?"

Monty gave me a withering glare.

"What do you think?" he asked. "This is my uncle."

I heard a loud laugh from inside.

"I'm going to guess that's a yes," I said, suppressing a laugh myself. "Good thing we don't have to get inside in a hurry. I could see where this would be problematic, given some of the enemies you've made."

"*I've* made? I'm not the one being hunted by a worshipper of a death goddess," Monty said. "If I recall, that would be you."

"Good point," I said. "Some of my fans have definitely veered over the edge into the lethal zone."

"You...mean you...you have fans that don't want...to kill you?" Monty said, finally getting the door open, and stomping inside to confront a laughing Dex. "Uncle, this sequence is completely unnecessary."

He was still wearing his bohemian mage look, except his

hair had done its usual thing and gone wild, hanging loose around his head.

"Why didn't you...why didn't you use your key?" Dex asked between gasps. "It's the shortcut. I seem to recall mentioning that."

Monty narrowed his eyes at Dex.

"When exactly did you mention that the key was the shortcut?"

Dex grew serious and scratched his chin, looking at us.

"It was...well, on the day...oh, I must have forgotten to tell you," Dex said, smiling apologetically. "Well, now you know. Using the key while touching the door is the shortcut. Don't forget to do both at the same time, or you'll be going for a nice trip."

"I'm glad to see this is amusing you so, Uncle. Having the sequence that long is an operational hazard. What if we were being chased?"

"I would expect you three would be able to handle whatever would be daring enough to chase you to your home," Dex said, still chuckling. "Lighten up, Nephew. Enjoy this while you still can. You two have some dark days ahead."

TEN

"That doesn't sound ominous at all," I said, settling into the kitchen which sat opposite the reception area. "What are you talking about?"

"I have news," Dex said as a scowl crossed his face. "We have a situation."

"What kind of situation?"

"Nana is currently out of the country," Dex said. "She'll reach out to you when she wants to meet."

"Nana is on vacation?" I asked. "That's the situation?"

"Don't be a smart arse, boy," Dex said with a growl. "It doesn't suit you."

I could tell from his response that something was worrying him.

"What's wrong?" I asked. "Really. Because I have several advanced degrees in smartassery, practically a doctorate even. It definitely suits me."

"Three things," Dex said, ignoring me and holding up three fingers. "My sources tell me York has become more unstable since I saw him last."

"How long ago was that?" Monty asked. "It's not like you regularly visit countries that want you erased."

"True. Give or take fifty years since the last time I was there," Dex said. "Seems the old noggin is failing him."

"Unstable how, exactly?" I asked, concerned. "What does that mean? Has he become eccentric in his old age?"

"Aye, it's more than that," Dex said, creating a large sausage for my eternally starving hellhound, who proceeded to inhale said sausage. "He left old age a few centuries ago."

"Then let's go see someone else who is still mentally capable," I said. "Isn't that an option?"

"Not really. He's the only one we can see," Dex said, turning to Monty. "That's your fault, Nephew."

"My fault?" Monty said, surprised, as he headed to the kitchen. "How is York's mental degradation any fault of mine?"

"Not his mental state, lad," Dex corrected, tapping his temple. "He's always been a bit daft. Too many archaic tomes. It's the fact that he's the only one we can go see about this situation. *You* used a lost rune. A lost *blood* rune."

I turned from Dex to Monty.

Monty remained silent and continued to prepare his tea.

"Care to explain?" Dex asked. "Those runes were lost for a reason."

"They weren't actually lost, they were hidden," I volunteered, glancing at the extra-silent Monty and immediately regretting it. "At least...that's what I heard."

Dex gave me a withering stare and turned to Monty.

"Aye, they were hidden for a reason," Dex said, his voice dangerous. "Did you tell him why they were hidden?"

"Blood runes are a shortcut to power," Monty said. "They use life force, blood, to impart significant power to the caster. They were hidden to prevent power-hungry mages and magic users from accessing these shortcuts."

"That's what we told the sects," Dex said. "The truth is worse, much worse."

"I beg your pardon?" Monty said. "What do you mean, the truth?"

"It's the same with each generation," Dex said, throwing a hand in the air. "Especially mages. Do you think the older generations did things because we were doddering fools?"

"Well...not fools, necessarily," Monty said, looking to shorten his life. "Perhaps overly cautious?"

"No," Dex corrected. "We hid those runes because they were—they *are* immensely deadly."

"It was my understanding that the lost runes were once common knowledge," Monty said, slipping into professor mode. I could see Dex bristle. "Most of the energy we manipulate has the potential to be deadly. Why are these runes any different? Energy is energy."

Dex formed a bright green orb in one hand. It was small, about the size of a golf ball. It gave off enough light to make me avert my gaze or risk being blinded.

"Energy is not just energy," Dex said, keeping his voice low. "Some energy is created for a purpose."

"You're saying the lost blood runes are evil?" Monty asked, prompting me to take a few steps away from Dex. Just in case. "Energy is neither good nor evil."

"Wrong," Dex said, looking at the orb in his hand. "Tell me what this is."

Monty narrowed his eyes at the orb for a few seconds and then visibly paled, stepping back away from Dex. How he managed to look at the miniature sun without losing his eyesight amazed me.

"How did you...?" he asked, fear lacing his words. "Why?"

"Tell me what it is," Dex said again, fixing his gaze on Monty. "Why do you sound so concerned? Energy is energy. Right?"

"That's...that's...a planar disruptor," Monty said, staring back at Dex. "Why would you ever create that?"

"It's only energy," Dex said, bouncing the orb in his hand. "What's the harm?"

"Uncle, please undo that cast."

"Are ye certain?" Dex asked. "I mean, I release this and this plane is disrupted. Major loss of life, unleashing of cosmic forces, ripple effects for decades, maybe centuries... Would you consider that evil?"

"Monty," I said, warily. "That orb can—?"

"Yes," Monty said, never taking his eyes off Dex. "That and more. A planar disruptor makes a void vortex look like a child's plaything. It has a collapsing cascade effect. The more power thrown at it, the more power it siphons, until, eventually, everything is gone."

"Everything? What do you mean—?"

"This plane would cease to exist, along with everyone and everything in it...everything is devoured and undone," Monty said. "It's a plane killer. I've never seen one up close. I hope to never see another. Uncle?"

"Dex?" I asked, careful not to upset the old mage holding an orb of utter destruction in his hand. "Would it be possible to put away the everything killer now?"

"I'm more than willing to oblige, once my nephew answers my question," Dex said, turning to Monty. "I don't pretend to be as educated as you, Nephew, so I'm hoping you'll set me straight. Does such a thing as evil energy exist?"

I knew where Monty stood on the subject. He had mentioned it earlier, and part of me agreed. Energy is energy. It wasn't necessarily good or evil. It all depended on how it was being used. Electricity could kill you, but it could also power your home. The electricity wasn't evil; it all depended on how it was used.

Looking at the glowing orb in Dex's hand gave me

another perspective. It was possible that some energy, just like weapons, may not be inherently evil, but we couldn't sugarcoat their purpose.

Some things were created to end life and kill.

I seriously doubted anyone who knew what was happening at the Manhattan Project thought they were building a life-saving bomb. Yet nuclear energy, when used properly, could replace other sources of energy before they ran out.

It wasn't an easy answer.

I saw Monty flex his jaw, and I knew he was sticking to his principles. I just hoped it didn't piss off Dex into making an example of this plane.

"No," Monty said. "Evil energy doesn't exist. Evil people using energy for evil acts *do* exist, but the energy itself is not inherently good or evil."

Dex reabsorbed the small orb, and I let out a long breath.

"Why?" I asked. "Are you trying to find out how immortal I am?"

"I doubt even you would've survived that," Dex said, looking at me before turning back to Monty. "A planar disruptor absorbs and destroys all energy. Did you understand the lesson?"

Monty nodded, his expression grim.

"Yes, I did. Thank you."

"Can you elaborate on this lesson without creating another plane-destroying orb?"

"Energy may be neutral, like the lad said." Dex glanced at Monty. "However all energy has duality. It can be used for both good and evil."

"Like the lost runes?" I asked. "They can be used for good?"

Dex nodded. "I'm old, boy," he said, rubbing a hand through his hair. "There's a reason for that. In my long life, there have been many mages stronger and more skilled than me."

"Really?" I said. "You seem pretty strong to me. Especially when you're using your axe-mace of insanity."

"Nemain doesn't require strength, just the courage and willingness to lose your mind," Dex said, glancing at me. "I have managed to outlive most of my enemies and peers. Do you know how?"

"Please tell me you're not going to go into some explanation about your extracurriculars with the Morrigan," I said. "If so, I pass."

Dex gave me a wicked grin.

"That's part of it, but there's more," he said. "When I was a young man, the lost runes *were* accessible to all mages, all the sects. They were known as elder runes back then."

"All the mages had access to blood runes?" I asked. "No matter their power level? Isn't that a recipe for, I don't know, disaster?"

"They weren't blood runes in the beginning," Dex said. "That came later. When they were first created they were still known as Elder runes."

"Who created the Elder runes?" I asked. "Someone did create them, right?"

"Aye, that would be before my time. I'm old, but I'm not *that* old."

"As you said," Monty said, "the elder runes were accessible to all."

"The elder runes, while accessible, still required immense skill and ability," Dex answered. "Only Archmages, or those close to that power level could use them."

"Wait, Monty's not an Archmage; how did he manage to use that rune against Mahnes?" I said, turning to Monty. "You're not an Archmage, are you?"

"Not in the least," Monty said, boiling the water for his tea. "Let him finish."

"The elder runes were inaccessible to the lower mages, who craved that level of power," Dex said, "Then, someone found a workaround. Something dark mages had known for some time."

"Life-force," Monty said, nodding slowly. "They used life force."

"Aye, and by using that, together with the elder runes, these inexperienced mages were able to access and use a level of power they couldn't before."

"That sounds like a bad idea," I said. "What happened to them?"

"They destroyed themselves, but the door had been opened," Dex said. "It was only a matter of time before someone found the right catalyst. The right combination."

"They found a way to stabilize the elder rune symbols," Monty said. "Without dying in the process."

Dex nodded.

"Life-force was too volatile, too difficult to control," Dex said. "They discovered something more stable and nearly as powerful."

"Blood," I said softly. "They started using blood."

"The blood mages became darker and stronger, a real threat," Dex said. "They were in the sects, and stopping them was almost impossible. Some of them splintered from the sects and formed new groups of dark mages."

"Did they survive?"

"Ach, dark mages don't play well with others, not even other dark mages," Dex replied. "Many of them died vying for positions of power and influence. The ones that remained... they couldn't move overtly against them."

"Why not?" I asked. "They had become dark mages using

forbidden magic. Why not just take them out? Boom. Problem solved."

"They couldn't, because too many of these dark mages were still part of the sects," Monty said. "It would destroy the Council of Sects. All of the sects would have been dissolved. It could have started a mage war."

"They arrived at another, more covert solution," Dex said, his voice grim. "A group was formed—a group of powerful mages who answered to no one as they quietly removed all those suspected of being dark mages."

"Verity," Monty said. "You're talking about Verity. I thought it was a myth?"

Dex shook his head.

"I wish it was," he said. "Some of the most powerful mages from all of the sects were chosen to form the three branches. The Eye, The Book, and The Blade, all led by Cain."

"Why does this group sound like bad news?"

"Because it is," Dex said. "Cain and Verity expunged the first dark mages accused of using elder runes. They were Judge, Jury, and Executioner."

"The Gloaming," Monty said. "You were there when it happened?"

"Aye, one of many," Dex said. "Those were dark times for mages."

"Many of those accused of being dark mages weren't," Monty said, an edge to his voice. "Many mages were falsely accused and killed because they were from the wrong sect, or had made enemies of the wrong family."

"I was there, Nephew," Dex said. "Whatever you've read doesn't compare to what really happened. Verity was merciless."

"The Gloaming made both the Spanish Inquisition and

the Salem witch trials look like a minor disagreement," Monty said. "Are you saying it was worse?"

"It's always worse. I lost friends and family to the blood runes and Verity," Dex answered. "Too many. Most of them good people, their only crime seeking to increase their power."

"To the blood runes?" I asked, confused. "How?"

Dex looked at me and nodded.

"I understand," he said, getting to his feet. "You turned down the offer. Power has no appeal to you. You're one of the rare ones, boy. Not everyone"—he glanced at Monty—"turns away from the lure of power. Verity knew this."

"What are you saying?" I said. "Monty used these blood runes once."

"To serve a greater good, yes?" Dex said. "Sounds quite noble, even."

"Because it is. What are you implying?"

"That, for many mages," Dex said, "my nephew included, it only takes one time to cause damage."

"He hasn't used the blood runes again after Mahnes."

"He hasn't used them again...yet," Dex said, narrowing his eyes at Monty. "But he'd be a lying fool if he denied the desire is there, just beneath the surface."

"What are you saying?"

"The power has a pull," Dex said. "It draws you into it. Next time, it will be to save a life. The time after that, to defeat an enemy. Every time there will be a good reason. Each one valid, each one a step closer to destruction."

"Monty?" I asked, turning to face him. "Is that where we are? Are you sliding into full Sith?"

"Of course not," Monty said after taking a sip of tea. "I have complete control of my faculties and choices."

Dex gave him a look and turned to me.

"Aye, Nephew, I've heard those exact words many times."

The knot in the pit of my stomach tightened.

"Where did you find the lost rune?" I asked. "The one you used against Mahnes."

"I told you, it—"

"You gave me a smokescreen," I said, cutting him off. "Don't bullshit me. I'm your shieldbearer. I'm supposed to protect you. That means from *all* danger, even if that danger is *you*."

"Aye, Nephew. Answer him," Dex said. "He, we, deserve to know."

The kitchen became charged with energy, and I could feel Dex's power slowly amp up. This was getting bad in a hurry.

"Very well," Monty said with a short sigh. "I managed to access Haven's Detention area. There, on the lowest level, which is currently empty, I discovered a portal access."

"You used the portal?" Dex asked. "You opened this access point?"

"Yes," Monty admitted. "I was bored senseless. Roxanne had effectively locked me into Haven."

"So you decided to do a little exploring?" I asked, slowly getting upset. "Are all mages insane? Nothing about this scenario screamed run away, don't open the portal?"

"Mages don't run away, and yes, we are all somewhat insane," Monty replied, glancing at Dex. "I'd say it's a prerequisite. My uncle is a prime example."

"Nay," Dex said, shaking his head. "I was insane long before I was a mage. Stepping into this world actually helped my madness."

"You were worse?" I asked. "How is that even possible?"

"Aye, I was," he said, turning to Monty. "Where did the portal lead?"

"Nowhere, or at least I thought so at first," Monty said. "After closer investigation I discovered I had found a passage to a sealed section of the Living Library."

"Ziller didn't sense you?" Dex asked. "How?"

"I don't know. Perhaps it was a self-contained section of the Library," Monty admitted. "I would assume the portal access didn't trip any of the alarms. It was there that I found the lost rune."

"Only one?" Dex asked. "There was only one?"

"Yes, only one, spread out among several tomes. It was monumentally difficult to decipher," Monty said. "Even when I was done with the research, I wasn't sure it would work. The first field test was against Mahnes."

"The first?" I asked. "You used an untested rune on Mahnes?"

"That rune wasn't exactly the 'try it out a few times' kind of rune," Monty said. "If I tried it and had copied it incorrectly, the consequences would have been catastrophic."

"If you had gotten it wrong, we could have all died."

"I didn't, and *you* wouldn't," Monty said. "After Mahnes, I realized the potential of what it was and opted to refrain from its use ever again."

I turned to Dex.

"Let me guess, it won't matter if Monty promises not to use that rune again, will it?"

"Not in the least," Dex said. "The portal access, lad. Tell me you sealed and destroyed it."

"Both," Monty said. "No one will be able to access the Library from that point ever again."

"I'll need to inform Ziller," Dex said. "This brings us to the second situation."

"I don't see it," I said. "Monty used a forbidden rune, but he's not going to do it again, right? Isn't that the whole point of this trip?"

"Doesn't matter," Dex said. "I told you, sometimes it only takes one use. In this case, my nephew seems unaffected, but his energy signature has been altered. Verity will see that and act accordingly."

"By act accordingly you mean—?"

"Expunged."

"Shit."

"Indeed," Dex said with a nod. "We need to get help before they unleash The Blades."

"What do you mean?" Monty asked. "I'm fine."

"In order for York to help you," Dex said, "you're going to need to be reset—realigned."

"Reset like a computer?" I asked. "Can you reboot a mage?"

"Reset like a dark mage brought back to the light," Dex said, his voice grim. "Only then can York help you."

"Help him do what, exactly?"

"York can help him achieve the Stormblood," Dex said, letting the words hang between us. "He's the only one I know who can in the time we have."

"The Stormblood?" Monty said, pensive. "Are you certain?"

"Ach, not in your current condition, no," Dex said. "That blood rune has mucked about with your energy signature. Ever since the schism you haven't been right. This has only made things worse. Much worse."

"How much worse?" I asked, recalling Dark Monty. "Are we dealing with a potential Darth Monty situation?"

"Get this boy out more," Dex said, giving me a look. "It means he needs to realign or York can't conduct the Stormblood ritual on him."

"What is this Stormblood?"

"It's not even worth discussing until he's realigned," Dex said, waving my words away. "There's only one person I know who will realign you and give you a chance of survival."

"Tempest?" Monty asked. "Will she do it?"

Dex nodded.

"Aye," Dex said. "I've spoken to her. She's done it before with some success."

"Some success?" I asked. "What are you saying?"

"She's managed to pull it off," Dex said. "Most of the times."

"And the other times?"

"The mage in question suffered a prolonged horrible death," Dex said. "It's still your choice, Nephew. You see her or I end it now."

"Whoa, what?" I nearly yelled. "How did we go from we need to see her to end it now? Slow down. What's going on?"

"What will it be, Nephew," Dex said, ignoring me. "Your choice."

"I'll go see her," Monty said after a moment. "I trust in her skill."

"Someone better explain what just happened, and fast."

"If he doesn't see Tempest," Dex said, "the alteration to his energy signature will unravel his mind over time. This will make the schism look like a mild cold. There's no coming back from blood-rune abuse."

"Abuse? He only used it once. How is that abuse?"

"The rune he used, the lost rune he used in his hubris, starts working after one use, especially after a schism," Dex said, his expression dark. "She's the only one that can help him now."

"If she fails?" I said. "What then?"

"Verity happens."

"What happens if they succeed?"

"Then my nephew will be given the burial a Montague deserves," Dex said, heading to his room. He cocked his head to one side and gave us a look. "It's not all bad news. You're going to go on an adventure, and that's always cause for good cheer."

"Even if it's full of death?"

"Especially if it's full of death," Dex said with small smile. "Speaking of death, that brings us to the third situation. Dealing with Verity."

"The third situation starts with death?"

"Aye," Dex said, looking at Monty. "You used the rune, with good reason, but you still used it. Verity will be hunting you. The Eye will be first. You need to be wary of their illusions. They are relentless."

"Bloody hell," Monty said under his breath. "The timing could not have been worse."

"What does that mean?" I asked. "What kind of illusions?"

"The kind that will have you believing your eyes instead of your instinct," Dex said. "The Eye uses a form of telepathy, limited as it is. Make sure you shield yourself."

"This mage is psychic?" I asked. "How are we supposed to deal with a psychic?"

"Not one person," Monty said. "According to my studies, they will try to capture me first. When that doesn't work, they use The Book—a group of highly proficient mages. If that fails, then they release The Blade—battlemages."

"You don't want it coming to that, lad," Dex said. "Cain leads The Blades personally."

"You know," I said, "I understood all of those words, just not in any context that makes actual sense."

"All three groups are part of Verity," Dex said. "The Eye are mages who are master illusionists. They will try to take my nephew without bloodshed."

"Without bloodshed sounds good."

"It won't work, but they will try," Dex said, glancing at Monty. "He'll see through the illusion, but they'll try it anyway. Mages find adapting to change difficult."

"Is that when The Book comes after him?" I asked. "What is that group, a bunch of angry librarians?"

Dex gave me a small smile and shook his head.

"The Book are the rank-and-file mages of Verity. What they may lack in power, and they are powerful, they make up for in numbers," Dex said. "They won't stop him either, but they will be difficult to deal with."

"You're worried about The Blade, aren't you?" I asked. "Please tell me it's a group of highly trained chefs, determined to make us eat delicious food, whether we want to or not."

"Always good to maintain a sense of humor, especially when death is staring you in the face," Dex said with a nod. "Best to face your demise with a grin...and a large blade."

"Okay, I'm guessing these people aren't renegade chefs."

Dex shook his head.

"If the sects had a police force, it would be The Blade," Dex said his voice somber. "These are elite trained battle mages, like my nephew, except with a few added centuries of experience. Those will be a substantial challenge. You don't want to face Cain."

"How do we deal with them?" I asked. "You have a strategy, right?"

"Aye, we present a difficult and fast-moving target," Dex said, clapping me on the shoulder. "Get your bags. We leave in a few hours."

Dex left the room.

ELEVEN

I looked at Monty, unable to form the words.

"Well, I think Dex finally discovered one way to make you speechless," Monty said with a small smile. "Miracles *can* happen."

"Oh, the humor," I said, deadpan. "Did you know you would trigger the Verity death squad by using that rune?"

"No," Monty answered. "I didn't believe they were real. Not much is documented about them, and what is written is contradictory. There is no documented connection between them and the lost runes. I would imagine this is by design."

"You think?" I asked. "Listen, I can appreciate gallows humor, but this isn't funny in the slightest."

"I don't think my uncle was trying to be funny," Monty said. "However, he has been known to pull a prank or two. Out of everyone in the family, he is certainly the one with the largest and most defined sense of humor."

"What you're trying to say is that he's the most deranged Montague in the family?"

"Well, there is that, yes," Monty said. "As far as I can

recall, he's the only one who possesses any semblance of humor, dark as it may be."

"That's depressing and scary all at once."

"That's my uncle. More on the scary side, though."

"I think Dex has been spending too much time with the Morrigan," I said. "She's beginning to rub off on him. Since when was he all Doom and Death and I'll have to end you now?"

"He's an old mage and a realist," Monty said. "Would you have preferred he lie?"

"Well, not exactly lie, but he could've softened the news a bit," I said. "One moment he's, 'We need to get you help.' The next, he's, 'Choose or die.' Are you sure the Morrigan isn't rubbing off on him?"

"I find that unlikely. My uncle is set in his ways of being. Not even she could alter his manner at this point."

"I'm just saying, hasn't he heard of breaking the news to someone gently?"

"How do you think he should have done it?" Monty asked before dropping into the best imitation of Dex I had ever seen. "You wanted him to say something along the lines of: 'Well, Nephew, aye. Your signature is altered. That's bad news for you. But, I have some good news. Instead of wiping you off the face of the earth, I could let Tempest attempt to help you, which may also kill you. If that fails—well, lad, I'll teleport you in pieces, before those Verity dogs get you. What will it be?'"

"Wow," I said, momentarily stunned. "That was actually a perfect Dex. Have you been practicing? How come you've never done that before?"

"I used to do it often, when I was younger."

"I've never heard you do a Dex. What made you stop?"

"I stopped because my uncle hates it, and the last time he

caught me and a group of friends doing our imitations of him, he violently teleported us out of his presence."

"How bad was it?"

"I do not enjoy being teleported to Siberia."

"Ouch," I said. "That sounds extreme."

"So was the weather," he said. "That experience ended my career imitating my uncle Dexter."

"Well, even though your imitation was spot on, this is horrible news," I said. "Why would one use of the rune affect you this badly?"

Monty rubbed his chin and gave it some thought before answering.

"Most likely because I began the use of the blood rune while still recovering from the schism," Monty said, after a moment. "My body and psyche were vulnerable. I had not fully recovered from the schism when I began my studies and deciphering of the lost rune."

"This is bad," I said, concerned. "Was he really ready to snuff you if you said no?"

"My uncle is a pragmatist," Monty said, looking away. "Do you recall how he showed up to our meeting at Ezra's?"

I shuddered at the thought.

"You mean the friendly neighborhood Harbinger Dex, complete with deadly axe-mace?"

"Yes," Monty said with a nod. "I think he is *always* prepared to remove us, or *anyone* close to him from the equation, if it means preventing us from becoming something worse, something evil."

"I totally understand that when it comes to you," I said. "But he's not *my* uncle. Why is he even looking my way when it comes to these things?"

"I did notice he didn't offer to end you earlier," Monty said. "That must have been a nice change."

"Easy for you to say," I shot back. "You've never had to face psycho Dex wielding that axe-mace, Nemain."

"True, but if it's any consolation, he reacts that way because he cares," Monty said after a brief pause. "You *are* family to him."

"That's comforting: he kills because he cares," I said. "Do you understand how insane that sounds?"

"Not as bad as his history," Monty said. "The rumors of my uncle in his dark days are troubling."

"Oh, troubling?" I said. "Is that what we're calling it these days? Dex is partnered with the Morrigan. I highly doubt he got *her* attention by being Kind Mage of the Year. Most likely it was through the deaths of many, many enemies across several battlefields."

"Most likely," Monty said. "As concerning as that may be, we will sort this out."

"Or you'll die," I shot back. "The options suck."

Monty stared at me.

"They're not optimal, no, but if this means I have access to the Stormblood, it's worth it."

"What exactly is it, this Stormblood?" I asked. "Is it some mage secret power?"

"Something like that," he said, heading down the corridor to his room. "I need to finish packing. I'll be right out."

I looked down at my hellhound, who glanced up at me for a second before padding to my room. I knew for a fact Monty had been packed about five minutes after he started earlier this afternoon. He was meticulous in the extreme and probably had a packed bag ready to go at all times.

"You're already packed," I said, raising my voice. "Why can't either of you answer a simple question? Maybe I'll learn Stormblood, and give it a proper name like Strongblood. You think I could learn this thing?"

"No," they both answered simultaneously from their rooms. "You're not a mage."

"Unbelievable," I muttered as I stepped into my room, grabbed my bag and headed back to reception. "You two are impossible."

There were a few things that were nagging at me. I was concerned about this realignment, even though I wondered if I could speak to Tempest to give Monty a sense-of-humor-alignment when she realigned him.

Mostly, I was concerned about him surviving not one, but two dangerous rituals and some ancient group of mages out to expunge him.

Whatever York had to do to access this Stormblood, I was certain it was dangerous and potentially lethal. It seemed to me that this was just the way things were in this world.

If you wanted to level up, there was a cost. There was always a cost. Most of the time it was steep. Sometimes, it was so steep it could mean your life. That brought me back to Kali and her wonderful new and improved mark.

What was she thinking?

Somewhere in our brief conversations, I had to have missed something. Some fine print I overlooked. I didn't recall ever agreeing to be the designated target for her successors. This was all an upside for them, but where was the upside for me?

As far as I knew, the curse and the mark were independent of each other. One kept me alive and the other made me a target for death. It was all very Kali-esque. Was she was getting her sadistic kicks by sending successors to kill someone who couldn't die? Why?

Dex appeared in the reception area and sat in one of the readily available Eames lounge chairs. He put his head back and closed his eyes with a low grunt and a loud sigh.

"These are very relaxing," he said. "That Roxanne really knows her chairs. I can fall asleep right here."

Roxanne had recently gifted us the chairs, having accused our reception area of being sterile and unwelcoming.

I told her it may have had something to do with the fact that no one was allowed to sit in the Hansen. She replied with two Eames lounge chairs and assorted smaller chairs, all ridiculously overpriced. The note attached to the pair of Eames read: *No one is allowed to sit on the Hansen. They can sit on these.*

Peaches padded into the reception area and parked between Dex and me. I made for the kitchen and grabbed my industrial-sized mug of Deathwish off the counter.

"Dex," I started after taking a long pull of javambrosia goodness that kicked my brain into overdrive, "can you see my new mark?"

"Aye," he said, keeping his eyes closed. "How many have tried to kill ye?"

"One, so far," I said. "A glowing ogre. Contestant number two in the Dust Simon Show is named Dira. She's a Black Rose. Ring any bells?"

"Mage assassins. Nasty bunch if I recall, hard to kill," he said. "They have neutralizing blades that nullify magic. You should be fine, though, not being a mage or anything of that sort."

"Well, now I feel so much better," I said. "Any ideas on how to deal with them that don't involve my being sliced and diced?"

"None come to mind," he said. "I've never had to deal with successors or a Mantle of Discord, although I've had plenty of enemies after me trying to relieve me of my life. What do you want to know? Don't beat around the tree, boy. Ask."

"How did they find him?" I asked. "How does Verity know he used the lost rune?"

"Everything is connected," he said, still keeping his eyes closed. "Energy is energy. The elder runes tap directly into the quintessence."

"Quintessence?"

"Everything comes from, and returns to, quintessence," Dex said. "Elder runes are closer to the source than any other kind of rune."

"And Verity could sense them?"

"Using elder runes sends ripples through everything. Verity's job, their purpose, is to make sure they *aren't* used. For them, it was like seeing the sun at night. There was no escaping their vigilance. Now, ask your *real* question."

I sighed, and took another pull from my mug.

"Why did she do it?"

"That's a broad question, boy," Dex said with a chuckle, eyes still closed. "I know many women who have done many questionable things. Narrow it down for me a bit."

"Why did Kali do it?" I asked, throwing a hand up in exasperation. "Why did she give me this insane bullseye on my forehead?"

"Ach, I understand," Dex said, opening his eyes and sitting up. "You think she just wants to make your life more difficult?"

"Kind of seems that way, yes,' I said. "You think I'm wrong?"

"You think, Kali, a goddess, is going to play this petty game just to aggravate you? Is that what you think?"

"I just said that."

"I'm just trying to understand," he said, holding up a hand. "What you're saying is that your existence is so essential to this goddess, that she spends *her* days pondering about *your* insignificant life?"

"Well when you put it that way—"

"*You* are so important to her, you, a human, that doesn't even worship her, that an immortal *goddess* lays awake at night roaming her realm, wondering what is on *your* puny mind?"

"Okay, there's no need to exaggerate. I mean—"

"You mean, Kali, *the* Kali, gave you this mark because she was bored? She wanted to spice things up and said: 'Hmm, why don't I curse this human alive and then give him a mark so everyone will try and kill him...but they won't be able to because I cursed him alive. What fun!'"

I stared at him.

"Well, yes," I said. "Why else would she do this if not to make my life hell?"

"That," he said, pointing at me. "Is the right question. Why indeed."

He rested his head back and closed his eyes again.

"Thanks for that profound and completely vague non answer."

"My pleasure," Dex said with a smile. "Ask yourself: why send successors to eliminate someone who can't die?"

"I have."

"What answer did you get?"

"I didn't get an answer. That's why I asked you."

"I gave you an answer, boy," Dex said, opening his eyes again as Monty entered the reception area. "Weren't you paying attention?"

"I'm ready," Monty said, placing his bag on the floor. "How are you going to do this, Uncle?"

"We start with debriefing the pup," Dex said, looking at me "You did debrief the pup, aye?"

"Yes," I said. "Do you want me to go over it again with him?"

"If you'd be so kind," Dex said. "Never hurts to be certain. Especially with hellhounds."

TWELVE

<Hey, boy. Do you remember when I told you we needed to go on a trip?>

<Where you go I go. We are bondmates.>

<True. But I'm going to need you to go with Dex for a little while.>

<Why? We are bondmates. I am not bondmates with the old man.>

<I know, and we are going to end up in the same place. We're just taking different routes.>

<Where are you going? Are you going to the bad-smell room?>

<No. I'm not going to the bathroom. It's just that we have to go to a certain place and we can't go together.>

<Why? If you ate more meat, you would be strong enough that we could go together. Ask the old man to make you meat. He makes good meat.>

<This has nothing to do with my diet. We have to try and sneak in somewhere, and you are too powerful. They will detect you.>

<If you ate more meat you could be as powerful as me. Why are we sneaking in?>

<Because dangerous people are looking for us, and if we go together they will find us and try to hurt us.>

<We can stop any dangerous people. Who wants to hurt you? The glowing orange lady?>

<Yes, and other people like her. If you go with him, Dex will make extra-large sausages for you.>

<Extra large? How extra?>

<You aren't worried about my being hurt anymore?>

<You said extra large, and you are my bondmate. I will not let anyone hurt you. How extra?>

<As big as you want them to be?>

<I want them to be very big. Meat is important. I am growing.>

<I'll make sure to remind him.>

<Don't forget to tell him extra. You said extra.>

"He's been debriefed," I said, looking at Dex. "You're going to have to make some extra-large sausages for him, though."

"Ach, a small price to pay to travel with such a fearless creature," Dex said, creating a large sausage. "This should hold ye for a few."

Peaches inhaled the sausage, so fast that for a second I thought my eyes were playing tricks on me.

<That large enough?>

<It's going to need to be extra.>

I shook my head and took another pull from my mug.

"Next?" I said. "How are you going to mask"—I waved my hand around my head—"this mark Kali graced me with?"

"I'm not," Dex said. "I'm powerful, but that mark is on another level. Besides, I don't want Kali coming after me for tampering with her Chosen. I have one dangerous goddess in my life, why would I want another?"

"Good point," I said with a slow nod. "What, then? Because this is not my department."

"I know," Dex said with a grin. "I'm going to give you a

temporary solution that might be slightly unpleasant, but should work."

"That sounds like a recipe for agony," I said. "Is that what we're discussing here?"

"You will feel slightly out of sorts, but it should be manageable."

Mages were the masters of understatement. If Dex was saying I would "feel out of sorts," it meant this was going to be total and complete upheaval, primarily of my digestive system.

"Explain it to me," I said, holding up a hand as he approached. "In plainspeak, not magespeak."

"Of course," Dex said, clearing his throat. "I will trace a multiphasic teleportation circle on your person. Said circle will last the better part of eight hours—plenty of time to get on your flight and land in Heathrow. In that time, your energy signature will appear slightly out of phase with this plane."

"Isn't that dangerous?" Monty asked, concerned. "He will be under a constant teleport."

"Well, if it were anyone else, I'd be concerned, aye," Dex said, looking at me. "Prolonged multiphasing is usually fatal, but it's not a worry in this case, is it? Not like he can die or anything."

"So glad to be the resident guinea pig you can test your theories on."

"Still," Monty said. "It's dangerous even if he is death-challenged."

Dex waved Monty's words away as he kept his gaze focused on me.

"It's harmless unless he tries to teleport while multiphasic," Dex said with a shake of his head. "Then that could get dicey, bits of you everywhere. It would be a bloody mess."

"Got it. No teleporting while multiplastic—"

"Multiphasic," Dex corrected. "This won't hide your

mark, exactly, but it will bounce you all over the place, making it nearly impossible to locate the real you."

"Teleportation doesn't really agree with my body."

"I thought you had worked that out?" Dex said. "In any case, by the time your flight is done, teleportation should never be a problem for you ever again."

"That bad?"

"Well, I won't lie, it's not pleasing, but try not to view it that way. See it as mostly mild discomfort."

"Can you elaborate on what you mean by 'mild discomfort'?"

"Upset stomach. Nothing major really—some dizziness, loss of balance, slurred speech, blurry vision, temporary blindness, headaches, nosebleeds, body aches, fatigue, and fine motor dysfunction," Dex said, rattling off the effects on his fingers. "I think that's all."

I stared at him.

"No spontaneous combustion?"

Dex looked at me, perplexed.

"Why would there be spontaneous combustion?" he asked. "There's no explosive component to this circle." He rubbed his chin. "Although, you may experience some hot flashes from time to time. Shouldn't be too severe, if I recall correctly. I think that's all."

"That's all? For eight hours?"

"Give or take," he said, wiggling his fingers. "Ready?"

"No," I said, quickly holding up a hand to block the finger wiggle of death. "What happens if I don't take this multi-destructive circle?"

"You want the bad or very bad?"

"Bad first, please," I said. "You can hit me with the very bad afterwards."

"Aye. The bad, then," Dex said with a nod. "The moment you land, the Penumbra Consortium will be waiting for you with open arms. They have agents stationed at all the major conventional egress and ingress points of the country. They will take you into custody, and because you two were such well-behaved guests of the country on your last visit, they will gleefully designate you both STACC. Then they will henceforth begin proceedings to convict you under said designation and sentence you to the highest punishment possible."

"What's that, banishment?" I asked. "What's a STACC?"

"Significant Threat Against Crown and Country," Monty said. "The penalty for this designation is death. I believe Mathers mentioned something about that when we saw him last."

"Well, shit," I said. "What's very bad?"

"You get on that plane," Dex said, putting an arm gently on my shoulder, "and while you're somewhere over the Atlantic, that successor of yours decides to strike, taking out the plane in an effort to end your life."

"You really think she would try to take out the plane?"

"If she thinks it will end your life, yes," he said. "She will fail, of course. You and my nephew will survive; I can't say the same for all those innocent souls on the plane. *You* will be solely responsible for their deaths."

"I understand," I said, my voice grim. "Circle me."

"Aye," Dex said, and began tracing symbols. "This will be a little uncomfortable. Brace yourself."

Dex stepped close to me and began gesturing.

His hands gave off a pale green glow, as he traced indecipherable symbols in the air in front of me. He began mumbling something under his breath, but I couldn't make out what.

After about a minute of this, he placed his hands together, as if in prayer, and then slowly spread them apart. An amazing circle of energy formed between his hands. I had seen his teleportation circles in the past, but this was different. This one rotated and shifted, the symbols juxtaposing over each other, turning one way then the other. Some of them switched locations, as the circle slowly, continually rotated in the air before me.

"That...that is amazing," I said, barely above a whisper. "How long does it take to learn something like that?"

Dex smiled at me and shook his head.

"You're immortal. One day, if you're still around for a few more centuries, we can discuss the *basics* of this type of circle."

"Not happening?"

"Don't feel bad," Dex assured me. "This one is beyond most. A few more things before I place this on you."

"More? More pain?"

"Don't be daft," Dex said. "There will be plenty of opportunity for more pain in your future. Tristan?"

"Yes, Uncle?" Monty asked. "Logistics?"

"Aye," Dex said with a nod. "Once I place this circle, the boy here will be about as useful as a wet napkin in a rainstorm. Cecil should have a car downstairs in a few minutes."

"You called Cecil?" I asked. "How did you manage—?"

"Robert will be downstairs," Dex continued. "I don't expect any trouble on this side, but when you get to London, expect to see Penumbra mages in the airports. They're standard now, thanks to your last visit."

"Will they sense us?" Monty asked. "My signature?"

"The boy here will stick out like a sore throat, but he will just have airsickness. You, on the other hand, will be masked. This should get you past them."

"What about Verity?" Monty asked. "They should be better than the Consortium at detecting masks."

"They are," Dex said. "I would expect them to appear at any moment, not just when you cross over. They take themselves very seriously. I would imagine an attempt before you get to the airport."

"Before?" I asked.

"Aye," Dex said as his circle slowly rotated in front of me. "It will be harder to apprehend my nephew in London. The Consortium and the BPD will curtail their movement. Remember, Verity doesn't exist. They like to keep it that way."

"Where are we going once we get there?" I asked, concerned that this plan seemed semi-flimsy. "I'm not getting a set vibe about this landing. Is there going to be anyone to meet us at the airport?"

"No, why?" Dex said. "Did you ask someone to meet you there?"

"Well, no. I mean——"

"You don't want anyone meeting you there," Dex said, poking me in the chest. "If there is someone waiting for you, something went terribly wrong. Understood?"

"Totally," I said, rubbing my chest. "No need for the violence."

"No casting on the plane, by either of you," Dex said, his voice soft as granite. "I'm going to say it again slowly for the hard of understanding. Do not, under any circumstances, cast on the plane——period."

"What if we're attacked?"

"By whom?" Dex asked. "No one will know who you are... unless you cast."

"Good point."

"Once you are out of the airport, SuNaTran will have a car waiting for you," Dex continued. "This car will take you to the New Forest, about sixty-five miles away from Heathrow."

"Why are we going to a forest?"

"It's the only way to find Tempest," Dex said. "The verderers will announce your presence at the edge of the forest and you wait. She will find you. Do not enter the forest alone if you want to exit alive."

"Are you telling me her address is The New Forest?"

"More or less, yes," Dex said, touching the edges of the floating circle. "Don't try and understand it. She likes her privacy, the forest, and the animals that dwell within more than she enjoys the company of people."

"She's an Earth Witch," Monty said. "Can't these verderers lead us to her home?"

"They won't help you," Dex said, "except to announce your presence. She fiercely protects the forest and the animals. Their loyalty is to her above all."

"What are verderers?"

"Think park rangers," Monty said. "People tasked with keeping the grounds and taking care of the animals within the park."

"Aye, New Forest is Crown land," Dex warned. "Try not to destroy anything while you are there. She won't be pleased, and I need not tell you what will happen if she becomes displeased."

"Where will you be?" I asked, suddenly aware that we were entering this place without Dex, and this Tempest seemed hostile at best. "Are you meeting us there?"

"Aye," Dex said. "I'll meet you at her house. I have a few stops to make first. One of my sources has a location for York. I'll be following up on that to make sure it's not a waste of time, and then I'll meet you at Tempest's."

"Does she know to expect us?" I asked, to reaffirm he had made the plans. "She does know we're coming, right? We're not going to crash this forest and end up as target practice for this Tempest?"

"No one in the Ten dares approach her home uninvited," Dex said, focusing on the circle. "Except perhaps TK, who is fearsome in her own right. Other than her, everyone in the

Ten respects the Tempest's privacy. If you are going to her forest, rest assured, I announced your visit first."

"So...she knows we're coming? I'm just making sure."

"She *knows*," Dex said with a sigh. "She may be a bit prickly at first, she never was a social one. I'm sure you two, on your best behavior, will win her over immediately. Ready?"

I nodded.

"Let's do this," I said, grabbing onto the counter. "Hit me."

Dex released the circle. It floated gently over to me and my world twisted in a flash of green.

THIRTEEN

"Give him a moment," Dex said, looking at me as I gripped the edge of the sink. "His body is adjusting. Now you, Nephew."

"I can mask myself," Monty said, holding up a hand and stepping back. His voice indicated he didn't want any of what Dex was selling. "Thank you."

"Stop being daft," Dex said. "I'm not placing a circle on you. Verity is after *you*. You need an inhibiting mask to throw off The Eye. Also, if the Consortium realize who you really are, who do you think they will hand you over to for questioning?"

"I haven't the slightest—"

"Head Inspector Matthew Mathers," Dex said. "Director of the BPD-London Office. I'm sure he'd be pleased to have you in custody, you two being such great friends and all."

"Wasn't that the officer that promised to hunt you down?" I asked. "He mentioned something about violently erasing you personally?"

"Mathers made Head Inspector?" Monty asked. "Impressive. Does this mean an increased BPD presence at Heathrow?"

"Aye, he's the one who pushed for the recent lockdown on London," Dex said with a nod. "Using your last visit as the reason to heighten security."

"It must have worked," Monty said. "Promotion and a lockdown? Matthew must be feeling quite full of himself these days."

"Do *not* cross him, lad," Dex warned. "I know you have history. Be the bigger man and let it go, understand? There's too much at stake to risk it for some childish rivalry."

"Understood," Monty said. "I had no intention of—"

My stomach decided that this was a good time to eject all of its contents. After about a minute, I looked up from the sink where it appeared I had emptied the contents of my stomach...several times.

It was not pretty.

"You call this adjusting?" I managed through the haze of blinding pain between my ears. I checked one of my ears and examined my hand. "Amazing."

"What are you doing?" Monty asked, grabbing me by the arm and keeping me upright. "There's nothing wrong with your ears."

"I was just checking to see if my brain was leaking out of them," I said, holding down the overwhelming desire to hurl whatever was left in my stomach as the earth tilted on its axis again. "Whoa...whoa."

I dry heaved a few more times before my body settled into what felt like an uneasy pre-hurl state: not quite there, but not far away either.

"Keep him near the sink, just in case," Dex said, giving me a concerned look. "He should be done by now, but you never know. Now, stand still."

Dex gestured and green symbols floated over to Monty, falling on him gently. He was briefly covered in a bright green aura which vanished a few seconds later.

"Did it work?" Monty asked after a moment of self-examination. "I still have access to my ability."

"It's a mask," Dex said, looking at Monty. "It's not for you. It's for Verity and the agents at the airport. Have you forgotten how inhibiting masks work?"

"I'm aware of their properties," Monty said. "I've just never had any use—"

"For being stealthy," Dex finished. "I know. Don't worry, next time I'll make you a disintegration mask. That way, any inanimate object you come in contact with will immediately explode into its component parts. That more your preference, lad?"

I nearly burst out laughing, but my stomach had other ideas.

"That's not remotely amusing," Monty said, raising an eyebrow at me. "How long will this mask last?"

"About as long as his circle," Dex said looking at me. "You're looking a little green, boy. Maybe you should sit down?"

Dex pointed to one of the Eames.

"I may be ill, but I'm not suicidal enough to sit even *near* the Hansen with my stomach like this."

"A valid point," Monty said as he opened the faucet. "Stay near the sink."

"I'm supposed to fly like this?" I asked, glancing at Dex. I didn't dare move my head too quickly. The chances of the nausea overtaking me were too great. "I don't...don't see it happening."

"No choice, boy," Dex said, looking at his watch. "Robert should be downstairs. Get your innards under control, say goodbye to your creature, and we'll catch up with you across the pond."

Peaches padded over to where I stood, propped up by Monty. He gave me a short whine and bumped my leg with his enormous head. Thankfully he was being gentle and I managed to keep my knee connected to the rest of my leg.

I reached out a hand and rubbed his head behind his ears.

<Hey, boy. Make sure you behave with Dex.>

<Do you need meat? I'm sure the old man can make you some meat. You look sick. Did you make some of your meat and eat it?>

The nausea threatened to make a comeback at the repeated mention of meat.

<No. I promise not to do that again. I'm good. This is all so I can hide. I'll be fine. Go with Dex and I'll see you soon.>

<You smell like old bad food. Is that so you can hide, too?>

<Yes, all part of the disguise. Now, I have to get on the plane. Be a good boy and listen to Dex.>

<I'm always good. I will know where you are. If you need help, call me.>

Peaches padded over to where Dex stood and waited.

I doubted his ability to track me extended over an ocean, but since we had never tested his range and he didn't come with a hellhound manual, I wasn't sure.

He sounded certain, and he was growing in power. It was possible that as he got older and stronger, his range to sense our bond increased. I'd have to ask Hades the next time I saw him.

"Done," I said, heaving as I grabbed my stomach. "Be safe."

"You may want to wash up before heading out," Dex said, giving me a once over and scrunching his face up in disgust. "You smell like putrid fish, the both of you."

"Wow, thanks," I said. "Not like *you* had anything to do with that."

"This thing you have with your bonds will be sorted sooner than you think," Dex said, narrowing his eyes at me. "Whether you want to face it or not."

"What's that supposed to mean?" I asked. "I thought I had it sorted."

"Sorted, my arse. If ye had, you wouldn't be trying to throw up your intestines all over the place," Dex said, wagging a finger at me. "Get it under control."

"Well, I can see the motivational speech gene is strong in the family," I said, fighting another wave of nausea. "I'm feeling more 'under control' by the second."

Dex nodded.

"If it all goes according to plan, we'll see each other in about eight hours," Dex said, forming a large circle under himself and Peaches. "Remember what I said—no active casting of any sort. None. Nephew, remember to shield your thoughts. The mask will help, but Verity is good. As long as neither of you cast, this should be easy."

"No casting from me, that's for sure," I said, turning to Monty, who averted his face from what I imagined was my pestilent breath. "How about you?"

"Right after I burn this jacket, and pack some mints, I'll make sure not to cast."

"Did I throw up on you?" I asked, gazing at the large smudge on his suit jacket. "Sorr...sorry about that. Dex kind of caught me by surprise."

"No apologies needed," he said. "I can always wear the new jacket Piero provided."

"Right, get it sorted and don't miss your flight," Dex said, taking the small bag that held Grim Whisper, my flask of javambrosia, and assorted items we couldn't carry on the plane. "See you soon."

A green flash filled the space around us. When I could see again, Dex and Peaches were gone. I let my senses expand

and felt the strong bond I shared with Peaches. Maybe he *could* sense me wherever he was.

"I suggest you don't do that on the plane," Monty said. "You may as well send out a beacon to the successor."

"You could sense that?"

"It's quite potent, though I think it has more to do with your hellhound's increase in power than your own," he said, walking me to the bathroom. "Even that simple act of expanding your senses to locate your creature can trigger the Consortium—or worse, the successor."

"I don't need or want that kind of attention, at least not on a plane."

"If you refrain from searching for your creature or creating your magic missile, we should be fine."

"What about Verity? They could be after you right now."

"According to my notes, scarce as they are, Verity is more bureaucracy than anything else," he assured me. "I doubt they even know where I am."

"Bureaucracies may be slow to get going, but once they gain speed, they're hard to stop, if not impossible," I said. "Dex seemed really concerned about them."

"My uncle occasionally worries too much," Monty said. "Ever since my father passed—"

"I get it," I said. "He's stepping in and looking out for you. That doesn't mean his concern is wrong."

"No, it just means it's misplaced," Monty said. "We have more to worry about with this York character than we do with any agents from Verity—which for the record, have not been sighted in the last five decades."

"Right," I said. "Well, for the record, that magic missile on the plane wasn't my fault."

"Of course not."

"I don't think I could create anything now even if I wanted to," I said, a vise grip of death squeezing my temples, as sweat poured from my brow. "Is it getting hot in here?"

"Focus, Simon. You're much stronger than you think," Monty said, leaving me at the bathroom door. "I'll bring you the new suit Piero sent over. Get out of those clothes and wash up. It should help alleviate the side effects."

I stripped and took a freezing shower to try and offset the effects of Dex's circle. When I was done, I felt almost human. Monty had laid out the new suit on my bed.

Piero, as usual, had outdone himself. I could tell the clothing was subtly runed. Nothing intricate, like Monty's Zegnas—I wasn't a mage, after all—but just enough to provide durability and protection.

I stepped out into the reception where Monty waited.

"How do you feel?" he asked when he saw me. "Piero did an outstanding job, as expected."

"I feel pretty normal, actually," I said, bending over to pick up my bag and slamming my head into the counter as I stumbled forward. When I managed to regain my balance, Monty was a blurry image in my vision. "Ow. I take that back. This is going to truly suck."

"Your curse will work to mitigate the worst of the effects," Monty said, helping me stand. "My uncle's ability is staggering. To be able to circumvent both Kali's curse and mark, and place your body temporarily out of phase with this plane—it's incredible."

"I'm pleased you find this torturefest so fascinating," I said, rubbing my head. "It's not so much fun from this side. Are you sure they won't sense Dex's circle when we land?"

"Not likely."

"Won't they pick up on the runes in the clothing?"

"No. Piero is a master craftsman," Monty said, straightening out a sleeve. "Even my jacket, which is heavily runed, is nearly undetectable."

"What about Kali's new mark of 'kick my ass'?" I asked. "Will they sense that?"

"Hmm...It's unlikely," Monty said. "None of the agents at Heathrow will be successors. They wouldn't know what to look for. Ready?"

"Not really, but it's not like I have a choice."

"Not true," Monty said, holding the front door open for me. "We can always stay here and face Chaos with our limited resources. He would most likely kill us and everyone we know and care for, but there is a choice."

I stopped walking for a moment and stared at him.

"That's not a choice, that's suicide," I said, before stepping into the outside corridor. "We have to level you up if we're going to have a chance of stopping him."

Monty turned and pressed parts of the door in sequence, locking it.

"I'm not the only one leveling up, *Aspis*," Monty said, double-checking the sequence before stepping back with a nod. "You need to get a handle on your power if we're going to have a chance at this."

I nodded as we headed to the stairs.

"You think we could take a vacation after all this?" I asked. "A real one. You know, a beach, crystal-clear water, and lots of quiet?"

"A beach?" Monty asked. "With plenty of sun?"

"Of course with plenty of sun, why would I want to go to the beach when it's cloudy?" I asked. "I mean, I get that you come from the land of little- to-no sun, but really, the beach and sun kind of go together. Don't you think?"

"Well, I was just considering how you were going to explain this vacation to your vampire," Monty answered. "Perhaps if she packed extra industrial sun block? I hear they make an SPF 100. Would that suffice, I wonder? Maybe you can get it doubled?"

"Oh, unleashing the drolltasticness?" I countered. "Well, at least Chi didn't pull a Rapunzel on me and lock me not into a room, but an *entire rune-covered wing* of Haven, with extra mage security for *my safety,* while I recovered from a schism. Can we say slightly overprotective?"

"No, your vampire went further," Monty said, narrowing his eyes. "She marked and claimed *you.*"

"I have news for you, Monty," I said, returning his look with a level-three Clint Glint of my own. "You're delusional if you don't think Rox—Miss Secure-an-Entire-Wing-With-Runes-and-Security—hasn't done the same thing to you."

"Good point," he said. "Well, if we can get over those *minor* obstacles, provided we are not in imminent danger, and as long as this plane of existence is safe, I don't see why a vacation would be contraindicated. Do you?"

"Basically, we're never going on vacation," I said with a groan as my stomach rumbled. "We could've gone somewhere warm and isolated."

"I could always speak to Hades," Monty offered. "I'm sure it's warm *in* Hades, and everyone there is deceased. It can't get any more isolating than being the only living among the dead."

"Your ideas are horrible," I said, stumbling down the last few steps and catching myself by grabbing the handrail. "Why do I even bother? Is it too much to ask for two weeks away where no one is trying to kill us?"

"You," Monty said as we stepped into the Rolls Royce Phantom waiting for us. "Where no one is trying to kill *you.* Hello, Robert."

The gentle pounding in my head stepped up to an Irish jig the moment I sat in the back. I rubbed my head to try and calm it down.

"Good evening, Mr. Montague, Mr. Strong," Robert said, tipping his cap and looking as dapper as ever. "We should be at the airport in one hour. There's some traffic in the Midtown Tunnel, but it's the fastest route."

"Excellent, Robert," Monty said. "The fastest route would be preferable."

"Hey, Robert," I said with a nod. "Long time no see. Can you make sure to take it easy on the turns? My stomach is a bit delicate tonight."

"Indeed," Robert replied with another nod. "Mr. Cecil sends his regards."

"Very good," Monty said. "I can use this time to—"

"To explain what this Stormblood is? That way there's no surprises later—you know, when we're running for our lives?"

"Don't be such a pessimist," Monty said. "Besides, you need to focus on those side effects of yours. Your body will only handle so much."

"You've got to be kidding me," I said, strapping in to my seat. "You're the realist. I'm just adopting your attitude. I'd rather be prepared than blindsided by this Stormblood."

Monty glanced at me, and then forward to Robert, who was dutifully ignoring us, but carefully listening to our every word. He was good, but not subtle enough. I got the hint.

"Not a subject to be discussed at this time," Monty said firmly."Better to wait until we land."

"Then what?" I asked. "You're going to use this time to...?"

"To get some much-needed sleep," Monty replied. "I'm certain it will be impossible on the plane."

A sharp pain ran down the back of my head and stabbed me in the neck. Bright lights flashed in my vision for a few seconds before calming down to excruciating. I could feel the sweat forming on my brow and the skin on my face felt clammy.

"You look dreadful," Monty said. "What's the matter? Is it your fear of flying?"

Something was wrong.

Monty knew I wasn't scared of heights or flying. For him to insinuate I had a fear of flying meant we were in trouble —now.

"You know how I get before a flight," I said. "It's just nerves. I'll be fine once we get airborne. It's the anticipation, that and not being able to see the ground."

"You know what they say, seeing can be overrated," Monty said, looking out of the window. "A shame we couldn't get better seats."

"Dex didn't put us in First Class?" I asked, as Robert pulled away. "You could have gotten plenty of sleep then."

"He wants us to blend in," Monty said, closing his eyes as he laid his head back. "First Class will be scrutinized by the Consortium. Mages, when they do fly, make sure to always fly First Class. They like to give the appearance of normalcy."

"Makes sense," I said, feeling another wave of migraine madness heading my way just as I lost sight in my right eye. "I'm just going to rest my eyes for a bit. My stomach isn't exactly settled."

"Refrain from evacuating your stomach in the car," Monty said, keeping his eyes closed. "Robert can stop if you do need to relieve yourself."

"It's not called relieving yourself," I said. "You *can* say throw up, or hurl, or even vomit. It's not like a trigger or something."

"Do tell," Monty said. "I'd rather not."

A small section of the Phantom opened next to me and a large plastic bag was exposed.

"Please feel free to hurl in the bag, Simon," Robert said with a nod. "I'll take care of it."

Monty sat up and raised an eyebrow.

"You, Robert," I said, putting my head back and closing my eyes, "are the man."

"Thank you, sir."

FOURTEEN

I focused on my breath and settled deeper into my surroundings. Something felt off about the Phantom, but I couldn't put my finger on it. The hairs standing up on the back of my neck kept giving me the nagging feeling that someone was following me. I turned and looked out of the rear window.

"How out of phase am I exactly?" I asked as I kept scanning the cars behind us. "Just out of curiosity."

"Why do you ask?" Monty said, opening his eyes. I noticed that he had begun tracing symbols slowly with one hand while pretending to rest his eyes. "What are you looking for?"

"A successor trying to kill me, for starters?"

"Impossible," Monty scoffed. "You should be completely invisible to the successor."

"Are you in imminent danger, sir?" Robert asked from the front. "I can assure you this vehicle has been given the Montague treatment."

"The what?" Monty asked, raising his voice. "What did you say?"

"Yes, Robert," I said, trying to hold back a laugh. "What did you say? The what treatment?"

"No offense, sir," Robert said, his voice worried. "It's what Mr. Cecil calls the extra-protection package."

"None taken," Monty said, his words clipped. "Please, get us to the airport as quickly as possible."

"Understood, sir."

Monty acted like it was nothing, but I could tell he was bothered, so I decided to help him. I mean, that's what shield warriors are for. Beneath it all, there was an undercurrent of wrongness.

It was like looking at a painting that was just slightly off-level.

You knew something was off, even if you couldn't put your finger on it immediately.

"So, Robert?"

"Yes, Simon?"

"Why does Cecil call it the Montague treatment?" I asked, glancing at Monty. "I'm asking for a friend."

Monty glared daggers in my direction, but I ducked and continued.

"Well..." Robert started, and I waved him on. "Mr. Cecil, after working on Mr. Stryder's car"—he shuddered—"and your recent car, he started repurposing some of the runes to make the new Phantoms stronger. He calls them his Indestructibles."

"I see," Monty said dryly. "I would imagine these *Indestructibles* all received the Montague treatment?"

"Yes, sir," Robert replied. "They are in high demand. I think Mr. Cecil plans to use the M-Treatment on all of the SuNaTran vehicles. It's very good."

"The same runes he used recently on our vehicle and Mr. Stryder's?" Monty asked. "The exact ones?"

"Yes, sir," Robert answered. "He said they were excellent and durable."

"He did, did he?" Monty said pensively. "Imagine that." He looked at me. "Using the same runes he used on Mr. Stryder's car for all his vehicles."

"They are excellent and durable," I said, picking up Monty's lead and running with it. "Do you know why he"—I did my best to refrain from smiling—"calls it the M-Treatment?"

"Yes, sir," Robert replied. "He said that the only thing that could damage one of his new cars was a Montague gone mad and let loose on the streets."

"That's quite an honor. Wow," I said, glancing at Monty, who was livid. "High praise indeed."

"I agree," Robert said, his voice serious. "The M-Treatment saved my life a few weeks back." Robert looked into the rear-view mirror. "Thank you, sir."

"You're welcome, Robert," Monty said, keeping his voice neutral. "When you see Cecil, after dropping us off, please inform him that he and I need to speak...face-to-face."

"Will do, sir."

Monty pressed the button on his side that raised the partition between us and Robert, effectively isolating us. He gestured, and a few seconds later I realized he had created a sphere of silence around us.

"You don't want to continue discussing the M-Treatment?" I asked with a wince, as the pain in my neck intensified. "Since when did Cecil want to rune every SuNaTran vehicle with death runes?"

"Caught that, did you?" Monty said, turning to look behind us. "Get ready."

"Get ready?" I asked. "I'm always ready."

"I'm sure you are," Monty said, gesturing again. "In the meantime, you may want to brace for impact."

"Brace for—?"

A large gray truck slammed into the rear of the Phantom.

I wasn't ready.

Nothing happened.

"This isn't a sphere of silence?" I asked, looking behind us. "What did you cast?"

"Does it appear that we need to discuss sensitive topics at the moment?" Monty asked, still gesturing. "How are you feeling?"

"Like shit," I snapped. "My head wants to split in two. You're asking this, because...? What did you do?"

"I placed an energy buffer around the vehicle," Monty said. "Think of it as an energy bumper." He looked to the front and raised his voice. "Robert, you may want to increase the velocity. Please."

"Right, sir," Robert called back. "Please, hold on."

I felt the Phantom leap forward as Robert stepped on the gas.

"Didn't Dex say no casting?"

"No *active* casting," Monty corrected. "This is a passive cast; a shield of sorts. It displaced the energy of the impact, which is why we didn't feel anything."

"A shield, like my dawnward?" I asked. "Should I try it?"

"No," Monty said, giving me a sharp look. "Your shield is an active cast, drawing from your energy, because you're not—"

"A mage, got it," I finished. "So this just stays in place?"

"Protecting the vehicle, yes."

"Why did you raise the partition if you didn't want to discuss something private?"

"Because this would be a good time to turn your attention to the *other* vehicle pursuing us."

"The what? Another vehicle wants to crush us?"

"Look beyond the truck," Monty said. "Don't just use your eyes, and whatever you do, don't expand your senses."

"Don't use my...oh, got it," I said. "Innersight is passive?"

Monty nodded.

I looked behind us and used my innersight. I let my gaze go wide and allowed the energy in me to increase my sight. It was similar to having several different types of vision at once, like night-vision overlaid over infrared, which was then over-laid over X-ray, creating a new way of seeing that depended on runic energy.

I peered into the night and focused, careful not to let my senses expand. Several cars behind the truck was another Rolls Royce Phantom. This one was gaining on us and swerving in and out of traffic with ease. Whoever was at the wheel was an expert in defensive and evasive driving.

I looked closer.

The energy signature of the driver was familiar.

Robert.

"Robert?" I hissed, bringing my sight back to normal. The migraine pain slammed the back of my head a second later, forcing me to sit back to alleviate the pounding. "How could that be?"

"Good question," Monty said. "Whoever is driving this vehicle is not Robert. I even doubt this is a real Phantom."

"Verity?"

"Without question," Monty said, examining the rear area. "This illusion is quite impressive. Not perfect, but nearly. It means The Eye has been watching me far longer than I imagined."

"So much for Dex overreacting."

"Indeed. They must have had agents stationed close enough to pick up on our conversations to know we were using SuNaTran."

"Then, what, a switch?"

"Most likely they sidetracked the real Robert on his way to us."

"How did you know?" I asked, rubbing my neck. "Ow—my head."

"Robert would never utter the word *hurl* in my presence," Monty said. "He certainly would never call *you* Simon, and Cecil never discusses details of the runing of the vehicles with his drivers, no matter how long they've worked for him. M-Treatment, indeed."

"Okay, that explains fake Robert," I managed through the haze of pain. "Who's in the truck trying to make us the meat in an auto sandwich?"

"The truck is shielded," Monty said, peering behind us. "Strong enough to render them invisible."

"Verity has that kind of ability?" I asked, trying to peer into the truck behind us. "I can't see the driver."

"Yes, it's part of the illusion," Monty said. "Rather than hide the driver, they create a distraction away from them. I'm certain there is some kind of augmenting rune in here somewhere, making it impossible to see the driver as long as we are inside this vehicle."

"Clever," I said as the pain stabbed my neck. "I think Dex's circle is reacting to the illusion. This headache is getting worse."

"It's possible," Monty said, opening the door. "I'm going to do something reckless."

"Reckless? You mean besides opening the door of a vehicle moving at speed?"

"We need to get you out of here," Monty said, gesturing. "It could be that the circle is conflicting with the illusion. If the illusion hinders the circle—"

"We'll get a visit by my favorite successor."

"Precisely," Monty said. "I'm going to try and shunt you out of here."

"Shunt? That sounds a lot like teleporting," I said warily. "Didn't Dex say no teleporting while I'm multiplying?"

"Multiphasic, and this isn't teleporting, exactly," Monty said. "You remember the Transporter?"

"The one you paid in chocolate? That one?"

"Yes, that one."

"The one you said that no mage could do what they do? Not even Dex?"

"Yes, that one," Monty said. "I'm going to try and copy her method."

"Wait, what?" I asked. "Are you insane?"

There was a slight pause which made me uneasy.

"Monty?"

"We'll discuss that later," he said. "Remember, whatever you do, do not cast. I have to deal with this."

"What are you talking about?"

He looked past me and nodded.

I turned to see who he was nodding at when my world flashed violet. When I looked back, I saw Monty in the fake Phantom unleashing a violet orb of energy at the truck. I was sitting in the real Phantom with the real Robert.

I hoped.

"Hold on, Mr. Strong," Robert said, and veered to the right. "Hold on!"

"What? No!" I yelled. "We need to go get Monty!"

"My instructions are to get you safe," Robert said. "Apologies."

He accelerated the Phantom as I turned to see the truck go up in a massive ball of flame worthy of Michael Bay. The fake Phantom veered off to the left and raced away from us as we headed east on the highway toward the Van Wyck and JFK.

Monty was still in the back.

"How could you leave him?" I said, my voice now calm with fury. "Turn back. Now."

"My deepest apologies, Mr. Strong," Robert said. "My instructions are clear. Get you to safety, no matter what."

"Who gave you these insane orders?"

"Cecil did."

"What the hell is Cecil thinking?" I said, gripping the door handle with enough force to make my knuckles white. "Where does he get off telling you to abandon Monty?"

"His instructions came from Dexter Montague, sir."

"What?" I said shocked, rubbing a temple and sitting back. "Prove it."

Robert reached down next to him and handed me a phone.

"Who is this?" I said into the phone. "Explain, and do it fast."

"It's me, Cecil."

"This isn't going to fly," I said. "We need to speak—"

"Face-to-face," Cecil finished. "I know. Robert is bringing you to me right now. I'll explain everything when we meet."

"I'm going to give you the courtesy of thirty seconds from the moment I see you before I forget my manners, Cecil. You better convince me that what you just did was for a good reason."

"I will."

He ended the call.

FIFTEEN

A few minutes later we pulled over to the shoulder of the highway and slowed down. The traffic raced by us as we stopped.

Ahead of us was what appeared to be a small tank.

Cecil stepped out and waved to someone who ran over to the Phantom. He was dressed in the typical SuNaTran driver uniform: a dark suit and cap. Once he got in the Phantom he took off his hat and replaced it with an F1 cap. He turned to face me and smiled.

It was Ayrton.

"Hello, Mr. Strong," he said, getting in as Robert raced to the small tank. "My uncle would like you to join him in the Jugger."

He pointed ahead at the heavily armored vehicle.

"The Jugger?"

"JuggerMaus, but no one calls it that," he said. "My uncle doesn't like it when I call it the Mouse. Are you okay? Can you move?"

"Give me a second," I said, getting my bearings. "I'm currently—know what, nevermind."

I opened the door, stumbled out, and closed the door.

Ayrton floored the gas and the Phantom sped off.

I made my way to the Jugger, careful to stay away from the speeding traffic. One stumble into the flow of vehicles would be an instant immortality test.

When I drew closer to the Jugger, Cecil grabbed me by the arm and escorted me into the back of the heavily armored vehicle through a thick door. He pounded the side of the Jugger with a fist, and I could feel us take off.

"Hello, Simon," Cecil said as he sat on one of the benches, strapping in a five-point harness around his chest. I sat opposite him, following his lead and strapping in. I rested my head against the cool interior of the Jugger. "You look like hell."

"Thanks," I said, glancing at him. "I've been better."

Cecil wore a black suit with a blue-gray shirt and a dark blue, almost-black tie. Every item he wore was runed, and these weren't like Piero's suits' runes. These runes, the ones I could make out, all looked dangerous. He ran a hand through his short, gray hair, and pulled on his neatly trimmed goatee before giving me a hard stare.

I still didn't know what he was, besides somewhat unstable for the death runes he inscribed in the Beast and Dark Goat, but his runes had saved me from extreme pain more than once, and for that, I was grateful.

The inside of the Jugger was covered with instrumentation that gave it away as a C & C vehicle: Command and Control. Two large screens dominated one side, while four smaller screens rested on the opposite wall. One of the large screens showed Robert and the front of the vehicle. The other large screen showed the rear of the vehicle.

The smaller screens were filled with maps of the area, traffic patterns, even the weather. One screen showed an image of a large plane sitting on a runway.

"Make sure that harness is tight; she may look like a tank, but she moves like a Lamborghini."

"Cecil," I said, staring at him. "What is all this about?"

He pointed at the second screen.

I looked and saw three Phantoms identical to the one I'd just left race past us. I saw them swerve in and out of traffic in pursuit of the Phantom Ayrton was driving.

"They won't catch him," Cecil said, proudly. "He'll drive them around for a few hours and then head back to SuNa-Tran. He'll lose them before then. No one can keep up with him when he sets his mind to it."

I looked around the interior again.

"Since when did SuNaTran start building tanks?"

"Since you started returning my vehicles as abstract art," Cecil said with a grimace before giving me a smile. "I'm sorry about the deception. We knew Verity was onto Tristan and couldn't risk divulging more of the plan. Their agents are good and they were close."

"How long did they know?"

"We spotted them a few days after he was admitted to Haven," Cecil said. "They kept their distance. It's possible they had been watching him before then, certainly after the cast against that mage."

"You're incredibly well-informed."

"Dexter brought me up to speed," he said. "In fact, Dexter is the only reason I know about any of this. Tristan isn't exactly the open and sharing type."

I nodded.

"You left him alone to fight that fake Robert," I said, letting the words fill the space between us. "I thought...I thought you were his friend?"

"This one time, and this one time only, I'm going to answer you as a courtesy," he said, his expression dark. "The bond between the Montagues and Fairchilds—my family—goes back centuries. We were fighting, dying, side by side on bloody battlefields for as long as there have been wars between men. Don't you *ever* question my fealty to any Montague, ever."

"I'm sorry...I didn't mean to question your bond," I said. "Why did you tell Robert to leave him?"

"Because we had to get *you* out of there," Cecil said, picking up a keyboard and tapping some keys. "We have the situation contained."

The rear screen changed to show another Jugger like the one I sat in pulling up behind a Phantom. I saw Monty get out of the Phantom and into the Jugger. He looked mostly intact, but one sleeve of his jacket was torn.

I could tell from the way he tugged at it that he was upset at the damage to his jacket. It brought a smile to my face.

"He always was a terror on clothing," Cecil said. "I keep telling him to don a suit of armor and call it a day. Would last longer."

"You know about Verity?"

"Yes," he said. "Few do, these days. They are experts at hiding in plain sight. Their greatest strength is convincing the mage world they don't exist."

"Makes sense," I said with a nod, which I immediately regretted as vertigo hit me. "Convince the world you don't exist and you can do pretty much whatever you want."

"Exactly," he said, typing on the keyboard again. "How's the Dark Goat?"

"Still intact," I said. "We recently took it through a stress test. Survived with flying colors—literally."

"Stress test?" he said, glancing up at me. "What kind of stress test? We put that vehicle through everything short of a nuclear explosion, and only because we couldn't do it safely within the city."

"Monty released an entropic siphon—"

"A what?"

"I don't know the details," I said "I only know that it turned into a whirlwind of death we had to drive—well, mostly fly—through. It tore the Dark Goat apart."

"Really?" Cecil said, hopeful. "You mean it's destroyed?"

"You didn't let me finish," I said. "It tore the Dark Goat apart, for all of ten seconds, maybe less. Then it leeched me of power and pulled itself back together, better than new."

"It's not destroyed?" he asked, disappointed. "It's not in pieces?"

"Sorry, no," I said. "I thought it was gone there for a second, but no such luck."

"I understand," he said, then brightened. "This is progress, though. If it was able to disintegrate the Dark Goat, even temporarily, that's good news."

"That's good news?"

"Yes," he said. "If I can get Tristan to share this entropic siphon, we can rework it to use on the Beast. That thing has proven invincible to everything we've thrown at it."

"About that," I said. "Have you created something called the Montague Treatment, or M-Treatment for short?"

"M-Treatment? No. What does that mean?"

"Just something I heard earlier," I said, knowing it had been too good to be true. "Would you consider creating a defensive runic package for your vehicles?"

"*All* my vehicles are defensively runed," Cecil said, narrowing his eyes at me. "Dex said you weren't yourself. Did you suffer a head injury?"

"No, no," I said, raising a hand. "The defensive runes on the Dark Goat are different from the rest, though, right?"

"Well, obviously," he said. "I'm not trying to kill my clients. You and Grey are special conditions."

"I would consider it a personal favor if you would consider

naming the rune package you used on the Dark Goat, the Montague Treatment."

"That would drive him absolutely mad," he said, and then gave me a wide grin. "That *would* drive him absolutely mad."

"Hey, fair is fair," I said. "I shared about the entropic siphon. All I ask in return is a slight renaming of the runes on one vehicle."

"It can be done," he said with a nod. "Thank you for letting me know. I'll ask Tristan to show me more about this entropic siphon when he has time."

"On that note, I really want to apologize for all the destruction to your vehicles," I said. "It's never intentional. You know that, right?"

"The abstract art that survived your 'date,' and was once the Aventador, still hangs in the shop," he said as I winced. "I know it wasn't you, but it stung. The Midnight Simone though; Tristan will have to replace that one. That one still hurts."

"That wasn't—"

"I know it wasn't either of you, but I really loved that automobile," Cecil said, his voice a mix of sadness and anger. "It cost a fortune to make her...and the time, the time it took to make. He brought me back a steering wheel—a steering wheel! You have no idea how much that one hurt."

I didn't know what to say.

He was right.

"You're right, I don't," I said. "But I know Monty feels horrible about it."

"He should. I'm going to let him simmer until we make a new one," Cecil said with a sly smile. "In the meantime, you need to find some way to destroy that Dark Goat. You owe me. The both of you do."

I nodded and looked over at the screen that showed a plane waiting on a runway and pointed.

"What's that?"

"That's your ride to London," Cecil said. "Like I said, we couldn't let you know what the real plan was."

"I'm going to guess, not JFK?"

"Not JFK," Cecil said with a nod. "Private airfield on Long Island. Owned by SuNaTran."

"I thought SuNaTran was just interested in vehicles?"

He gave me a look that said, *How many times did you smack your head tonight?* before continuing.

"A plane *is* a vehicle, Simon."

"I meant, you know, indestructible cars and such."

"That's only one facet of what we do and provide," Cecil said. "Our security measures extend way beyond vehicles. We've just created a new branch of the company—SuNaTran Security."

"Sounds upscale," I said. "You're runing vehicles and heading security? When do you sleep?"

"I don't."

"You don't sleep?"

"I don't run the security division," Cecil said. "I leave that to professionals, like Elias."

"Elias?" I asked, confused. "Elias Pirn?"

"You know him?"

"He's your head of security?"

"Recently appointed, yes," Cecil said. "He came with an impressive set of recommendations. Aside from being an accomplished sorcerer."

"I can only imagine," I said, shaking my head. "Yes, I know him. He's good, one of the best. Last time I saw him, he was head of security at Haven."

"Which is now secured by SNT-SEC," Cecil said. "We upgraded the facility considerably. That last attack could have been prevented."

"Don't know about that," I said, thinking back to when

Evers and Monty were going at it. "At the very least, I'm sure they won't see rampaging ogres loose through the place."

"Certainly not. We take our security seriously."

"Speaking of secure, couldn't Verity just listen in while we're in here?" I asked, taking another glance at the interior. "I mean, I feel physically secure in here, but is it shielded?"

Cecil pressed a button on what I thought was a watch. Turns out it was much more than a watch. The inside of the Jugger exploded with different colored runes over every surface of the interior.

"Whoa," I said, looking at the amount of runes. I couldn't decipher any of them. "This is major rune work."

"The interior of the JuggerMaus is runed against any kind of energy attack or intrusion. In addition, it has runic ablative designs inscribed on the exterior."

"Like the stealth planes?"

"Similar," Cecil said with a nod. "It's pretty complicated. The designs allow any runic energy that impacts the vehicle to slide off without detecting what the vehicle actually is."

"You're describing runic camouflage," I said, surprised. "What does this vehicle look like to anyone searching for it, runically?"

"Well, if you're standing in front of it, it looks like what it is—an armored AFV," Cecil said. "But the runes diffuse even its outward appearance. Verity is good, but not *this* good. Now, if they were searching for it without visual confirmation, well, it would look very different and very ordinary."

"What would it look like?"

He gave me a mischievous grin.

"A 1966 Volkswagen bus."

SIXTEEN

I laughed despite myself, stopping when the pain in my head advised me that laughing harder would only trigger my nausea.

"That's just evil," I said after a few gasps. "Do they know?"

"Does who know?" Cecil asked innocently. "Who are you referring to?"

"Bango and Cash," I said. "I mean, Bangers and Mash. The duo of cluelessness?"

"I'm sorry, I've never heard of this 'Bangers and Mash' duo you speak of," he said with a slight smile. "But, if I had heard of them, I would never admit their existence, or the fact that they drive a formidable SuNaTran vehicle known as the Pumpkin, on principle alone."

"Understood," I said, dropping the subject with a smile of my own. "Is Monty meeting us there?"

I pointed at the plane on the screen.

"That's the Shrike," Cecil said. "One of my newer projects."

"Looks like a mini C-130."

"Close," he said. "The Shrike is one of our cargo and

transport planes. We'll drive the Jugger right into the cargo bay, creating a double-shielding effect for you and Tristan."

"SuNaTran runed that thing?"

"Every vehicle we own is runed."

"Monty is in that?" I asked, looking at the screen again. "Is it runed against explosions?"

"I'm aware of Tristan's propensity for, shall we say, detonations," Cecil said. "He'd be hard pressed to bring down the Shrike."

"Sounds like famous last words," I said. "How far away is that?"

"We'll be there shortly," Cecil said. "Once we arrive, I'll take the other JuggerMaus back, and you two will take your flight while remaining *inside* this JuggerMaus."

"Doesn't exactly look comfortable for a 6-7-hour flight," I said, examining the interior closely. "Not seeing many seating alternatives besides these benches."

"There's a living module that will be attached to this vehicle once we arrive, securing you in place," he said. "It will make the flight more comfortable."

"More comfortable sounds perfect right now."

He nodded.

"A few things," Cecil said. "You can't leave the JuggerMaus until you land in England. That will throw off Verity and your successor and buy you time."

"You know about the successor?"

"Simon?" Cecil said, giving me a look that told me to keep up. "Focus."

"Focused, sorry. Go on."

"The flight will take considerably less than six hours," he said. "The Shrike is a VTOL subsonic aircraft, but its top speed is just a hair short of Mach 1."

"VTOL? Vertical Takeoff and Landing? Like a Harrier?"

"Better than a Harrier, but yes, no runways needed."

"Impressive."

"Necessary," Cecil answered. "Some of our clients need to be across the globe as fast as possible, and certain areas don't or won't allow for alternative means of transport."

"Like London?"

"Exactly like London," Cecil said. "You can avoid detection as long as you remain inside this vehicle. Once outside... they will find you, eventually."

"We're landing this beast in London?"

"Not exactly," Cecil said, shaking his head. "Outside of the national incident landing in London would create, that's not your primary destination. You're headed first to the New Forest."

"We're landing this beast in the New Forest?"

Cecil nodded.

"An area designated as Blackwater, to be precise," Cecil said. "You'll have access to London via the A35 a few kilometers away. That leads into the M27, which connects to the M3. After that, it's a fairly straight shot to London, about a ten-kilometer trip." He must have caught my expression of mild confusion. "And...you have no idea what I'm talking about, do you?"

"Not in the slightest. A35, to M27, to M3 and London," I repeated. "Sounds simple enough."

"It is," he said with a short nod. "Don't worry—your driver, Adam, will get you to London. After that, Tristan is familiar enough to prevent your getting lost."

"Any particular reason we're landing in a forest?"

"You'll have to ask Dexter that."

"Of course," I said. "Just seems odd to land in the middle of a forest."

"The New Forest is protected land," Cecil said. "Your equivalent would be an area designated a wildlife preserve."

"I may be mistaken, but I doubt you can land something

this large in any wildlife preserve in the States," I said. "How are we doing this, and are we going to encounter an angry military when we do?"

"The Shrike has state-of-the-art stealth technology along with runic defenses and camouflage. No one will see us coming or going, but it was Dexter who pulled this off. Don't ask me how. That old mage got us clearance to land for thirty minutes, provided we don't destroy any of the trees and leave a zero footprints behind."

"You can do that with a plane that large?"

"We can and will."

"I would imagine this has something to do with the witch."

"The Witch of New Forest?"

"You know her?"

"I know *of* her," Cecil said, his voice grim. "She's not to be trifled with, that one. There are rumors of her causing massive lightning strikes in New Forest. Got so bad, the government ceased all air traffic over the protected land."

"This is the area we're flying into?"

"Dex informed me Blackwater was as close as we could get to your target destination in the Forest," Cecil answered. "He wouldn't give me precise coordinates, which means this is the best we can do. Remember, once you step outside of the plane, you'll become visible to trackers...eventually."

"Verity and my successor," I said. "That makes it easy not to leave the Jugger. Anything else?"

"When you land, your car will be waiting," he said. "Once you conduct your business in the New Forest, try to get moving as quickly as possible. The longer you stay in one place, the easier it will be to find you."

"That would be great if I knew *where* we were going in the Forest," I said. "Hold on, what *kind* of car?"

"Why do you ask?" Cecil asked with a wry smile. "SuNa-

Tran has always provided you top-notch vehicles—for you to demolish, I might add."

"Except that one time you were super-pissed about the experimental Urus," I corrected. "I still have nightmares about a small red Vauxhall Astra."

Cecil laughed.

"I recall that one," he said with a chuckle. "I was feeling especially vindictive that day. How did it drive?"

"Cramped," I said. "Those things aren't meant to be driven by humans of average height."

"They are a bit limited in the space department," he said with a smile.

"Tell me it's not an Astra, please."

"No, you'll have an Urus waiting to take you to your destination," Cecil said. "Adam will leave you the vehicle. Do I need to say it?"

"No," I said, shaking my head. "You want us to return the vehicle in the state in which we received it?"

"If you would be so gracious as to do so, just this once, I'd really appreciate it," he said, with a short nod as he glanced at one of the screens. "We're here."

The JuggerMaus came to a slow stop. I saw Robert tip his hat to me in the front screen. I looked up as a loud hiss was followed by a large clang, rocking the Jugger for a few seconds. This was followed by another quieter hiss.

I looked at Cecil.

"What was that?"

"That would be the module being attached," Cecil said, checking a screen with his keyboard. "We're inside the Shrike. There are accommodations, complete with amenities, behind that door"—he pointed to a door off to the side of where we were sitting—"that will, I'm sure, meet with both your and Tristan's approval."

"A pleasure as usual, Mr. Strong," Robert said, as his voice coming over the intercom as he exited the driver's seat. "Moving to Jugger 2, sir. Have a good flight, Mr. Strong."

"I'll be with you shortly," Cecil said, pressing an intercom button on the wall. "A few more things to sort here before I join you."

"He has some excellent driving skills," I said. "Please tell him I said thank you."

"I'll pass on the message," Cecil said, unstrapping his harness. He tapped the keyboard again and the rear door opened with a quiet hiss. "Tristan is here."

The door opened and Monty peered in with a nod.

"I'm pleased to see the shunt worked," he said, looking at me before turning to Cecil. "Cecil, my deepest thanks."

"Stuff it, Tristan," Cecil said angrily as he turned his head and winked at me. It was all I could do to keep a straight face. "You brought me back a steering wheel?"

"It wasn't my intention—" Monty started, but Cecil cut him off.

"I lend you an automotive work of art, a rare classic, and you bring me back a bloody steering wheel? Have you lost your bloody mind?"

"I understand you may be upset—"

"I may be upset? I *may be* upset?" Cecil said, raising his voice. "You better believe I'm upset." He closed the distance on Monty and poked him in the chest as he spoke. "I expect you to cover the full costs of the new Midnight Simone version 3. Complete with the Montague Treatment."

"Montague Treatment?" Monty said, glancing at me. "*You* did this."

"No idea what you're talking about," I said, deliberately looking away. "I hear this new M-Treatment is the best, though. Makes cars indestructible."

He gave me a glare before turning to Cecil.

"You're really going to use this M-Treatment nonsense?"

Cecil nodded.

"Didn't you hear? Makes vehicles indestructible."

"Cecil..."

"I'll begin building her once I'm done here," Cecil said, pointing at Monty's face. "On *your* commission this time."

"Of course," Monty said, looking down at Cecil. "I wouldn't have it any other way. Are you done now?"

Cecil paused and crossed his arms.

"Mostly, yes," he said with a smile, then grew serious. "I take it you dispatched the Verity agents?"

"You killed them?" I asked, shocked. "Wouldn't that—?"

"No," Monty said. "This was The Eye. Killing them would have escalated things needlessly. We need them to follow their protocol. It will buy us much-needed time."

"Dex is on the ground and headed to the New Forest," Cecil said. "Says he knows where this York person is, but it won't be easy getting to him."

"I never expect easy where Dex is concerned," Monty said. "I doubt he knows the meaning of the word."

"What did you do to them?" I asked, looking at Monty. "The Verity agents? If you didn't kill them, where are they?"

"They are both bound uncomfortably in the boot of their fake Phantom with some immobilization runes," Monty said, turning back to Cecil. "I had to actively cast. I take it this vehicle is shielded?"

"Both the vehicle and the Shrike," Cecil said. "I can offer you a blanket of invisibility until you land."

"The Shrike?" Monty asked, surprised. "You actually made it? I thought it was an avionic nightmare."

"I've dealt with the likes of you two," Cecil said with a small smile. "Design nightmares are child's play and actually calming in comparison. Once you land, we can't provide air support, unfortunately. I've been informed that if the Shrike is in the New Forest for longer than thirty minutes, it will never leave. You have that window of time; after that, you are on your own."

"Not on my own," Monty said, glancing at me. "I have an *Aspis*."

"An *Aspis*?" Cecil repeated, glancing at me. "Sounds like a chronic condition. You should get that examined before it gets worse."

"I'll take that under advisement," Monty said. "Thank you again, Cecil. For everything."

"You can thank me by christening the new Duesenberg when it's completed," Cecil said, serious. "Don't underestimate Verity, Tristan." He looked down at Monty's jacket. "There's a change of clothes in the module."

"Thank you. I appreciate it."

"Don't thank me, thank your uncle."

"Of course."

"If it weren't for him," Cecil said, "this whole thing would have gone pear-shaped. I'm glad he's on our side. I'd hate to face that devious mind in battle."

"Agreed," Monty said and held out a hand. "We won't keep you any longer."

Cecil reached out and the two clasped forearms.

"You show them it's a mistake to cross a Montague," Cecil said with a grin. "First rune on the Duesenberg is yours when you return. Make sure you return."

"I will," Monty said with a nod. "As soon as I can."

"Strong, you keep an eye out for him," Cecil said. "Better than you do my cars. We still have a few Astras in the garage."

"Astras?" I said with a wince. "No, thank you. I'll keep an eye on him."

"See that you do," he said, giving me a short nod and leaving the Jugger.

Monty closed the thick door behind him and sat on one of the benches, letting out a deep breath.

"Astras?" Monty asked, following Cecil with his gaze. "Do I want to know?"

"Not really," I said. "How was your trip?"

"That was a little more complicated than I expected," he said as he looked around. "Did Cecil mention anything about tea in this tank? I could use a good cuppa right about now."

I sat there and stared for a good five seconds.

"A *little* more complicated?" I asked raising my voice. "I feel like I stepped into a Bond film."

"That's a bit dramatic, don't you think?" Monty said. "Besides, we don't have any of his useful gadgets."

"Car chase to secondary vehicle, to large armored vehicle, which is now inside some super plane," I said. "When do I start drinking the martinis?"

"Why would *you* be drinking the martinis?" he asked. "If anyone is Bond in this film of yours, it would be *me*. Bond is British; always was, always will be. If you're anyone, you would be Leiter—classic CIA, clueless, well-meaning, but just a few steps behind the action."

It didn't surprise me he was up to speed on his Bond. He was English, after all. From what I understood, Bond was some kind of cult hero over there.

"Says the person who didn't see the Verity illusion until it was almost too late," I countered. "What took so long?"

"I didn't expect The Eye to move so quickly," Monty said, removing his jacket with a scowl. "Their deception was well planned."

"What was the plan?" I asked. "They would kidnap you and then what? Hand you over to...?"

"No one," he said, his voice somber. "I'd be taken to a secondary location and dealt with."

"Dealt with? That sounds like a polite way of saying exterminated."

Monty nodded.

"Verity has a High Tribunal from what I managed to gather tonight," Monty said. "Final arbiters and all that. They have, in their infinite wisdom, determined that my use of the lost rune requires my expunging with extreme prejudice."

"You can't plead your case?" I asked. "You know, explain why you used the rune?"

Monty shook his head as the plane began to move. He sat opposite me and strapped in.

"They seemed pretty dead set about the 'expunging with extreme prejudice' part," he said, looking at his jacket. "There is no pleading or explaining. They pass judgment, declare a sentence, and I'm supposed to die."

"Harsh," I said. "Mages really need to relax a bit. This Verity Tribunal sounds a bit high strung."

"Beyond harsh. You'll find not all mages are as calm and relaxed as I am," he said with a straight face, which astounded me. "Some of them are particularly prone to violence first, then asking questions."

"You don't say?" I said. "Calm and relaxed? This is how you view yourself?"

"Of course," Monty said, gesturing and incinerating the jacket to ash. "How else would I view myself? I always maintain my composure."

I was about to answer when the intercom interrupted me.

"This is your pilot, Daniel," a deep bass voice said through the speakers. "We will be airborne in five minutes. Please strap in and make yourselves comfortable. We should arrive at your destination in four hours."

"Four hours?" Monty said, raising an eyebrow. "A flight to London usually takes hours longer."

"This plane is a little faster than the norm."

"I see," Monty said, giving me a once over. "How do you feel?"

"Right now? Fairly human as long as I don't make any sudden movements."

"Good plan," he said, looking around. "Are we expected to sit on these benches for the entire flight? Is Cecil still punishing us for the Duesenberg?"

"Accommodations in the module, according to Cecil," I said, pointing to the door next to us with my chin. "Though he really was hurt by the steering wheel you gifted him as the remains of the Duezy."

"I'll make it up to him," Monty said, and leaned back. "The next version will be even better than the one he loaned us. I'll make sure to give it a true M-Treatment."

I barely felt the acceleration of the plane as we lifted off.

"We will be reaching our cruising altitude of sixty thousand feet shortly," Daniel said in a smooth airline pilot voice. "Feel free to enjoy the amenities in the module connected to your vehicle, once we achieve our cruising altitude."

"Is this a plane or a rocket? Sixty k shortly?"

"The plans for the Shrike were quite radical," Monty said. "I'm surprised he actually built it."

"You think pilots get special voice training to sound calming like that?" I asked. "You know, to prevent passenger panic?"

"I don't think having a soothing voice is one of the qualifications for attaining a pilot's license," Monty said. "You prevent panic by knowing how to fly...and land."

"I don't know," I said "I'm pretty sure I could pull off a decent pilot voice. 'Good evening, this is your Captain speaking. We've just lost both our engines, but rest assured, I'm an experienced pilot. You're in good hands."

"Both engines, really?"

I continued in my pilot voice.

"I'll make sure to glide us over that string of active volcanoes, into that large body of shark-infested waters, where we will be momentarily safe before the weight of our craft sinks us to the bottom of the ocean."

"I think no matter how smooth your voice is, people would lose their minds in that scenario," Monty replied. "Shark-infested waters seems a little over the top, don't you think?"

"I disagree," I said. "*My* passengers will stay cool and collected, because my voice is uber calming."

Monty stared at me for a few seconds, before shaking his head.

"I doubt you could pull it off," Monty said, examining the interior of the Jugger. "I'm sure there's a switch on their console somewhere that automatically provides perfect pilot voice."

"No need to get snippy," I said. "You can just admit my voice puts Barry White to shame."

"I can see my uncle's circle has clearly destroyed what remaining neurons you had left," he said, looking at the ash that used to be part of a very stylish suit. "Do you realize my jacket didn't even last a day? Not even an *entire* day."

"I noticed. That must be some kind of record, even for you," I said, glancing at the small pile of ash. "What happened?"

"The Verity agents moved faster than I anticipated," he said, shaking his head. "Blasted me in the side before I could react. The jacket took the brunt of the impact."

"Piero does make good jackets," I said. "Maybe you should ask him for something in the mage Titanium Zegna line? Might last you a little longer."

"Your humor leaves much to be desired. Starting with actual humor."

"Ouch," I said "The illusion was good—had me for a moment, until fake Robert started calling me Simon." My vertigo and stomach informed me the plane had stopped climbing. "We hit sixty k already? Is that even possible? I thought normal planes flew at thirty?"

"I would imagine this is anything but a normal plane, knowing Cecil," Monty said. "What's this module the pilot referred to?"

"Through that door," I said, pointing to the small door next to us. "Cecil doesn't want us to leave the Jugger."

"The what? Excuse me?"

"Jugger," I said, motioning to the vehicle around us. "This tank-like vehicle we are currently sitting in is designated as a JuggerMaus."

"JuggerMaus? Ah, understood," Monty said, unstrapping his harness. "Cecil always loved his tanks. Be right back."

He opened the door and disappeared from view. I remained strapped in on the bench. Getting up and introducing my head to the various hard surfaces of the interior of the Jugger wasn't my idea of a good time.

Staying put on the bench seemed to be the most I could manage at the moment. At the very least, my stomach wasn't doing flip-flops, keeping time with the jackhammer of a migraine at the base of my skull.

Small favors and all that.

Monty returned a few minutes later with a new jacket and a cup of tea, looking pleased with himself—well, as pleased as his face would allow. He was currently in semi-scowl mode.

The tea must have been exceptional.

"See you found your cuppa," I said. "All must be right with the universe now."

"Nothing a good cuppa can't fix," he said, taking a sip. "Excellent."

"I don't recall Piero sending suits to the JuggerMaus," I said, examining his new Zegna jacket. "Dex?"

Monty nodded.

"My uncle can be quite resourceful when needed," Monty

said. "I'm sure he anticipated our need for a change of clothing and planned accordingly."

"More like *your* need," I said, getting to my feet unsteadily. "Is there a place to lay down in the module?"

Monty nodded.

"Full kitchen, restrooms, and beds, yes," he said, raising a finger. "Before you go, we need to discuss something."

"Can it wait? I feel like something Peaches threw up." At the mention of his name, I missed him immediately. "Although I doubt he would throw up anything. Probably against the hellhound code. Why couldn't he be here? This place is double shielded and all that."

"For *us*," Monty said. "Your creature is exhibiting a particular energy signature that makes it difficult to mask. He would give us away."

"Won't it be the same thing when we land?"

"Not exactly," Monty said. "The lockdown around London has dampening effects. It will be harder to locate him and us. I would imagine that's why The Eye tried for me sooner, rather than later."

"Makes sense," I said, gripping a convenient handle bolted into the wall to prevent my falling. "What did you want to discuss?"

"Stormblood."

SEVENTEEN

I sat down and strapped in.

"Right, Stormblood," I said. "Spell it out for me."

"Interesting choice of words," Monty said, putting the tea cup down on a small shelf beside the bench. "It is, indeed, a spell. A very ancient and obscure cast."

"How obscure?"

"Obscure enough that York may be one of the few living practitioners of this particular cast," Monty said. "Do you recall my uncle mentioning quintessence?"

"Yes, it's like the ultimate source of energy for mages and magic?"

"Yes and no," Monty said. "It's the ultimate energy source, period."

"Is that what mages manipulate when you do your finger wiggles and trace symbols in the air?" I asked. "You're playing with quintessence?"

"No, mages cannot manipulate quintessence directly, not without placing themselves in mortal danger. It's like electricity."

"Quintessence is electricity?"

"Do you want me to explain Stormblood or not?"

"I do, but I can feel you entering deep magespeak territory and my brain is leaking out of my eyeballs," I said. "Or at least it feels that way with this circle Dex hit me with."

"I'll speak plainly, if you'll listen."

"I'm all ears, and for the record, I've never heard you speak plainly about anything when it comes to mage topics," I said, raising a hand. "You started this conversation with quintessence. Is that plainspeak?"

Monty sighed and I smiled as I closed my eyes and leaned back.

"Very well, I'll speak even more plainly," Monty said after taking another sip from his cup. "So plain even *you* will understand."

"One can dream," I said, motioning him to continue. "Please, go on."

"Electricity," Monty said. "You're familiar with the concept?"

I opened my eyes.

"Seriously?"

"Just making sure," he said. "Would hate to be accused of making this convoluted. Electricity is an energy source, but it needs conduits. With me so far?"

"So far, yes," I said. "Cables and wires and the such allow us to use electricity. That where you're going?"

"Yes," Monty said, slipping into professor mode. "Quintessence is like electricity. Runes, words of power, and artifacts are like the cables and wires. They allow mages and other energy practitioners to tap into and manipulate the energy at will."

"I'm actually understanding you," I said, sitting up, curious. "Where does this Stormblood come in?"

"When you want to power, say, an enormous sign in Times

Square, you can't use a small wire," Monty said. "That much energy requires massive cables, correct?"

"Correct," I said. "Jumbotrons are huge in the electricity expenditure department, especially the ones at Times Square that never turn off."

"Now, imagine you could circumvent the need for cables at all," Monty said, lowering his voice. "What would happen if the electricity could flow directly into that jumbo sign without the use of cables or wires?"

"Jumbotron. I'd call that a lightning strike and one destroyed sign," I said. "That's what would happen."

"That is what the Stormblood allows."

"It allows for lightning—?"

"It allows a mage to tap directly into quintessence," Monty said. "Without runes, gestures, artifacts, or symbols."

"You forgot without sense," I added. "I'm not an electrician or a mage and that sounds batshit crazy even to me."

"It does pose some risk," Monty admitted.

"Some risk?" I said, pinching the bridge of my nose. "You're comparing this quintessence to electricity. Okay, well, here's what *I* know about electricity. When a regular person grabs a live wire, a couple things can happen: they either get launched away as the electricity, looking for ground, stops their heart as it blazes through their body, because—too much power."

"That is one scenario, yes," Monty confirmed. "Electricity *is* highly volatile, unless harnessed correctly."

"Thanks for the confirmation, Tesla," I said. "The other scenario is that the person becomes part of the path for the electricity looking for ground. They get rooted in place as their insides get cooked, because, again, too much power. The end in both cases is bad. It's a lose-lose scenario all the way around."

"What if there was a way to harness the electricity?"

Monty asked, after another sip of his tea. "A way your body could withstand the electricity and harness it?"

"Harness it?" I said in disbelief. "Impossible. I'd call that person—"

"A mage with Stormblood."

"No way," I said, still having trouble processing his words. "It sounds like suicide."

"I know what it sounds like," Monty said. "It's possible."

"Tell me this isn't like that lost rune you somehow forgot to field test," I said. "Tell me you have something concrete, something empirical. A mage you know who is alive and can use this quintessence."

"Not a mage," Monty said after a pause. "This person is a powerful magic-user, though."

"Is this a living being?" I asked. "Not someone from six centuries ago that was known for being a badass on the battlefield."

"I'm pretty sure they were formidable six centuries ago... and today."

"Who is this person who can harness quintessence without barbecuing his body and brain?"

"Her," Monty corrected. "Her body and brain."

"What are you saying?" I asked, confused. "Her, who?"

"Stormblood? Tempest?" Monty said, extending his hands and bringing them together. "Do I have to spell it out for you further?"

I glared at him.

"No need to be patronizing," I snapped. "I'm still getting up to speed with quintessence. You're saying Tempest can harness this Stormblood?"

"I thought I just did."

"Then why do we need to see York?" I asked. "She already has it. Have her give you the electroshock therapy boost and we're good."

"Not quite that simple," Monty said. "She's not a mage, and the Stormblood she exhibits is inherent to who she is. She can't just impart her ability any more than you can share your immortality."

"Does she know the ritual?"

Monty shook his head.

"Stormblood came naturally to her," he said. "She ascended into it the way a mage would ascend into Archmage, except she's—"

"Not a mage," I finished. "I can relate. Is this why the rest of the Ten stay away from her?"

"She exhibits resonance," he said. "It's also the reason she lives in the New Forest, away from modern civilization."

"Resonance? Which means what? She vibrates? Speaks in echoes?"

"Not *that* resonance," Monty said with a scowl. "She's not a violin."

"Well, that's good to know," I said. "Care to clarify your definition of resonance, then?"

"She...leaks...power and magic," Monty said. "I'm sure you've heard the stories about some mages; babies grow quiet when they walk by, streetlights flicker, electrical devices of all sorts mysteriously stop functioning properly, animals flock to them?"

"Same applies to some of the very scary creatures we've faced," I said after giving it some thought. "You're saying that's resonance?"

"Precisely," Monty said, taking another sip. "When a mage begins shifting and growing in power, the energy in and around them becomes more pronounced, encompassing their surroundings."

"But she's a witch, not a mage."

"I know, and she is beyond formidable," Monty said. "*That*

is why the rest of the Ten stay away from her…except TK, of course."

"Are you saying TK has this Stormblood too?"

"I'm not certain, actually," he said, placing his cup down. "When I faced her in combat, she was definitely holding back an immense portion of her power. I'm sure the potential is there."

"Okay, how about we never find out about TK and her capacity for Stormblood?" I said nervously. "At least for the immediate future."

"Agreed," Monty said. "We'll have enough to deal with when we meet Josephine."

"Josephine?" I asked. "Why not Tempest?"

"Josephine is who she is," Monty said. "That's her name. I'd add a 'Miss' in front of it, if I were you. It never hurts to be overly polite."

"You and Dex call her Tempest."

"I would never address her that way," Monty said. "Not if I wanted to keep full use of bodily functions. My uncle, on the other hand, is a unique case."

"No shit," I said. "Talk about the understatement of the millennium."

"He has a history with her," Monty said. "She's older than my uncle, and I daresay, just as strong if not stronger."

"That makes me feel so much better," I said. "And we get to meet her in this isolated New Forest in the middle of nowhere, where she could just blast us and no one would know or interfere if they did?"

"An accurate assessment, yes."

"Why Tempest, then?"

"Josephine is *who* she is," Monty said, his voice low. "Tempest is *what* she is. A side of her I hope we never have to face."

"You really need to broaden your circle of acquaintances,"

I said, shaking my head. "Why can't we meet some pleasant mages of phenomenal comedic timing? Tell some jokes, have some laughs, maybe even exchange limericks. No, you have to belong to the circle that deals with the Stormbloods and Death Goddesses."

"Limericks?" Monty said, giving me a look of disdain. "I do not engage in limerick exchange."

"Exactly what I mean," I said. "Every Montague I've met has been on the far side of deranged, dour, or destructive. You fall into the latter category, of course. Most of the time, it's a mix of all three."

"You haven't met that many of us."

"Am I wrong?"

"Not entirely, no. I was merely stating that your exposure to mages, and Montagues in particular, has been quite limited."

"I've met enough mages and Montagues to last me a few lifetimes, trust me."

"We can't choose the family we're born into," Monty said with a small shrug. "I suggest you try and get some rest—let your body deal with that circle Dex gave you while you try to get some sleep."

My head was spinning with the words Monty had shared about quintessence and Tempest. It was all jumbled and too hard to figure out at the moment.

"One more thing," I said, heading to the module door. "If she's a witch, how did she manage to attain Stormblood naturally? I thought it was a mage thing only."

"Imparting it is a mage thing," Monty said. "How she attained it is a mystery."

"A mystery to you, or a mystery period?"

"I think it has to do with her affinity," Monty said, tapping his lips in thought. "She's an Earth Witch. They happen to be some of the strongest of their kind. That may have something to do with it. If you really want to know, you could always ask her."

"I just might," I said, heading into the module as he crossed his legs and closed his eyes. "Wake me up when we land."

"Of course," he said. "Have a good rest."

I found the nearest bed and collapsed into it, letting the darkness overtake me.

EIGHTEEN

"Simon, it is time," I heard Monty say from a distance. "Wake up."

"What? I just put my head down five minutes ago," I complained. "What could be so damn urgent that I can't get some shuteye?"

"That was four hours ago," he said. "We've landed."

"Four hours?" I said with a groan, refusing to believe him. "Are you certain?"

"How do you feel?" he asked. "Headache?"

"Achy, but no headache," I said. "My body feels gently mauled by a large and very angry ogre. Are you sure four hours have passed?"

"This is Daniel, your captain, speaking," Daniel said in his smooth-as-silk voice over the intercom. "We are currently sitting in Blackwater, England, one of the regions of the New Forest. We are scheduled to remain here for no more than thirty minutes before takeoff. A SuNaTran vehicle will arrive shortly, and Adam, your driver will take you on the next leg of your journey. It has been an honor and a privilege flying you both."

"As I said," Monty replied, "we're here."

"Thirty minutes isn't very long," I said. "I wonder what happens if he stays longer?"

"I'm certain Daniel doesn't want to find out."

"Cecil said Dex was the one who managed to allow us to land in the New Forest," I said, still slightly amazed. "How does he do things like that?"

"My uncle is very connected and very old," Monty said. "I'm sure it wasn't difficult to arrange this landing, provided the land wasn't damaged."

"That's what Cecil said," I replied. "No trees damaged and zero footprints when they left."

Monty nodded.

"Sounds like an arrangement between my uncle and Josephine."

"Is it safe to assume that the Penumbra Consortium leaves Josephine alone?" I asked. "I mean, they don't even acknowledge that Nana is alive somewhere. They must really not want to deal with a witch as powerful as Josephine."

"The Consortium stays away from the New Forest. The *entire* New Forest," Monty said. "I believe they operate under the 'cut your losses and live and let live' method of dealing with her."

"So we won't run into them in the New Forest."

"I would imagine not, no," he said. "I'd say the same for Verity and your successor. The latter two because we've been off their radar for several hours."

"Several hours and crossed an ocean."

"True. Once we step outside we have at most a few days in the Forest, and perhaps a week in London, before they pick up our energy signatures."

"Oh, joy," I said, rolling out of bed. "I'm going to douse my face with some ice water and try to wake up. Give me a sec."

Monty nodded and headed out of the module. I reluctantly shuffled to the restroom and splashed my face with frigid water. My internal clock, which had been out of whack since Dex circled me, was back online.

Four hours and ten minutes had passed since I crashed into the bed.

I made my way out of the module and into the Jugger. Monty was typing on the keyboard and looking at one of the screens. He tapped some more keys and I saw text scroll across the screen he was facing.

"BPD is on high alert at Heathrow," he said, reading the scrolling text on the screen. "Seems like they were expecting some trouble on British Airways Flight 1220. All passengers on the plane have been detained."

"How did they find out?"

"Verity must have given them an anonymous tip," he said. "There's a good chance Mathers knows to look for us."

"So that means the Consortium probably knows too," I said. "Not a reunion I'm looking forward to."

"Nor I," Monty said. "But a confrontation with the BPD is inevitable while we are here."

"Inevitable? Really?" I said. "London is a huge city. Can't we avoid Mathers and the BPD?"

"No," Monty said, his voice firm, catching me off guard. "Matthew and I have unfinished business. I intend to finish it this time."

"Just a suggestion," I said, putting a hand up in surrender. "We have Verity after you, my successor fan club trying to kill me, and we need to find York so you can get turbo charged. I don't think you settling a score with Mathers can fit conveniently into our scheduled missions of mayhem."

"This has to be resolved *before* we leave the country," he said. "We will do what we came to do, but I *will* deal with Mathers before we leave."

"As long as that doesn't mean we have to die in the process, I have your back," I said. "After all, I'm the Aspis. You know, I think I need some kind of intro line. Something to instill fear and awe."

"A what?"

"An intro line. You know, like Muhammad Ali?"

"I know I'm going to regret this," he said. "What kind of intro line would denote *you* being the cause of fear and awe?"

"How about: Float like a butterfly, sting like an Aspis, mess with Tristan Montague and get your ass kicked." I finished off with a quick demo of Ali-esque shadowboxing and a menacing bite of my lip. "What do you think?"

He stared at me before turning back to the screen.

"I was right," he said as he tapped the keys.

"Right about what?"

"That I would regret asking," he said. "Let's go."

He pressed a few more keys and the back door opened. We headed out of the Jugger and down the wide ramp of the plane.

"I think it can work," I said as I followed. "It needs some polish—"

"Several centuries worth."

"You saw what I did, though, with sting like an Aspis—get it, asp, Aspis?"

"If you have to explain it, it doesn't work," he said and stopped halfway down the ramp. "If your goal is to strike fear and awe, nothing speaks louder than silence following the utterance of your name."

"I don't understand."

He began walking down the ramp again.

"Does the Morrigan have one of these 'intro lines'?"

"Not that I know of, no."

"Does she strike fear and awe in those she meets?"

"She's the Chooser of the Slain," I said. "It kind of comes with the whole 'goddess of death' territory."

"Fair enough," he said with a short nod. "What about my uncle, the Harbinger? When you faced him with Nemain. Fear and awe?"

I shuddered.

"Both, in ample doses," I said. "But, I'm not following the whole silence thing."

"In many circles—most of them powerful, dangerous circles—the name of the Harbinger is followed by a moment of silence," Monty said. "Do you know what that silence is filled with?"

"Fear and awe?"

"The word you're looking for is dread," he said as we reached the bottom of the ramp. He turned to me and stared into my eyes. "You don't need an intro line. What you need is to make everyone and *everything* who hears the name of Simon Strong, the *Aspis*, dread encountering you."

I paused for a moment, surprised by the intensity of his words.

"I understand," I said, matching his intensity as I looked around. "Like the *Dread* Pirate Roberts, who takes no prisoners and leaves no one alive. Do you think Piero can make me a runed Aspis cloak?"

"You are incorrigible," Monty said, stepping off the ramp and onto the grass. "Let's see if we can find one of the verderers."

I followed him off the ramp and turned to look at the Shrike. SuNaTran wasn't fooling around. The Shrike was enormous—not C-130 enormous, but big enough to fit one, maybe two, more Juggers in the cargo bay.

The large rectangular module that was attached to our Jugger sat squat to one side of the cargo bay. The VTOL engines were massive, and I was fairly certain no air force on the planet had a plane like this.

"I'm really glad Cecil is not a maniacal evil genius bent on taking over the world," I said, still taking in the Shrike. "He would be a serious threat to anyone who came up against his creations."

Monty turned and glanced up at the plane. A small smile crossed his lips at some triggered memory.

"Cecil has an extensive creative genius," he said, gazing at the Shrike. "I much prefer him creating things like this, than weapons of war."

"Me too," I said, looking around at the clearing we stood in. "Where do we find these vertebrates?"

"Verderers," Monty said, pointing forward. "I would imagine we head deeper into the forest. They won't be out here in the clearing. They'll find us."

I saw the black Lamborghini Urus pull up around the plane, careful to stay on the road that circled the clearing where we stood.

"We have to walk or can we take the car?"

"Walk," Monty said, peering at the vehicle that closed in on us and slowed down. "This is protected land. Besides, you can't drive through a forest without causing damage, no matter how runed the vehicle."

"Hello, Mr. Montague, Mr. Strong," the driver said, getting out of the Urus and walking to us. "Welcome to England. I've been instructed to wait here until you conduct your business in the New Forest, and then escort you to the city proper."

Adam was tall and wiry, with sharp eyes. He wasn't overly massive, but I could tell he trained from the way he carried himself. His brown hair was cropped short, and he wore the typical black SuNaTran driver uniform, minus the cap. I noticed the small, silver shield on his left shoulder with the red letters SNT in a stylized font in the center of the shield.

"Adam?" I asked. "Simon, not Mr. Strong, okay?"

"Of course, Mr. Strong."

I turned to Monty and shook my head.

"I give up," I said and noticed the thigh holster complete with weapon attached to his leg. "You're not just a driver—you're SNT-SEC, aren't you?"

"Yes, sir," Adam said with a hint of pride. "My job is to get you to London safely, no matter what."

"SNT-SEC?" Monty asked. "What has Cecil—?"

"I'll explain on the way," I said, before turning to Adam. "You could probably restock in the plane."

"Thank you, Mr. Strong, but I'm fully stocked," he said. "The vehicle is keyed to your signatures. Please rendezvous on my location when you have concluded your business."

Adam headed back to the Urus and waited.

"Will do," I said and started walking for the trees. Monty was still looking at the Urus. "Monty? You coming?"

He snapped out of whatever thought he was having and started walking in my direction.

"The runes on that vehicle are extraordinary," Monty said when he caught up to me. "Cecil has nearly managed to create an indestructible vehicle without the runes of death. It's quite elegant, yet so simple."

"Maybe you can have him call it the M-Treatment?"

He gave me a short glare.

"I'll have to ask him how he did it," Monty continued "He's used runes in ways I didn't think possible. Fascinating."

"You two can compare notes," I said. "He wants to know about your entropic siphon since it almost destroyed the Dark Goat."

"Who said it almost destroyed the Dark Goat?"

"I did," I said. "Tornado of death ring a bell? Pieces of the Dark Goat whirling around us?"

"It didn't almost destroy the Dark Goat," Monty said as we walked. "The runes on that vehicle are too strong, even for an entropic siphon."

"It tore the Dark Goat to pieces. I remember, I was in it at the time."

"The entropic siphon should have disintegrated the Dark Goat to atoms in seconds," Monty said. "The runes on the vehicle, coupled with your life force, dispelled the siphon without much effort."

I gave him a sideways glance as we kept walking.

"You are a scary individual," I said. "Don't you ever worry one day you'll go too far and unleash some world-destroying cast?"

"No," he said. "I'm not my uncle. I don't possess anywhere near the power he exhibited with that planar disruptor."

I shuddered at the memory of the golf ball of obliteration Dex had formed in his hand.

"Have I ever told you that you have a scary family?"

"Says the immortal, hellhound-bondmate, time-bending, Aspis, Marked of Kali," he replied. "I think the pot calling the kettle black applies here."

"Hey, most of those—"

"Stop where you are or die where you stand," a voice said from the trees. "State your purpose."

We had been walking for close to an hour and stood in the middle of a thick growth of trees. We immediately stopped walking.

"Wow," I said raising my hands. "They take protecting the land seriously here."

"This isn't just the land," Monty said under his breath. "This is Josephine's domain. They are loyal to her because *she* protects the land."

"These are the verdere...verderrieres?"

"Verderers, and yes," Monty said with a nod. "I suggest you call them rangers. I don't think they would appreciate being called verderrieres."

"Right," I said, making a mental note. No one enjoyed being called the green asses, even if they worked in an over-sized park. "We're here to see Ms. Josephine."

"Liar," one of the voices said. "She doesn't see anyone, and if she *did,* she wouldn't see the likes of you."

"What's that supposed to mean?" I said, turning toward the voice behind me. "That's just rude."

"It appears there's been a misunderstanding," Monty said. "My uncle arranged this meeting."

"Turn around and go back the way you came."

I was starting to get upset.

"I'm afraid that won't be possible," Monty said calmly, and lowering his arms. "Please inform Witch Josephine that we seek an audience. We will be remaining here until we hear from her, directly."

"We'll see about that," a voice said.

That's when I saw the trees move.

NINETEEN

"Are trees supposed to do that?" I said as I noticed some of the trees closing on us. "This isn't some side effect from Dex's circle? You're seeing the moving trees, too, Right?"

"Trees aren't usually ambulatory, no," Monty said matter-of-factly, while remaining still. He raised his hand and formed a blinding white orb in his extended palm. "Whatever you do, do not harm the trees."

"Are you referring to the menacing trees that are coming our way? Those trees?"

"Yes," he said and turned to the moving trees. "This is an orb of runic flame." He lowered his hand slowly. "If you attack either of us, this orb will find its way into that part of the forest."

Monty pointed to the dense growth of trees to our right.

"If you unleash that orb," a female voice said, "neither of you will live long enough to take your next breath."

"Monty," I said, keeping my voice low. "I'm really fond of breathing."

"As am I," he answered in the same tone. "But we've

slowed their advance. It seems we have Witch Josephine's attention."

He was right.

The trees had stopped moving.

"This may not be the kind of attention we were looking for," I said. "This is the kind of attention that gets us blasted into atoms."

"We mean you or your land no offense," Monty said, ignoring me. "I am—"

"I know who you are," the voice said, interrupting Monty. "Your words are meaningless while you hold destruction in your hand. Douse the flame, and I *may* allow you to leave here with your life."

"This would be a good time to douse the flame," I said. "She sounds pissed."

Monty reabsorbed the orb.

The forest grew still as if holding its breath. I hadn't noticed it before. There were no sounds of animals scurrying in the underbrush. I didn't hear one bird singing in the distance. It was probably because they didn't know any elegies.

All we got was silence.

It was the kind of silence that filled you with dread.

"Well, this doesn't look good," I said. "Maybe opening with an orb of flame was a bad call?"

"Trees don't like fire," Monty said. "It's not like I was actually going to set the New Forest aflame."

"Holding a loaded orb and demanding an audience seems a little pushy, I think," I said, looking around for the rangers. "The verd—rangers are gone too."

"They're not gone," Monty said. "They're hiding. Waiting for orders from her."

"This would be a good place to use that famous diplomacy of yours," I said. "The one that doesn't get us killed."

"The method may have been heavy-handed, but we have the desired result," he said with a look around. "We have her attention."

"I'm just pointing out that the approach could've been a bit smoother," I said. "Super powerful witch who's touchy about her forest, and you open with, 'Come any closer and I'll burn it down?' And you wonder why people talk about the Montagues' destructive tendencies?"

A woman stepped out from behind one of the trees.

My first impression was—power.

She was dressed like an average person. She wore a green blouse with long flowing sleeves over a pair of dark jeans. Her long brown hair was pulled back in a loose ponytail and she was barefoot.

She didn't look a day over thirty.

Her medium-sized frame blended well into the background of trees. Everything about her seemed ordinary until you looked *around* her.

Reality itself seemed to be bending around her.

The space around her body seemed warped as she stepped forward. If I had any doubt about her mood earlier, the angry waves of energy coming from her removed all doubt.

She was pissed.

She stopped about twenty feet away and stared at us calmly.

Her eyes pulsed with an iridescent blue energy, the color of a deep ocean. Small bolts of blue-white energy arced all around her. Surprisingly, they didn't cause damage to the trees or the grass beneath her feet.

"He's certainly dense enough to be your kin," she said to no one in particular. "He nearly earned himself an early grave."

"Aye, he gets it from his mother's side," said another, familiar voice. "Fiery she was indeed."

"I told Connor to stay away from that one," she said, sizing up Monty. "Did he listen? Of course not. You Montagues never listen to the voice of reason. At least he has his mother's looks."

"Don't blast them," the familiar voice answered. "They'll behave."

Dex.

"What of the cursed one?" she said, turning her powerful gaze to focus on me. "He is bonded to the hound and marked by the dark goddess? A curious pair, these two."

I wasn't exactly squirming under her gaze, but I suddenly understood how ants felt right before the boot stomp.

"He's a babe in this world," Dex said. "They both are. I take responsibility for them both while on your land, with my apologies."

"You do?" she said, staring at Monty again. "They must mean much to you for you to make such a pact."

"They do."

"On your word as bond," she said, still looking at us. "An accord has been created. Their words and actions fall upon you."

"Understood."

A green teleportation circle floated in the air next to her and Dex stepped forward into the New Forest with an angry expression. Next to him I saw Peaches, who bounded over to me and nearly knocked me down.

<I missed you, boy. How was your trip?>

<The old man made me some meat, but it wasn't extra. I'm still starving. Do you have meat with you?>

<Great to see you, too—and no, I don't walk around with meat.>

<You should. Then I wouldn't starve.>

<It's good to see your priorities haven't changed in my absence. The polite thing would've been to ask how I'm doing. For all you know, I could've been lost during my trip.>

<You were never lost. I know where you are all the time. You are my bondmate. Please ask the old man to make some extra meat soon.>

<I will.>

I rubbed my hellhound's massive head and then took a good look at Dex.

"Shit," I muttered. "This just got worse."

"By orders of magnitude," Monty said. "He does *not* look pleased."

"Come to the house," she said, and turned to walk away. "I will be waiting. Do not delay."

A few steps later, she melted into the forest and vanished from sight.

Dex turned to face Monty. His expression was neutral, but his intent washed over us.

The intent in his body language read: shred to little pieces, then incinerate said pieces. I half expected him to draw Nemain and pound Monty across the forehead.

"What *exactly* were you thinking, lad?"

"I was thinking—"

"Stop right there," Dex said. "Wrong."

"Wrong?"

"You weren't thinking," Dex said. "You threatened her trees. Are you mad?"

"They were about to attack us."

"You have faced mages bent on destruction and controlled by old gods," Dex said. "Are you standing there telling me you were in fear for your life...from some twigs?"

"Those are some enormous trees," I said, glancing at the now innocent-looking trees. "They were moving, closing in on us. I mean, one swipe from one of those branches—"

He gave me a withering glare that froze my words mid-thought and stepped closer to the both of us. I realized he was well within axe-swinging range.

"Josephine...is my *friend*," Dex said evenly as he focused

on Monty. "You behaved like some first-level apprentice, who jumped at his shadow because the fearsome trees were coming for him. You are a Montague and an experienced mage."

Monty remained silent, but his face turned bright red.

"We're sorry," I said. "In Monty's defense, he wasn't going to set the New Forest into an inferno."

"When I left you earlier," Dex said, glancing at me, "my nephew possessed the power of speech. Are ye his shieldwarrior *and* spokesperson now?"

I remained silent, properly chastised.

"The orb was merely a deterrent," Monty said. "A way to buy time."

"This is *protected* land," Dex said with a small sigh. "Do you understand what that means?"

"The government has designated it special land to be preserved?" I said. "It's a place they care about and have the verderri—rangers patrol to keep people from damaging anything?"

"Yes, and more importantly, there is a person—a very powerful person—who will *actively* protect this land by raining deadly power on any who would destroy her domain."

"Oh, *that* kind of protected."

"Aye, that kind of protected."

"I was not going to incinerate the New Forest," Monty said, keeping his voice low. "It was never my intention."

"I should think not," Dex said, narrowing his eyes at Monty. "The reason, the *only* reason, you are standing here is because I advised her against destroying you."

"Thank you," Monty said. "I acted without thinking, and for that I am truly sorry."

"Aye," Dex said shaking his head. "A modicum of restraint is required when dealing with her. Did I not explain this?"

"Restraint?" I said, coasting over the thin ice I stood on

and blissfully ignoring the cracking sounds around me. "I'm surprised Montagues even know the meaning of the word."

"Oh, I'm familiar with the term," Dex said, turning to me. "Right now, I'm exercising large amounts of it. That's why you two are still standing in the New Forest and not freezing in the Arctic Circle. See? Restraint."

Peaches whined next to me.

"Us *two*?" I protested. "I'm not the one who formed a flaming orb of destruction."

"You're not wrapping your brain around who you are, are ye?" Dex said, pointing a finger at me. "*You* are *his* shield warrior. His Aspis. *His* actions reflect on *you*. *Your* actions reflect on *him*. He gets sent to the Arctic, so do you. It's a package deal."

I took a few steps back.

"I want to formally state that this package deal sucks."

"It's called life," Dex said with a growl. "Deal with it. Now, let's move. Let's not add the insult of making her wait to the attempted incineration of her home."

He turned and walked ahead, grumbling to himself. I caught something about "royal pains in my arse," but lost the rest as he led the way deeper into the forest.

TWENTY

"He seems really upset," I said as we followed Dex. We were close, but not too close, in case he decided to reflexively teleport us out of the country—like distance was an issue for a mage who could throw teleportation circles at you. "Why is he so upset? The orb?"

"No," Monty said after a pause. "We caused him to lose face with someone he respects. He had to personally vouch for us to save our lives. It puts him in her debt, which I'm sure is considerable by this point."

"What do you mean?"

"Aside from my realignment, she allowed the Shrike to touch down on her domain," Monty said. "She's also the one who knows where York is. I can't imagine how many favors my uncle called in to get us to this point. After all that, he risks his life."

"That's what the pact was about?"

Monty nodded.

"He basically guaranteed our lives with his own."

I looked up at the old mage, who was moving quite fast despite his age, with a newfound respect.

"I can understand her blasting *you*, Mr. Flaming Orb," I said. "I don't see how that translates into my getting a death sentence. Not that I would allow you to go down alone, just seems excessive."

"It's a matter of death by association in this case," Monty said. "If I do something to damage the land—in this case, burn the trees down—she has to assume, because you are with me, that you're a threat. The prudent thing would be to be preemptive and remove you before you attacked."

"Witch logic makes less sense than mage logic."

"It's a matter of show me who your friends are, and—"

"I'll show you who you are," I said. "I get it, but it seems like an overreaction."

"Actually it's quite simple," he said. "She's an Earth Witch. Any threat to her land is met with zero tolerance and overwhelming force."

"That would explain *her* reaction, but this pact Dex made? That doesn't make sense."

"Yes," Monty said. "I've never heard him do that before. He must hold her in high esteem. Or prefers we don't die here."

"Are you saying that if we—according to what Dex said—if we do something wrong, something that violates her rules, he takes personal responsibility?"

Monty nodded.

"I don't imagine that would go well," Monty replied as we moved forward. "Can you understand why he's upset? She's his friend, but we're his family and we put him in the difficult position of standing against his friend to protect us."

"Family always comes first," I said, mostly to myself as we walked. "Sometimes your family isn't always blood, though."

"Precisely," Monty said. "My uncle doesn't have many people he can call friend *or* family. Mostly because he's so powerful, he scares those close to him. Actually, he and Tempest are very similar in that regard."

"Or it could be that little matter of dating the Morrigan," I said. "I mean, that would make it hard to make friends. Can you imagine the dinner parties? Who's that? Oh, this is my date, the Morrigan, Goddess of Death, Chooser of the Slain. Can't imagine she would be the *life* of any party."

"A valid consideration," Monty said. "The heart is a complex and tangled thing. I can't pretend to understand his attraction to her and, even less, *her* attraction to him."

"Is that why he's always so grumpy, or is that part of the DNA of the Montague mages?"

"I think it's a mage thing, actually," Monty replied. "Mages don't really relax— or *cut loose,* as you like to say. There's too much at stake if we lose control."

"Smiling is not the same as losing control," I said. "Even laughter would be good for you from time to time."

"You're fairly new to this life, so I can appreciate your position," Monty said. "Most of the mages I've known have very little to smile or laugh about."

"Is this because he's old?"

"It's also because many of his friends have died," Monty said, glancing at his uncle's back. "He's older than any mage I know, and Josephine is even older than him. Can you imagine the history between the two?"

"Aren't the Ten his family? What about the Morrigan?"

Monty kept walking in silence for a few seconds.

"You just mentioned more reasons for people to fear him," he said. "He's too dangerous for the Ten. Think on that for a moment, knowing what you know of that group. He is basically...alone."

"I can't imagine what that would feel like."

"You will, sadly."

"What are you talking about?"

"If Kali doesn't lift your curse, what do you think will happen to you?"

"You mean if my successors don't dust me first?"

"Provided you survive every encounter, what is the end result?"

"I'm alive," I said. "I like that end result. That is a good end result."

"Now it is, yes," Monty admitted. "What about in one hundred years, one thousand, ten thousand? When everyone you know is a memory, and it's just you, alone, in a different era?"

I remained silent for a few moments.

"That would utterly suck."

"*That* is what Kali has cursed you with," Monty said. "My uncle may not be immortal, but he is ancient. I'm sure this is why he has some affinity to you. He understands what lies ahead for you, at least to a small degree."

"This is why his friendship with Josephine is so important," I said, glancing ahead at Dex. "How are *you* going to make it up to him?"

"*We*. We are going to make it up to him."

"Fine," I said with a short sigh. "How are *we* going to make it up to him?"

"I don't know yet, precisely, but I have an idea," he said. "I'll start with profuse apologies to her, and then... There is a cast I've been working on that may be just the thing. It's something I was experimenting with while at Haven to accelerate my healing."

"That sounds like a mistake," I said, shaking my head. "Can we stay away from any experiments while we're in the scary witch's forest?"

"This will be fine," Monty assured me. "It's a small spell and should help us gain her favor."

"Ugh. Let's just stick to apologies, that sounds safer."

"We owe him that much and more," Monty said serious. "We have to at least try to repair what is broken. This is no small matter, Simon."

"Okay," I said, giving in. "When she's blasting us to little bits, understand that I'm going to remind you that it was all your fault."

"It won't come to that."

"You'll forgive me if your track record prevents me from believing you," I said, looking ahead and realizing Dex was gone. "Where's Dex?"

"Inside," Monty said, pointing. "We're at her home."

"Her home?" I asked, confused. "All I see is a huge grass-covered mound. What home?"

"Look carefully," he said. "The mound up there."

I used my innersight. A cascade of light and power bombarded my vision, nearly blinding me.

"What is that?" I asked in awe. "It's like an energy generator."

"That"—he pointed to the large grass-covered mound surrounded by large rectangular stones—"is her home."

Each of the stones, which stood three feet tall, contained complex and ornate decorations on their surface. As we approached, it felt like getting closer to an electrical power plant. I could feel the hair on my arms and back of my neck stand on end.

The air around us felt charged, like standing outside right before a thunderstorm. The air was clean, and crisp, the smell right before a hard rain in the spring.

"It looks like an enormous hobbit home," I said, taking in a deep breath. "What are those stones?"

"It is not a smial or hobbit-hole," Monty said. "You do realize that is a story, yes?"

"Of course," I said. "It's not like hobbits are *real*."

"Correct," Monty said, looking at me sternly. "Josephine is

not a hobbit. I strongly suggest you remove that thought from your brain. The stones, if I'm not mistaken, make this mound the center of a circle henge."

"Like Stonehenge?"

"Similar, but different," Monty said. "This is a henge of immense power, one that no one visits. Stonehenge has power, but it's been diluted by becoming a tourist attraction. This henge has retained all of its power. Within that circle of stones, Josephine's power is magnified."

"Great, the uber scary powerful witch is even more powerful in her home," I said. "This doesn't feel like walking into a trap at all."

"It's not a trap."

"It's not dangerous?"

"I didn't say it wasn't dangerous," Monty said. "We're walking into the home of an upset witch. It's quite dangerous, but it's not a trap."

"Thank you for making that much clearer," I said. "I feel so much better about walking into the not-trap home of an offended witch."

"Where her power is magnified."

"Right, where her power is magnified," I said. "Can't forget *that* part."

"The difference is always in the details," he said and stepped forward to touch one of the stones, which thrummed with power. "The entrance is on the other side."

"Are you sure?" I said, examining the mound. "I'm not seeing any kind of entrance...anywhere."

"I believe that's the point," he said, circling the mound and touching some of the stones, but not the others. "There is an entry sequence with the stones."

"What happens if you get it wrong?" I asked warily. "Do you have any sort of experience with henges?"

"Considering whose home this is, I would imagine something unpleasant."

"Oh, just something unpleasant like getting turned around or finding yourself outside the New Forest?"

"Something unpleasant like an energy blast rendering us to dust."

"I think I'll leave the stone keys to you then," I said, eyeing the runed slabs as Monty placed his hands on them. "Try not to make a mistake."

"I will endeavor to do my best," he said. "Silence really helps my concentration."

"Really? Mine too. I find that I concentrate best when things are quiet," I said. "I have the best focus when I'm surrounded by silence. It's important."

Monty stopped walking and stared at me.

"I was referring to our immediate circumstances," he said, moving to the next stone. "The runes are archaic and some of them I barely recognize."

"Do you need help?" I asked. "My rune reading is getting better."

"That's a kind offer, really, but I think I'll soldier on with my limited literacy, thank you."

"Well, you say the word and I'm here," I said. "I'm sure I could pick up some of these runes given time."

"Simon," Monty said when we reached the next stone. "Are you eager to test the limits of your immortality?"

"Am I what?"

"Eager to see what it would take to kill you?"

"Not particularly, no."

"If I get this sequence wrong, I'm fairly certain you will," he said, examining the stone. "Do you want to have a conversation, or are you going to let me focus on these runes?"

I stepped back a few steps.

"Sorry about that," I said, waving him on. "Focus away."

"Thank you," he said keeping his eyes on the stone. "This should only take a few more moments."

I paused for a moment and let him examine the stone.

"Are you sure you want to do this?" I asked.

"I'd rather not stay out here all day," Monty said, still deciphering runes. "I think finding the door would be a good idea."

"Not that," I said. "I mean this whole Stormblood thing. What if it kills you? Or turns you into a Darth Monty permanently?"

Monty stopped examining the current stone.

"Those are probabilities, though I'm not so certain about the whole Darth state."

"You know what I mean," I said. "You weren't exactly yourself during your schism. You and your dark side were getting a little too close for comfort."

"The key is, I didn't succumb to my darker nature."

"During a schism, this is something else," I said, looking around. "This is stepping into the big leagues. Josephine is on another level of power."

"I understand your concerns, but we have to look not at what may happen, but what we know will happen. Chaos is not going away, especially not after what happened with Mahnes."

"He's not going to drop this, is he?"

Monty shook his head and went back to examining the stone. He crouched down to get a closer look.

"I would assume ancient beings of power are accustomed to getting their way," he said, dusting off the surface of the stone. "We have now stopped him more than once. He's not going to agree to disagree. Beings like Chaos tend to lean more toward the 'destroy everything in their path' method of resolution."

"He's acting like a spoiled brat," I said. "Aren't there any beings stronger than Chaos we can call on to set him straight?"

"Of course," Monty said without looking away. "I'll just use my phone and call them. I'm sure I have several beings of mind-numbing power stored in my contacts. Why didn't I think of that?"

"Not funny. If Chaos is out here on a rampage, where is Order?"

"The same as Chaos, Order is always present and on occasion uses agents to confront the personification of Chaos."

"I'm sorry; I didn't see any personifications fighting alongside us when we faced Mahnes," I said. "It was just us, with help from Dex."

"Yes, it was."

"It would be nice if we could summon an old god to step up on our side from time to time."

"I know," Monty said, glancing at me. "It's not that easy. If you want to 'speak' to Kali, how would you go about it? Can you simply call her? She doesn't seem like the type to be summoned on command, does she?"

I gave it some thought. I'd only gotten her attention the first time because I stumbled into and screwed up a 5000-year-old trap she'd been about to spring on Shiva.

That hadn't go so well.

"I don't know," I said. "Outside of that temple in Jersey, she's more the 'don't call me, I'll call you' type of goddess. Not that I'm complaining."

"It's difficult," he said. "This is a goddess you have some connection with and you can't access her easily. When they reach that level of power, they rarely interact with humans unless they want to"—he waved a hand in my direction—"curse you or something similar."

"Kali, I can understand," I said. "We interfered in her plan, ruining 5000 years of preparation."

"That does have a tendency to create animosity, yes."

"But what did Chaos expect?" I demanded. "That we were just going to let him do whatever he wanted, whenever he wanted?"

"In a word, yes," Monty said, pressing the symbols on the stone, before standing. "There, that should do it. Chaos *is* chaos: he expects to disrupt, and destroy. It's what he does and who he is. He doesn't expect to be thwarted by what he deems creatures of insignificance."

"Isn't this Stormblood thing going to put a larger target on your back?"

"You mean larger than walking around with the Aspis of Kali who currently has successors after him, while dealing with Verity who would prefer I cease existing, based on some archaic rule about runes?"

"Yes, larger than that."

"After Mahnes," he said, rubbing his chin, "I would imagine we both have sizable targets on our backs. Our options are limited."

"Oh? We have options?"

"Of course. We can hide, which would only delay the inevitable."

"Not so big on hiding in fear, pass."

"We could capitulate and perish," he continued. "I doubt even your immortal state would protect you in that scenario."

"I'm aware of the power levels we are facing. Surrender isn't an option...ever."

"That leaves our final option: become a greater threat by increasing our power. The side effect of this option is that it brings us unwarranted attention from beings we'd prefer to avoid."

"The more of a threat we become to them, the more we stand out?"

"Succinctly put," he said, heading to the far side of the

mound. "Take your hellhound for example; a puppy is not that dangerous."

"Are we discussing the same hellhound I know?" I asked. "Because the hellhound I know is mostly all danger, destruction, and digestion."

"Your creature has the *potential* for danger, but is currently easy to neutralize," he said. "Providing you aren't in imminent danger, a large amount of meat can easily distract him."

"True," I said. "He does have a one-track mind."

"Now, compare your creature to Cerberus," Monty said, coming to a stop. "Do you think a bowl of pastrami is going to stop him from rending you to pieces, no matter how large?"

I thought about the last and only time we'd faced Peaches' father. Even Hades, a god, was uncomfortable with the thought of facing his hellhound in combat.

"Not even for a second," I said. "So you're saying I'm becoming a serious threat now? I get it."

"Not entirely," he said, touching the mound. "You are like your creature. The potential is there—"

"Are you calling me a puppy?"

"In the best sense of the word," Monty said as a large section of the mound opened, allowing us entry. "Those we face would prefer to eliminate you now, before you grow into your power."

"What about you?" I asked. "Are you a puppy, too?"

"Did you miss the display of power from Josephine, or my uncle with that planar disruptor?"

"No, both were pretty incredible and frightening."

"Did you happen to notice either of them using symbols or tracing runes in the air the way I do?"

"Now that you mention it, they slipped into fearsome mode pretty easily," I said giving it thought. "No gestures or symbols."

"That should answer your question," Monty said, pointing. "This is the entrance."

I looked into the entrance that sloped down into complete darkness. It resembled a large mouth about to swallow us whole.

"This isn't creepy at all," I said, looking down the mouth. "I'm not seeing any switches to turn on the cave lights."

Monty formed a small orb of light. I gave him a look.

"Don't worry, this is luminescence only," he said, walking forward. "Wouldn't want you to lose your footing and stumble into Josephine's home. That would send the wrong impression."

"Right, because we've made such a good impression so far," I said. "After you."

TWENTY-ONE

We traveled down into the mound for a few minutes.

The dim light from Monty's orb provided just enough light for us to see several feet ahead of us. Outside of that radius, the passageway in the mound was pitch black.

After a few more minutes of walking in the dark, we found ourselves in a foyer. This was one of those cases when the inside was much larger than the outside.

I could overhear Dex and Josephine speaking as we entered.

"You left them outside?" Josephine asked. "Are you mad?"

"Of course I left them outside," Dex snapped. "If he can't find the blasted door, he has no business being here."

"The door is hidden for a reason, Dexter," she said. "He could be out there lost, wandering the Forest."

"My nephew can be impetuous and prone to destruction," Dex said, "but he *is* a Montague."

"Is that supposed to make me feel better?" she replied. "Do I need to remind you about *your* plan to hide the New Forest?"

"No need," Dex grumbled. "I still hold that it was a good plan."

"That would have worked once," she said with a sigh. "Lining the border of the land with explosive runes would have destroyed the entire Forest."

"I was young."

"Yes, impetuous and prone to destruction," she said. "It seems to be a trait in your family. Your father was the worst, by far."

Dex chuckled.

"He did have a destructive streak," Dex said. "Still, Tristan will find the door."

"Or blow a passageway in," Josephine said. "Which, if he does, you will be responsible." There was a slight pause. "Never mind—they did find the door."

We walked into a large comfortable room, and Dex turned to us with a tight smile.

"Did you find the door or make one?" Dex asked warily. "Tell me you found it."

"We used the stones, Well Monty did, and then a door appeared."

Josephine looked at Monty and nodded.

"He has promise after all," she said. "Follow me, both of you."

We were standing in a large sitting room. There were a few stone tables with books opened and flasks with different-colored liquids. Next to the flasks, I noticed some mortars and pestles with various powders in them. Leaves were spread out near them, arranged in small groups.

Dex sat on a stone bench at another table that held more books. He was currently reading a large book covered in runes with pages that gave off a subtle green glow. The room itself smelled of freshly cut grass and moist earth after a rain.

Josephine led us out of this room and into a small corridor

which opened into another room. I looked back to see Dex sitting at the table, waving us on after Josephine.

"Get a move on, lads," Dex said. "We haven't all day."

"What does that mean?" I asked. "We just got here."

"There are elements pursuing you both," Josephine said. "Our time before your discovery is limited. We must make haste."

"Even here?" I asked. "In your domain?"

"There are deterrents in place, but neither of you is invisible," she said, glancing back at me. "The beacons placed on you would require you to leave this plane to hide effectively. Even then, that would be a short-term solution. You have been marked by a dark goddess and Tristan used an elder rune. These things tend to attract attention."

"No kidding The wrong kind usually."

"Once the realignment is complete, they will know where you are."

"I left my successor across an ocean. Same with Verity."

"Distance is not a factor here," she said. "The realignment will broadcast your location to those pursuing you. The same for Tristan. There is no hiding from this. They are coming."

She remained silent as we kept walking.

We followed her into the next room. Peaches padded silently next to me. For such a large animal, he could be surprisingly stealthy when he wanted to be, unless meat was involved.

This room was twice the size of the sitting room. It was made entirely of stone and was empty, except for a large rune-covered circle etched into raised stone which dominated the center of the dark stone floor. I looked around in awe. All of the walls were stone, but the entire space felt warm and cozy.

"How did you build all of this?" I asked, still looking around. "This construction is amazing."

"Thank you," Josephine said. "I had help."

"So, Josie," I started as I felt the air escape my lungs while my throat constricted. "Jo—"

The circle in the center of the floor pulsed with green-white energy as Josephine glanced my way with a small smile.

"You were saying?" she asked. "Please continue."

I pointed to my neck, trying to form the words but lacking the air to do so. It became harder and harder to take a breath. Monty looked at me, his expression dark with concern. Peaches whined, standing by me, and looked up at Josephine.

"Witch Josephine?" Monty asked.

"I'm sorry, is something the matter?"

"Josephine, would you kindly release him?" Monty asked. "He does need to breathe." Monty gave me a short glare. "He's immortal, not intelligent."

She flicked her wrist and the vise grip around my neck vanished. I took a huge breath and gasped.

<Don't make the tree lady angry.>

<I wasn't trying to.>

<Try harder. She is very strong. If I bite her, it will be bad.>

<Do not bite the tree lady. She will hurt you.>

<We are bondmates. If she hurts you, I will protect you.>

<I won't make her upset again. Promise.>

<Good. Maybe she makes good meat?>

<I don't think we should ask any time soon.>

<Ask later when she is happy with you.>

She took a step closer and faced me.

"The name is Josephine or Witch Josephine, until I say otherwise. Understood?"

I nodded.

"You're entirely too familiar, and where I come from it's considered rude. You don't hear me calling you Simon the smart arse, do you?"

"I'm sorry," I said after a few more gasps. "It won't happen again."

She gave me an even stare, easily a four on the glare-o-meter. I was impressed. I think even Clint would give her the nod of approval for a glintastic glare capable of stopping anyone in their tracks.

"See that it doesn't," she said, turning back to the center of the room. "Words have power. That mouth of yours is going to get you killed one day, if you're not careful."

"Not the first time I've been given that advice," I said, rubbing my neck.

"Heed it. There are many beings with less patience and considerably more power than I possess, who would destroy you with a glance."

"Understood," I said, keeping my voice low. "Thank you."

She turned to Monty.

"Very well," she said. "Let's take a look."

This sounded like the beginning of a medical examination and I suddenly felt like I should be in the other room with Dex.

"Should I be here?" I asked. "I mean if you're going to do an examination, I could wait in the other room."

"You're his shield warrior; where else should you be?" she asked. "Watch and learn. You're next."

"I'm what?"

"Is he hard of hearing," she asked, looking at Monty, "or simply overwhelmed?"

"Mostly overwhelmed, but I'd say he's adjusting well," Monty said. "He hasn't lost his mind... yet."

Josephine turned to me, and glanced down at Peaches.

"You bonded to a hellhound," she said. "This tells me you have considerable potential. That, and Kali's curse has privileged you with life. You stay. This involves you as much as it involves him."

"She also marked me with a bullseye and then sent successors after me," I said. "Not feeling especially privileged these days."

She narrowed her eyes at me and nodded.

"A test," she said with a smile. "You do know how to make enemies. Kali does not like you."

I was about to answer in my typical manner when Monty gave his head a slight shake, warning me and probably saving me from another breathless episode.

"No, she doesn't," I said, finally. "I don't understand why she didn't just kill me."

"You will, but not for many years," she said. "In the meantime, we will prepare you both."

"Prepare us both?" I asked, pointing at Monty. "I didn't go through a schism, he did."

"In order for Tristan to ascend to Stormblood, you must accept who you are. You are both linked, stronger together than apart."

"I don't see the connection," I said. "He's a mage and I'm...not."

"Neither am I," she said and waved an arm, causing the room to burst into green-white light as the circle filled with energy. "Mages are not the only ones who can manipulate energy."

"I understand that, I just don't understand why I'm a part of his Stormbloodiness," I said. "It doesn't make sense."

"We will make some of it clear today. First, Tristan," she said, turning to Monty, "please step into the circle."

Monty stepped into the center of the circle.

The green-white light pulsed for a few moments before turning violet with hints of black and red. Then it turned only violet and black.

"Unleash your power," she said. "All of it."

"All of it?" Monty asked. "I don't think that would be wise. I could damage your home."

"Where was this prudence when you stood in my forest?" she asked, crossing her arms. "You could unleash ten times what you currently possess and it would barely tax this circle. You are powerful, but not *that* powerful. Unleash your power. Use gestures if you must, but make sure it's all of it."

Monty nodded and began tracing symbols in the air. Josephine nodded as he created violet runes in the air. She extended a hand for a few seconds as a column of violet energy shot into the air surrounding Monty.

Monty grimaced as he stood in the middle of the column of power. I could feel the power filling the room as the violet energy shifted from pure violet to violet with black and red sections.

The circle remained green-white in the center. The violet-black energy filled the circumference of the circle and slowly crept inward to the center.

Josephine looked at him and shook her head.

"Your schism is not fully healed," she said. "Then you used an elder rune? It's a wonder you're still alive."

She extended her arm again.

The green-white energy increased and completely filled the circle in the floor. The violet energy Monty stood in transformed from violet-black to only violet.

I saw a trickle of blood flow from Monty's nose.

"This is hurting him," I said. "He's bleeding."

"This isn't hurting him, not yet," she said her face grim. "It will hurt in a moment, once you do your part."

"My part?" I said, looking at Monty. "I don't have a part in any of that."

"Which is why your strongest bond is blocked."

"My strongest bond?"

"As above, so below. Inside as it is outside."

"That makes no sense," I said, concerned. "Can we stop this now?"

"Kali and your hellhound, your undead, and"—she looked at Monty—"him."

"I wish I understood what all of that meant."

"Above, below, inside, and out," she said tersely. "This last bond is not yet reconciled and needs to be set right."

"How am I supposed to do that from out here?"

"You can't," she said, focusing on Monty. "You have to step inside."

TWENTY-TWO

"I have to step inside of that?"

The violet beam shot through Monty and into the ceiling, filling the room, and casting nearly everything in a purple light—everything except the floor, which blazed green-white.

"If you don't, he dies," she said. "The schism and elder rune have done extensive damage. That energy is slowly killing him. He will either succumb to the darkness or the schism will overtake him. Either way, he dies."

I took a step forward and she placed a hand on my shoulder.

"You must know that if you step in that circle, you can die," she said firmly. "If the balance isn't restored, you will both end here. Your curse will not protect you."

"What do I need to do?"

"You do what you are meant to do," she said. "That is all I can tell you."

"That's not vague at all."

She gave me a small nod followed by a sad smile. "The world you now walk in is defined by the uncertain. Nothing is promised, and little has explanation."

Peaches whined by my feet.

"It'll be okay, boy," I said, rubbing his head, then looked up at Josephine. "If something happens to me and I don't—"

"He will be cared for," she said. "I won't let him transform, and he can stay here if he chooses to do so."

I nodded.

"Thank you."

"Remember, together you are stronger than each alone."

Witchspeak was worse than magespeak when it came to being cryptic—not that I shared that with her.

I took a deep breath and stepped into the circle.

The first thing I noticed was the sensation of power running through my body. It felt like stepping into a waterfall of energy. My brain was overwhelmed with sensory input. I took a few breaths to calm down and managed to get my breathing under control.

How was I supposed to help with the balance? I looked at Monty who was staring off into space somewhere, lost in pain. If he noticed my presence, he gave no indication of it.

Do what I'm meant to do? What did that even mean?

In the back of my mind, I heard Monty begin to scream. I turned to look at him and saw more blood flowing from his nose.

I was running out of time.

Somehow firing a magic missile at the violet beam seemed like the wrong move. It wasn't like my repertoire of casts was extensive. I had my magic missile, Ebonsoul, and my recently acquired dawnward. Other than that, there wasn't much else I could do to stop this energy beam from killing Monty.

Then I remembered my mark.

My first mark.

I looked down at my hand and saw it softly glowing white. *When did that start?*

An idea began forming in my mind. The issue was time, but I had a way to buy some time—at the very least, a few seconds. I'd seen Monty do incredible things with a few seconds of time.

I pressed my mark and felt time slow.

The heady smell of lotus blossoms and earth after a hard rain filled my lungs. This was followed by the sharp smell of cut oranges and an aroma hinting of cinnamon permeating the air.

It was one of the only times when I actually welcomed the smell of approaching Karma.

She appeared dressed in black jeans and an off-white Chanel sleeveless blouse. Her feet were bare as she walked past Josephine and Peaches, stepping into the circle beside me. On one shoulder, I could see a deep red letter B tattoo.

Her hair was pulled back in a tight ponytail with red lace intertwined throughout its length. I didn't see the several small sharp-looking knives as accessories, but she wore two long hairpins which looked deadly.

"Hello, Splinter," she said, taking in the room. "You never cease to amaze me." She glanced at Monty. "Are you trying to kill him? That's a little dark, even for you. I thought you were friends?"

"I'm trying to save him," I said. "Josephine said this was the best way."

Karma turned to look at Josephine.

"Best is a relative term," Karma said, looking at me again. "Did you summon me?"

"Yes," I said honestly. "I don't need you to do anything, except point me in the right direction. If you want to implement some karmic justice later, fine. I'll take whatever I deserve. I need your help now or Monty dies."

She narrowed her eyes at me and crossed her arms, gracing me with a small smile.

"You do realize death is the natural order of things for those who haven't been cursed alive?"

"I do," I said. "Monty shouldn't die for trying to help me stop Chaos."

"That's not what this is about," she said. "Look deeper. Did Chaos force him to use blood magic?"

"No."

"Was it Chaos that caused his schism?"

"Not to my knowledge, no."

"I know, it was Chaos that forced him to enter a forbidden area of the Living Library, and borrow an elder rune to stop a deranged mage. That must be it."

"No, he did that of his own volition," I said. "He made his choices."

"Choices, action, or inaction, always have consequences, Splinter," she said, glancing at Monty. "He's here because of his choices. Why are *you* here?"

"I choose to help him," I said, my voice firm. "I choose to help him live."

She nodded.

"You may end up regretting this choice," she said. "Then again, that in itself is a choice, isn't it?"

"Yes," I said. "Can you help me stop this?"

"You can't stop it," she said, stepping close to the violet light around Monty. "You really don't want to. If he gets through this, his schism will be repaired. All you need to do is establish—"

"Balance," I finished, interrupting her and forgetting myself for a moment. "How? How do I establish balance?"

"You do what only you can do. It's simple."

"Could you make it a little clearer?" I asked. "That's what Josephine said."

"I have to admit, I'm impressed," she said. "You meeting

Tempest? She's not even actively trying to kill you. That is exceptional."

"Right now she isn't."

"True. This is you after all," she said. "I give it another ten minutes max before she threatens to erase you from existence."

"We already did that."

"Really? And yet here you stand...alive," she said, giving me a once over. "You really never cease to surprise me."

"Balance?"

"You're not thinking this through. You can't stop this process, so what can you do?" she said and began fading out. "What are the few things you can do, besides give me attitude? How do you balance something like this?"

"I need to bleed off some of that power, give Monty a chance to deal with the energy around him," I said, still confused. "I don't know how to do that. I'm not a mage."

"Stop thinking in absolutes," Karma said. "Neither is Josephine, and yet she manipulates vast amounts of power. Now, if only you had something that let you siphon power."

"No."

"Yes," she said. "All choices have consequences. It's not making the choice that's difficult, it's living or dying because of the choice made. You know what you have to do; the choice is yours."

Karma disappeared and time snapped back into its normal flow.

I knew what I had to do, I just didn't know what would happen if I did. This had the potential to make things so much worse.

"Nothing ventured, nothing gained," I said under my breath. "I'm going to apologize now in case I kill you, Monty...sorry."

I reached out to the energy within me and formed the

silver mist that would become Ebonsoul. It enveloped my arm, forming the blade in my hand. The red runes along the length of the blade gleamed with vibrant energy.

I stepped close to Monty, letting the violet energy wash over me. I could feel the power trying to undo me. This was the schism in action. If left unchecked, it would kill him.

I took a deep breath and really hoped I was right about this. I used my innersight and saw what I needed to do and where.

I hefted Ebonsoul in my hand and plunged the blade into Monty's chest.

TWENTY-THREE

Monty's body arched as he was lifted off his feet and began floating in the center of the circle, arms outstretched and still screaming. I felt more than saw the black energy flow into Ebonsoul.

Then into me.

My blade siphoned the energy of the schism and elder rune. The backlash slammed me into the wall, breaking ribs, and still it flowed, pinning me to the wall.

The violet energy around Monty intensified, blocking him from my view. My body flushed hot and I was confused. Kali's curse was working to keep me alive, but the damage was too extensive, the power too great.

The pain ratcheted up to eye-gouging level as my body tried to deal with the extra power. It flowed in and through me, the sensation of internal burning covering my entire body. I forced myself to look down, and I was shocked to see my skin intact and not peeling off in layers.

At some point, I lost my vision and sense of hearing. I floated in a void of endless pain as my body fought and failed to contain this power. I felt Ebonsoul dematerialize and rush into my body with a fresh wave of agony.

I screamed then, a silent wailing against power I had no way of understanding or controlling.

After what felt like an eternity, I collapsed to the floor, keeping my face against the coolness of the stone. I lay as still as possible, careful not to reactivate the pain coursing through my body.

A few choice words came to mind, but I was conscious of Josephine next to me. Somehow I didn't think the words I wanted to unleash would be respectful of her hospitality. I opted for agonized silence, broken with the infrequent groan every few seconds.

"You saved his life," Josephine said, crouching down next to me. I felt a warm hand touch my face as a green glow filled my vision. "Along with your own."

"I thought I could die in here," I rasped, my voice refusing to cooperate. "I felt the curse trying to heal my body. You said I would die."

"No," she corrected. "I said you *could* die. It wasn't a foregone conclusion for you. For Tristan, yes—but you, you had to make a willing choice. You had to be willing to risk your own life."

"Why?" I asked. "Why couldn't you save him?"

"I don't share the bond of brotherhood with him," she said. "You do. This was something only *you* could do."

I tried to sit up and my body screamed at me, informing me it was a fantastically bad idea. I laid my head back against the cool stone.

"My pain has pain," I said with a groan. "That was beyond unpleasant."

"How did you figure it out?"

"Karma," I said. "She pointed me in the right direction."

I expected her to scoff at my mention of Karma.

"I thought I recognized the endless knot. Did Kali give you that mark?"

I nodded and my vision swam for a second.

"That was the first mark she gave me," I said. "I think Karma is the added bonus."

"No," she said. "Karma is part of the mark. You've been cursed alive; who better to be exposed to Karma than an immortal?"

"It...it makes sense," I managed. "Kali never explained it that way."

"She wouldn't," Josephine said. "Consider: your actions lead to consequences which lead to actions, which lead to more consequences."

"An endless knot of choices."

Josephine nodded as she moved her hand to my chest.

"I haven't seen Karma in ages," Josephine said. "Is she still a bitch?"

"I can neither confirm nor deny that characterization of the personification of causality," I said, trying to sit up and failing. "She knows you, though. Called you Tempest."

"I'll take that as a yes," she said with a slight smile. "I haven't been called Tempest in over half a millennium. Those were different times, requiring constant violence."

"Is it true you have a type of Stormblood?"

She looked at me in silence for a few moments.

"Being a witch means my power is primal, of the earth, not refined like a mage's. My power acts like a living thing. That doesn't mean it isn't as strong as a mage's use of power, just different and more volatile. Witches possess a different body of knowledge compared to that of mages; older, less orderly. This power is why we have always been feared throughout history."

"Knowledge is power."

"No," she said, tapping me in the head. "Power is power. Knowledge allows you to use that power correctly. When it comes to my power, it needs a vessel. The greater the power, the larger the vessel needs to be to contain it."

"Are you saying the New Forest is your vessel?" I asked, trying to comprehend the extent of her power. My brain seized after a few seconds. "The entire forest? How is that even possible?"

She nodded.

"I'm old," she said, "even by witch standards. I've channeled my power into my land over centuries, using it to protect those living in my domain."

"How do you have Stormblood? You're not a mage."

She gave me a smile.

"Who told you I have Stormblood?"

"Monty did. He said you have a version of it."

She glanced over at where Monty lay.

"He must be misinformed; I never told him I had Stormblood."

"Because you're not a mage?"

"Neither are you, and yet we both use energy in different ways," she replied. "Don't let the mages convince you that only *they* know how to wield power effectively. You should know better by now."

I made to get up again and she pushed down firmly on my chest.

"Lie still," she ordered. "Let the healing do its work."

"The balance?" I asked, glancing over where Monty lay. "Is it restored, or did I turn him into Darth Monty? Will he be okay?"

"He is scarred," she said. "Your method was...brutal, but effective. In time, there will be no trace of the damage from the schism."

"What about the elder rune?" I asked. "I felt the power of it flow into me."

"Not into you," she said. "Into your blade."

"The elder rune is in my blade?"

"Part of it is, yes," she said "The rest of the rune's power resides in Tristan."

"It's still active?" I asked worried. "Does that mean this didn't work?"

"The elder rune is dormant," she said. "For now. The elder runes require the user to relinquish them entirely. You have made it easier, but the attraction is strong—"

"He has to refuse its hold over him, doesn't he?"

"Yes," she said. "For now, he will not feel its effects, but it's there, waiting. May I see your blade?"

"Sure, but I don't know if I can—"

She tapped my chest and formed Ebonsoul, holding it in her hand. My blade, which was usually a black blade with red runes, now contained a band of silver down its length.

"I don't remember seeing that silver part before."

"That is the effect of the elder rune," she said, admiring it. "This is a siphon and a seraph blade. Your bond to this blade and the undead who presented it to you is powerful."

"Undead? You mean Michiko?"

"How many undead are you bonded to?"

"Just the one," I said. "I was making sure. How did you do that?"

"Do what?"

"Materialize it like that, effortlessly," I said. "I'm bonded to it, but even I've had issues with materializing it."

"You'll find it to be much easier now," she said, placing Ebonsoul on my chest. It vanished a second later and I could feel it within. "Your bonds will grow stronger now."

"My bonds?" I asked. "Is that a good thing?"

"That will depend on you, in the end. Today you made a

difficult choice." She looked at Monty again. "The conse-quences of that choice won't be known for some time."

"Karma said something similar," I said. "I can't believe you've met her."

"We've all met her at some point or another," she said. "How do you feel?"

"You mean aside from being battered, bruised, and broken?"

"Yes, aside from that."

"I feel whole, actually."

"Above, below, inside, and out," she said, getting to her feet. "You must be vigilant. The balance can be disrupted and must be maintained."

"Can Monty still use the Stormblood?"

"That will be up to him and York," she said. "My part is done. He's certainly ready to do so, physically. His body and energy are aligned. His mind is another matter entirely. The Stormblood is as much in his mind as it is in his body. I don't know what will happen when he undergoes the ritual."

"Can it kill him?"

"Of course," she said, gently. "Life is risk. If you want to stand against the forces of darkness, you must be prepared to accept every part of life. That includes death, even if it is not your own."

"Life has been mostly pain ever since I met Kali."

"I have walked through oceans of pain to get where I am today...some of it has even been mine," she said, looking away. "You will grow stronger. Pain has a way of shaping you, the way a blade is formed in the heat of the forge."

"Repeated hammering?" I said. "Because I've been hammered plenty by life. I'm ready to do some hammering of my own at this point—as soon as I can stand without falling over."

"You are a peculiar man, Simon Strong," she said,

motioning to Peaches, who padded over. "You will need that attitude soon. The Consortium has encroached on my land. They will be here shortly."

"They would dare approach against you?" I asked. "On your land?"

"The Penumbra Consortium is led by mages who are young and foolish," she said. "I have kept away from them for the most part, and they leave me alone. Today, they are here for you and Tristan; today, they will learn why they should have stayed out of the New Forest."

"Maybe you can get Dex to divert them from the Forest?"

"He would do it with explosives and deadly circles," she said, shaking her head. "Subtlety is not his strong point. He's a Montague. I will deal with the Consortium. Dexter will take you to Mage York."

I heard footsteps and saw Dex enter the room.

"We have company," he said. "Want me to—?"

"I will deal with them," Josephine said, cutting him off. "Get these two to York. He is sleeping with the four lions."

"Bugger, really?" Dex said. "He couldn't have picked a more public place? That's going to be nearly impossible to access."

"Perhaps that is why he chose the location?" she said. "Get moving as soon as you're able. You have a vehicle waiting nearby. It's not far to the motorway."

I got to my feet unsteadily and Dex helped Monty, who was still shaky, up to his feet.

"Bloody hell," Monty muttered as he dusted himself off. "I'd rather not do that again...ever."

"Did it take?" Dex asked Josephine, before looking at Monty. "He's ready?"

"He is," she said, waving a hand in Monty's direction and covering him with green energy. "I doubt you'll need to explain the situation to York, but you should, to be on the safe side."

"Aye, he's not exactly in his right mind these days."

"He hasn't been in his right mind for several centuries now," she said. "Make sure he understands what he is doing before he begins the ritual. You may need to assist him."

"I will," Dex said, turning and handing me the bag with my flask of javambrosia, Grim Whisper, and extra magazines of both entropy and Persuader rounds. I switched the magazine to Persuader rounds. "I see you cleared up those bonds, finally."

"Not fun," I said with a wince as I tightened the holster, placing the flask and extra ammo in my jacket. "Some warning would've been nice."

"I did warn ye, boy," Dex said with a grin. "More than once. You weren't paying attention."

"They have crossed the border of the Forest," Josephine said. "Let's go greet our uninvited guests. Dexter, I will keep them occupied while you—"

"Head to London," Dex finished. "Understood. Will you be fine on your own?"

"I was old when you were an irritating child," she said. "I think I can handle a group of mages with inflated egos who have come to challenge my power."

"Don't kill them, Josephine."

"Are you giving me instructions now?"

I felt the level of energy around us increase.

"I would never dream of telling you what to do," Dex said quickly, with a smile. "It was a mere suggestion. You kill this group, the Consortium will see it as a challenge and send more."

"I will educate them as to why they should stay out of my forest," she said, her voice filled with menace. "Repeatedly, if necessary."

"Aye, that's what I'm afraid of," Dex said, helping the glowing Monty out of the room. "Let's go. Best not to get in the witch's way when she's about to conduct a class in pain."

She gave him a glare and then smiled before leading the way out of the room to greet the Consortium.

TWENTY-FOUR

Josephine led us out of her home.

We stood inside the stones circling her mound and found that the Penumbra Consortium was taking our presence in the country seriously.

The morning sky was brilliant with sunlight. I squinted as my eyes adjusted to the brightness.

A small group of five stood about thirty feet away from the stones. I could feel the energy they radiated. Especially the center figure. Beside him, on either side, stood two mages, a man and woman.

Around us, I could sense thirty more mages.

Powerful mages.

The ones in front of us were dressed in typical mage uniforms. Runed Zegna as far as the eyes could see. I wondered if they had some sort of bulk discount arrangement with Ermenegildo regarding the suits.

"Does Zegna hold a monopoly on runed bespoke mage attire?" I asked under my breath. "Seems like all these mages discovered the Zegna Outlet."

"The House of Zegna is an ancient mage sect," Dex said. "They specialize in runed garb, always have."

The center figure took a few steps forward and cleared his throat.

"I am Mage Ben Logan," the center figure said, focusing on Josephine. "You are harboring fugitives on this property. By order of the Penumbra Consortium you are hereby commanded to surrender them to our custody."

The sky began to darken and I heard a rumble in the distance. The smell of ozone filled my lungs.

"What's that smell?" I asked. "It smells like—"

"Death, if these mages don't leave soon," Dex said, looking around. "Where's that vehicle?"

"I know what you are, Mage Logan, and whom you truly serve," Josephine said, narrowing her eyes at Logan, then turning to us. "Look closely; you will have to confront this mage very soon. His name is Balugan."

"You know nothing, hag," Logan said, with a twisted smile. "Your time will come soon enough. I will see you beg for your life before you die."

"Did he just call her a hag?" I asked in mild shock. "I didn't realize the Consortium had a suicide squad."

"He doesn't serve the Consortium," Monty said. "Bloody hell, this can't be happening. Is that really Balugan?"

Dex nodded.

"It's happening," Dex said as I heard the Urus approaching. "The Consortium didn't send him. Clever use of the name. He must be undercover."

More rumbling reverberated around us. I looked up to the sky to see lightning arc across the clouds.

"Your special effects do not impress me, witch," Logan said, taking a few more steps forward. "Hand them over and we will consider letting you stay on protected land, for now."

The sky became overcast, blocking out the sun and plunging us into an early night.

"Josephine," Dex warned, "if you kill him, he will just find another."

"I'm well aware of the consequences," she said without taking her eyes off Logan. "You two really know how to make enemies. Dexter, best to take your leave now, before I get started."

"Aye," Dex said. "Are you sure you don't—"

"Now, Dexter!" she snapped. "Your circles will be neutralized until I'm done. You'll have to run to the car."

"Confound it, woman," Dex grumbled. "First you want me to me leave in a hurry and then you neutralize my circles?"

"You could stand to do some exercise," she said, glancing at Dex. "I will keep him alive and contained for as long as possible. That should give you enough time to leave my domain."

"There's too many of them," I said, letting my hand drift to Grim Whisper. "We can stay and help."

"That's admirable, but you will only get in the way," she said. "Dex will explain the threat you face on your way."

"The threat?"

Logan unleashed a beam of black energy aimed at us.

Josephine extended a hand, diverting the beam into the ground several feet away from us where it blasted out a four-foot crater, sending dirt and debris into the air.

"That beam looked familiar. Monty?"

"I think it's safe to say that Mage Logan serves another, darker power, and not the Consortium."

"You have got to be kidding," I said, backpedaling. "Are you saying he's—"

"No," Monty said. "That's not Chaos, but I can confidently say he serves him."

"Well, shit," I said, looking around at the rest of the mages closing in. "Is Josephine going to be...?"

I never finished my sentence.

A flash of light blinded me as lightning cascaded around Josephine, striking the mages and incinerating them where they stood. They didn't even have a chance to scream. When I could see clearly, Mage Logan stood immobilized in a lightning cage.

The rest of the mages were piles of ash.

"It's time to go," Dex said his voice grim. "Josephine."

She nodded in his direction, which he returned.

"He will remain here until you leave my domain," she said, her voice dark and filled with death. "Once you cross my borders, he will be freed. Rest assured, his master still pursues you."

"You...you killed them all," I said, shocked. "Why?"

"Simon—" Monty began.

"You question me?" Josephine asked as lightning arced around her body. "Heed my words, Marked of Kali. The time will come when you will have done far worse than this."

"No," I said, shaking my head. "Never. I won't kill indiscriminately."

"Who said this was indiscriminate?" she said as the blue energy filled her eyes. "You still stand and breathe. I know exactly what I am doing. No one violates my land with the intent to kill and leaves unscathed...*no one*. Now, go. I must unleash the storm."

"Oh, hell," Dex said, grabbing me by the arm. "Let it go, boy. This is one battle you can't win. We go, now."

We ran to the Urus where Adam waited.

Peaches bounded ahead of us and made his way to the rear. I opened the door to let him in before heading to the driver's side. Adam was standing on the right side of the vehicle and for a moment it threw me. Then I remembered: the steering wheel was on the wrong side.

"I can't drive this!" I said, raising my voice. "Who places the steering wheel on the wrong side anyway?"

"No one said you were driving," Monty said, getting behind the wheel. "I'm driving."

"Pardon me, sir," Adam said. "I've been tasked with—"

"Listen, young man," Dex said, jumping into the Urus as I slid in next to Monty. "In about ten seconds this entire forest is going to be covered in deadly lightning. You can stay here and argue about who should drive, or you can get in and leave this place with your life. Your choice."

Adam jumped in the Urus next to Dex. Peaches sprawled in the rear of the SUV with a low whine.

"Good choice," Dex said. "Drive, Nephew."

Monty floored the gas. The Urus lived up to its Lamborghini name and leapt forward, accelerating away from Josephine and toward the edge of the New Forest.

A crack of thunder deafened me for a few seconds, followed by what I could only describe as a wall of lightning. I always thought thunder came after the lightning—seems like I was wrong. The wall of lightning was immense, stretching out behind us.

"What is that?" I asked, surprised. "Is that—?"

"Yes," Dex barked. "Tristan, go!"

The wall of lightning was gaining on us.

TWENTY-FIVE

"Monty," I said, glancing back at the lightning wall. "This is a Lamborghini. It's designed for speed. We need to go faster or we're going to be microwaved by that storm."

"What is that dreadful sound?" Monty asked, searching the dash. "More importantly, how do I shut it off?"

"What are you talking about?"

"Apologies for the music, Mr. Montague," Adam said from the back. "That was me."

"You call this music?" Montague scoffed. "It's horrendous."

"Is that MB?" I asked Adam. "The new album?"

Adam nodded.

"You know them?" Adam asked with a look of surprise. "They are the best."

"It sounds like screeching cats engaged in combat," Monty snapped. "Stop it, before I destroy the dash."

"You'll have to excuse Monty," I said, accessing the radio controls. "He's really big on popular music from the 1800s. He would never understand MB."

"Of course I understand this cacophony you call music,"

Monty snapped. "I understand that whoever is being recorded is experiencing torture. Do I want to know what MB stands for?"

Adam shook his head, but I felt it was my duty to educate the cranky mage and expand his musical tastes into the current century.

"Misaligned Buttcheeks," I declared proudly. "Best punk group ever."

Adam tried to shrink in the backseat and Dex chuckled.

"Simon," Monty said, glancing at me. "We are trying to outrun a deadly lightning storm. I will not race against death to the sound of *Misaligned Buttcheeks*."

Dex burst out laughing because, well, Dex. Even Adam suppressed a chuckle. I nodded solemnly and turned the radio off.

"Would you prefer some Wagner?" I asked, barely maintaining my composure. "I'm sure I could find *Ride of the Valkyries* if I searched."

"Silence is preferable," Monty said. "Uncle, do not encourage them. Can you deal with that storm?"

"Aye, but if we slow down and try to fight that storm, we'll be forced to kiss our misaligned buttcheeks goodbye," Dex said with a grin as he glanced behind us. "There's no 'dealing' with that much power." He shook his head. "I've forgotten how dangerous she truly is."

"Are you sure you can't teleport us out of here?" I asked. "I'd even risk digestive destruction if it meant getting away from that."

"Aye, boy I'd love to, but I can't. That contrary witch shut down my circles in her forest. Nephew, drive faster."

"I'm pushing this vehicle as fast as possible," Monty said. "Unless you have a cast that can add velocity, this is our top speed."

Monty was right. We were redlining the speed and the

lightning was still closing in on us. We needed a new strategy, fast.

Adam cleared his throat.

"Excuse me, Mr. Montague?"

"Out with it, child," Dex said from beside Adam. "This is not the time for formalities."

"See that red toggle switch next to the steering wheel?" Adam said, pointing to the wheel. "The one labeled Emergencies Only? That will activate the speed boost. Cecil said he equipped this one special because I was driving you both and may need to race away for my life. I thought he was joking."

"Racing away for your life is a feature with the Montague & Strong Detective Agency," I said. "Did Cecil say what kind of boost it is? Nitrous, or something else?"

"He didn't say," Adam admitted. "He only said to make sure we had plenty of road before I flipped that switch."

"I'd say this qualifies as an emergency," Dex said. "Push the button, Nephew."

"We're still on grass," I said. "You flip that switch and we'll lose control. Adam, how far from the road are we?"

"A35 is about half a kilometer straight ahead," Adam said, pointing. "That leads into the M3."

"Which leads to the M27 and London," I said, turning to Monty. "Can you stay ahead of the lightning for half a kilometer?"

"I don't know," Monty said, glancing in the rear-view mirror. "It seems to be gaining on us. Knowing Cecil, I doubt it will be something as simple as nitrous oxide. He would tie it to some sort of runic component."

"Then we better have a road under us when you flip that switch," I said, my mind turning over solutions to increasing our speed. "Runic NOS sounds scary fast. You hit that while we're on this grass and there's a good chance we flip right before the lightning barbecues us."

"That would be bad," Monty said, death-gripping the steering wheel. "I can't cast and drive, and your dawnward is a fixed defensive cast."

"I don't think my dawnward could hold up against that much power," I said. "We need to go faster."

If we couldn't increase our speed, we needed to decrease the weight of the vehicle somehow. I turned to the backseat.

"Dex, any ideas?"

"If I try to make us go faster, we'll not withstand the stress. The vehicle will fall apart, SuNaTran or not, then that lightning will chew through us."

"How about instead of making us faster, you make us lighter?" I asked. "Long enough to reach that road?"

Dex rubbed his chin.

"Aye, that I can do," he said, gesturing. "It won't be long, but it should do."

As he gestured, green symbols left his fingers, enveloping the vehicle. We shot forward as the interior filled with green energy. The Urus began outpacing the approaching storm as the road raced up at us.

"You're going to have to slow down to get on the road," I said, putting my finger on the switch. "Slow down just enough to straighten out, and then I'll hit the speed boost."

Monty nodded without answering, keeping the steering wheel steady as we sped across the grass. It was one of the few times I saw him appear concerned. It was taking all his focus to keep the Urus steady. I don't know how light Dex had made us, but I knew we suddenly had more engine power as we crossed the grassy fields.

Monty pulled a hard right onto the road, causing us to drift for several feet as I hit the switch. The interior of the Urus flashed blue as runes bloomed to life across the dash in various shades of red. The entire vehicle descended about a foot as we picked up speed and blasted down the road.

The Urus began shuddering as we left the lightning storm and the New Forest behind. When it felt like the SUV was going to shake itself to pieces, I flipped the switch back to the off position. The last thing I wanted was explaining to Cecil why his Lambo was in pieces along the A35.

The Urus slowed down to a manageable speed. I checked the speedometer and we were clocking in at just under 190 miles per hour.

"You can slow down now," I said, glancing behind us. "I don't even see the storm."

"This is slowed," Monty replied. "Between what my uncle did and that speed boost, we easily exceeded the speed tolerances of this vehicle."

"Good point," I said, leaning my head back in my seat. "That was too close. Adam, how long until we get to London?"

"At this velocity? I'd say thirty minutes, if Mr. Montague doesn't slow down."

"Will this speed attract attention?"

"This isn't an autobahn," Adam said. "The A35 is a road, not a motorway. Going this fast is bound to get some attention."

"Monty?"

"I'll decrease our speed," he said, slowing down as the Urus rose on its suspension. "We should be leaving the New Forest in its entirety soon."

"This place feels like an oversized Central Park."

"You can fit eighty-four Central Parks in the New Forest," Monty said. "Witch Josephine's domain is vast."

"How do you even know this?"

"The New Forest has been the site for megaflashes in the past, and studied extensively," Monty stated. "I thought it natural phenomena, until today."

"Those megaflashes do sound like Josephine's lightning

storms," I said, glancing back at Dex. "Why did she kill those mages?"

"Josephine is complicated," Dex said, looking out of the window. "In her domain, her word is law."

"Was it necessary?" I asked. "Couldn't she have stunned them or bounced them out of the Forest? Without killing them?"

"No," he said. "She deals in absolutes. They came to kill; she just beat them to it. The Consortium didn't send those mages. Balugan was evidence of that."

"I thought he said his name was Ben Logan?"

"Balugan is an agent of Chaos, one of the first and most powerful," Dex said. "I don't know how he found you. He shouldn't be able to track your mark."

"I think I have an idea of how he found us," I said, looking behind us at three black Rolls Royce Phantoms giving chase. "I don't think that's SuNaTran."

Adam looked back and shook his head.

"Those don't belong to us."

"You probably want to let Cecil know Verity is using Phantoms for nefarious purposes," I said. "It's going to give SuNaTran a bad name."

"Verity?" Adam asked. "What's that?"

"Verity isn't exactly common knowledge," Monty said. "Did you just use the word nefarious?"

"I did," I said. "I think, considering their activity as of late, that it fits."

"Agreed," Monty said. "*They* must have informed the Consortium regarding our location."

"Which means they informed Logan and his crew," I said. "Those other mages with him, were they...?"

"They were most likely rogue Consortium mages," Monty said, his voice somber. "It's safe to say Balugan has infiltrated the Penumbra Consortium."

"How could they not know?" I asked. "Josephine and Dex saw right through him."

"Josephine is easily as powerful as the entire leadership of the Consortium combined," Monty said. "My uncle is adept at seeing through illusions."

"Judging from the energy signature on those vehicles," Dex said, "it's safe to say The Book has been tasked with bringing you in."

"What does that mean?"

"They've moved to the next phase of apprehension," Monty said. "The Book will use casts to take us down."

"Why does that sound painful?"

"Because it is," Monty said. "Brace yourself, we have incoming."

He swerved the Urus from left to right. Several bright yellow orbs, crackling with power, flew by our vehicle. They impacted the road beside us, carving up huge chunks of asphalt and launching debris into the air.

"They're not here to talk," Dex said. "Slow down, Nephew. I'll deal with this."

"Don't you need to take us to York?" I asked. "We don't know where he is."

"My nephew knows as surely as I do," Dex said. "York is sleeping with the four lions; use the entrance where Nelson fell."

"The key sequence?" Monty asked. "I don't know it."

"You do," Dex said. "It's lost."

"How does he know it if the sequence is lost?" I asked. "For once, could you mages just speak in English?"

"I thought that's what we've been speaking all along," Dex said. "Don't think too hard on it and it will come to you, Nephew."

"You two are impossible," I said throwing a hand in the air.

"Once The Book gets wind of where you are, they'll come at you hard," Dex said. "Show no mercy and don't get caught. Now, slow down."

Monty slowed the Urus and Dex opened the door, giving me a grin.

"Are you insane?" I yelled. "We're still moving."

"You can't stop," Dex said. "You don't stop until you get to London. Once there, the dampener will make you difficult to locate. Probably can't keep this vehicle either, as it'll be marked by Verity. Call Cecil to provide another. Understand?"

"What are you going to do?" I asked. "I mean, besides break something when you land?"

"I'm going to go deal with The Book," Dex said, looking behind us. "I'll buy you some time and meet up with you in the city."

He crouched down and jumped out of the Urus. Adam pulled the door closed with a look of shock on his face. I almost felt sorry for him.

"He jumped," Adam said, looking behind us. "He really jumped."

I saw several green flashes, followed by the figure of Dex in the middle of the road. He extended his arms wide as the three Phantoms sped at him.

The next moment I saw him crouch and slam both hands into the road, causing an enormous semi-circle of green energy to block it. The Phantoms were moving too fast to evade his roadblock.

Each one slammed into his energy barrier and crumpled.

"Those were definitely not SuNaTran Phantoms," I said as the doors to the Phantoms opened and mages stumbled out. I counted nine mages against one Dex. "Well, that's not going to end well...for them."

"We should go back," Adam said nervously. "He's seriously outnumbered. There's nine of them and he's alone."

"It's only nine," I said, turning around and settling into my seat. "He won't even break a sweat."

"Nine against one and you're going to leave him alone?" Adam asked, confused. "He's one old man. What can he possibly do?"

As if on cue, the sky behind us flashed a deep green, followed by a deep *thunk, thunk, thunk.*

"I'd say he dispatched them," I replied, closing my eyes and rubbing my temples. "All nine."

"He...he killed them?"

"No, Adam," Monty said. "My uncle is many things, but a coldblooded killer is not one of them. I can sense their vague energy signatures from here. They're alive, in pain, and probably regretting taking this assignment at this very moment."

"Care to clarify about York sleeping with the four lions?" I asked. "If you tell me we have to head into a jungle or visit the zoo, you can stop the SUV right now and drop me off."

"My uncle was referring to a particular set of lions," Monty said. "The Landseer Lions."

"Landseer?" Adam asked. "You mean...?"

"York is hiding in Trafalgar Square," Monty finished. "Or, more accurately, under it."

TWENTY-SIX

"Trafalgar Square?" I asked. "You mean the same Trafalgar Square that's constantly packed with tourists? That Trafalgar Square?"

"Are you going to destroy Trafalgar Square?" Adam asked warily. "We're very fond of those lions. It will not go over well if something were to happen to them."

"We have no intention of destroying anything," Monty assured him. "We need to access the tunnels beneath them."

"Are you referring to the Tube?"

"No," Monty said. "Beneath the Square lies a network of tunnels that lead into the National Gallery. We need to access those tunnels."

"From the square?" I asked.

"The entrance is on the square," Monty said with a nod. "Under Lord Nelson's column and between two of the lions."

"Are you serious?" Adam asked. "There's a secret entrance between the lions?"

"He's always serious," I said. "How exactly is this going to work? The place is filled with people, all the time. You plan on pressing some button and opening a door?"

"This isn't the States," Monty said. "Trafalgar Square closes by 6pm."

"It's nearly noon now," I said. "No way to open that door without getting attention."

"Noted," Monty said. "We'll wait until after closing, make sure there aren't any stragglers, and then make our approach."

"Isn't Trafalgar Square close to Downing Street?"

"Yes, why?"

"Thinking about security," I said. "That close to the Prime Minister means an armed response if something explodes."

"Explodes?" Adam said, nervously. "What do you mean. explodes?"

"I know Monty said he has no intention of destroying anything," I said glancing at Monty. "It's best to expect the worst and plan for the default contingency."

"What does that mean?"

"It means that if we get attacked, which is highly probable, there will be explosions," I said. "Which means an armed response."

"We won't approach until a few hours after closing," Monty said, rubbing a temple. "I could use a good cuppa right about now."

"What you really need is some Death Wish," I said. "That would make everything right."

"No thank you."

"Does this secret gallery entrance have any other defenses?" I asked. "Can you press some buttons and open the door?"

"Not that simple," Monty said. "York isn't in the Gallery proper, he's beneath it, in a mage stronghold. Think Churchill's bunkers, but for mages."

"The Gallery has war bunkers?"

"Not for the conventional wars, and yes," Monty said.

"The Gallery Bunkers are one of the most secure locations in the country."

"How difficult is it going to be to open this door?" I asked. "It seems involved and complicated."

"It is," Monty said. "Or at least it was when the bunkers were in use. I don't know what alterations York has made to the access point. It could be impossible now."

"How long ago were those bunkers in use?"

"They were last active close to a century ago."

"You're going to try to open a door that's been closed for a century?"

"It should be possible, if York hasn't tampered with the runic sequence."

"That's a big if," I said in disbelief. "Will you be able to cast in London?"

"That depends on how strong the dampener field is," Monty said, his voice pensive. "Mathers and the BPD would err on the side of excess and make it as powerful as possible."

"We may need a distraction," I said. "Even if the Square is closed, your abilities may be impacted. You sure you can open this door without blasting the place?"

"Blasting *would* be easier."

"I strongly suggest against blasting anything in Trafalgar Square, sir," Adam advised. "Nelson's column is a national treasure, as are the lions."

"They are a bit touchy about the historical monuments," I said with a nod. "You recall what happened after our last visit? All those bridges, the Eye, Big Ben, Hyde Park, even the Castle of London."

"Tower of London," Monty corrected. "That was mostly the—"

"I remember the damage," Adam said, looking from Monty to me with shock. "They said those were terrorist attacks. Are you saying it was you two?"

"Not entirely," Monty said. "The Fomor was responsible for most of the damage."

"The Morrigan had a part in that too," I said. "She really unleashed the fury."

"That she did," Monty said. "Your hellhound was quite impressive as well."

"Hellhound?" Adam said. "You have a hellhound?"

"The sprawltastic meat vacuum in the back," I said, motioning to Peaches who momentarily perked up at the word "meat" before going back to sleep. "He's a hellhound."

Adam turned slowly and looked at the currently snoring beast.

"That damage was caused by you three?"

"And his uncle," I said. "The old man who jumped out of the vehicle earlier."

"How could three, four people and a hellhound be responsible for so much damage?"

"You don't know the Montagues too well, do you?" I asked. "Blasting things is a family trait. It's like breathing to them."

"That's an exaggeration," Monty said. "I will refrain from blasting anything if at all possible."

"That means there will be *some* blasting," I said. "Have you never dealt with mages?"

Adam shook his head.

"This is my first time," Adam said. "I was tasked with getting you to London, nothing more. Seemed simple enough."

"Cecil really threw you into the deep end," I said. "Did you do something to piss him off?"

"Not to my knowledge," Adam answered. "He did say something about a trial by fire for the security firm, but it made no sense at the time."

"I'm sure it's making some sense by now."

Adam nodded.

"I thought Cecil was being humorous when he mentioned the speed switch," Adam answered. "I didn't believe him when he said this vehicle needed more runes to deal with you two."

"I only know of one vehicle—well, two—that have enough runes to deal with us," I said. "Both of them are across an ocean. Both of them are lethal."

"Adam, we seem to be out of immediate danger," Monty said, sounding tired. "Why don't you take over the driving duties? London is close."

Monty pulled off and stopped on the shoulder of the road. They switched positions with Adam taking the wheel. Monty sat in the back and closed his eyes as Adam pulled away and kept us under flee-for-your-life speed.

"You okay?" I asked, turning back to look at Monty. "You're looking a little peaked."

"I need more rest," Monty said. "Whatever process Josephine facilitated in her home has left me drained. Nothing some rest and a good cuppa can't fix."

We merged onto the M3 and Adam slowed further to blend in with the speed of the traffic around us. I kept looking behind us from time to time to make sure Verity wasn't on our tail.

"If Verity knows where you are," I said, "does that mean—?"

"That your successor knows your location? Likely."

"Wonderful," I said. "Will the dampener hide me?"

"I don't know," Monty said. "Once we get to London, I'll be able to assess how diffuse your energy signature is. Until then, it's best we keep moving."

TWENTY-SEVEN

We arrived in London without another welcome committee.

"You would be safer if you left us here," Monty said, looking around. "We'll blend in with the tourists. It won't be long before Verity and the BPD will be on the alert."

"I could wait," Adam said. "Provide a quick escape if needed."

Monty shook his head.

"No need," Monty said. "I'll inform Cecil of your exemplary service. Thank you."

"No thanks needed, Mr. Montague," Adam said. "If I'm not being too forward, may I ask a favor?"

"Of course you may ask."

"Would it be possible to limit the destruction this time?" Adam asked. "Your last visit caused considerable damage and the construction was impossible to deal with."

"You can rest assured that I will keep any and all destruction to a minimum," Monty answered. "I realize how important the monuments and places of historical importance are to the citizens of the Commonwealth."

"Thank you," Adam said with an audible sigh. "I'll let Cecil know where I dropped you off."

"Please do," Monty said as we exited the Urus. "Thank Cecil again for me."

Adam nodded and pulled away, leaving us on the sidewalk. We walked to the river's edge, making sure no one was following us. I looked up at the horrendous building that stood behind us.

"Out of all the places he could have left us, you picked here?"

"It allows us to hide in plain sight and places us close to our target destination," Monty said. "Besides, didn't you mention you wanted to revisit when we weren't being chased?"

"I said no such thing," I answered with a growl. "This place needs to be renovated...permanently."

"Keep your creature close," Monty said. "No need to attract undue attention."

I stepped closer to Peaches and crouched down to rub his back, all the while maintaining situational awareness.

"How far away is Trafalgar Square?" I asked, looking across the Thames. "I can see Saint Paul's."

Angry memories of Thomas bubbled to the surface as I gazed upon the dome of the cathedral.

"It's just across the Thames," Monty said, pointing to our left. "The Hungerford will lead us directly there."

"I see a bunch of bridges—all intact, by the way," I said. "Which one is the Hungerford?"

"This is the Millennium," he said, pointing directly ahead of us. "Next over is the Blackfriars, Waterloo, then Hungerford."

"All of which will remain intact this time?"

"Of course," Monty said. "I have no intention of summoning a Fomor."

"Just making sure," I said. "The Consortium may be tied up in mage madness, but I'm sure Mathers would love to get a shot at you, if you give him one."

"That will be resolved before we leave," Monty said, his expression dark. "We may as well blend in and find somewhere to get a good cuppa that isn't overpriced."

"I thought we *were* blending in?"

He stared at me and glanced at Peaches.

"There are few scenarios where you and your creature blend in," he said, turning and walking toward the building behind us. "We'll blend in while in there; also less of a chance to encounter your successor. The dampener is strong, but that mark of yours is still quite visible."

"You're doing this on purpose," I said, following him. "This is some form of sick torture you cooked up."

"I have no idea what you're referring to. I do, however, think it's only fitting, considering I was subjected to that assault on my hearing in the SUV," he said with a hint of a smile. "Think of this as embracing culture."

"I can't believe how well they reconstructed the place," I said, looking up. "It looks brand new."

"I'm sure the Consortium had a hand in its reconstruction," Monty said. "I heard it was restored in a few weeks. Apparently the damage wasn't as extensive as we thought."

"Pity," I said. "I kind of enjoyed it as a crater."

"The Consortium would not allow it to remain destroyed," he said. "It's too important a structure, due to its proximity to certain ley-lines."

He crouched down and traced some symbols into the ground.

"What was that?" I asked. "Those runes looked scary."

"Precautionary insurance," he said, walking some distance away and repeating the sequence. "It's very likely Verity or your successor will show up. I'd prefer not to be caught unawares or unprepared."

"What exactly is this insurance?" I asked, concerned. "Those runes look volatile."

"Impressive," Monty said, repeating the sequence several more times in different spots along the river. "You *have* been studying. These runes tap into a major ley-line that runs under St. Paul's and crosses through this location."

"I seem to recall you saying tapping into a ley-line would be suicidal, even for an Arch Mage," I said. "How exactly are *you* tapping into this line?"

"I'm not *tapping* exactly," he said. "This is more of a redirection. I can't safely use the power of a ley-line, but I can redirect some of its power if it's not too radical a deviation from its usual location."

"Redirect it where, exactly?"

"In there," he said.

"Is that why you picked this place?"

"Well, my power is halved, but this ley-line remains a source of vast energy unaffected by the dampener," Monty said, turning to look at the building behind us. "Energy that can be leveraged. That, and this visit will be good for you. It will expand your horizons."

"The only thing that needs to be expanded across the horizon are the remains of this building," I said under my breath as we approached the ticket-purchase area. "I could wait outside, while you embrace the culture."

"It's not the same if it can't be shared," Monty said, looking at the ticket agent. "Two tickets, please. This is his emotional assistance animal. I do hope that's acceptable."

The ticket agent glanced at Peaches and paused, before smiling with a nervous nod.

"What a beautiful animal," he said as he handed us two tickets. "Please keep him under control."

"Definitely," I said, rubbing Peaches' enormous head. "He's a good boy, always under control."

"I'm sure you'll enjoy the exhibits," the ticket agent replied, taking a step back from the counter and Peaches. "Welcome to the Tate Modern."

"To call this place a museum is a crime against all real museums," I said as we descended down a ramp to a large open space. "This place looks like an abandoned warehouse."

"Power station," Monty said absentmindedly as he looked at the brochure describing the exhibits. "This used to be a power station."

We had reached the lower level when I felt her presence.

Peaches whined a second later.

<The orange lady is here.>

<I know, boy. We'll deal with it.>

"Shit," I said, looking around. "She's here."

"We need to move somewhere less populated," Monty said, moving rapidly across the floor to another large open space. "In there."

"I thought that was the plan when we came in here?"

"This is contained," he said, gesturing. "Better than facing her on the Thames with plenty of collateral victims for her to choose from, don't you think?"

"That opening looks pretty accessible if you ask me," I said. "How are we going to contain—"

A violet lattice shimmered down from the ceiling and blocked off the entrance to the enormous exhibit hall we were currently standing in.

"Like that," Monty said, moving over to the remaining people in the hall. "I'm afraid this exhibit is currently closed for cleaning. Would you be so kind as to visit another of our fascinating exhibitions?"

The small group of people walked through the lattice, causing it to shimmer again before disappearing from sight.

"Can you cast anything else besides that?" I asked, adjusting my holster and Grim Whisper. "I don't think a colorful wall is going to stop her."

"My abilities to cast are halved while in the city," Monty said with a frown. "Mathers has made it nearly impossible to cast anything truly powerful within London."

"The ley-line?"

"Insurance," he said, still scowling. "Activating that will create a destructive cascade. It's best if we aren't in the building when that happens."

"If your abilities are halved, does that mean she's handicapped too?"

"I don't know," he said, looking around. "Successors seem to operate under different rules of engagement. They seem to derive their power from being successors, not magic users. The Black Rose is not comprised of mages. They are mage killers."

"It would be great if we could lose her, at least until this thing with York was over."

"Do you still have Piero's vial?"

I searched my jacket and pulled out the small vial of blood.

"Right here," I said, holding it up. "You think we can make her drink it?"

"It's not for her, it's for you."

"You want me to drink this now? When all she wants to do—"

"Is kill you."

The realization dawned on me.

"All she wants to do is kill me."

"I say you should oblige her," Monty said. "It would buy us some time before our attempt to locate York tonight."

"If everything goes according to plan, you mean."

"Five minutes until you 'die' and then six hours of being

technically dead," he said, calculating the time frame. "If you can keep her busy for five minutes, you can convince her she dispatched the Marked of Kali. At least until the effects of the blood wear off."

"Then she'll be back."

"If you make it convincing, it will be some time before she realizes the deception," Monty said. "Perhaps if you let her stab you a few times?"

"Stab me a few times?" I asked and glanced at him. "You do realize that my stabbing you at Josephine's was necessary?"

"I'm well aware," he said evenly. "I do not hold grudges, Simon. You did what you had to do. I'm grateful and fully healed."

"Okay, just checking," I said. "It's not like I go around randomly stabbing people, you know."

"I should hope not, but you will have to face her, eventually," Monty said. "This tactic is delaying the inevitable for a good reason, but it is inevitable."

"What about Peaches?" I asked, concerned. "That blade of hers sounds dangerous to him."

"Can you keep him out of this fight?" Monty asked. "Is that possible?"

"I don't know," I said, glancing down at my amazing hellhound protector. "He takes being my bondmate seriously. I might be able to bribe him, though."

"Try."

<Hey, boy. I'm going to go fight someone right now.>

<The orange lady? Can I bite her?>

<No, I don't want you to get close. She has a dangerous weapon that can hurt you.>

<Is she going to try to hurt you?>

<Yes.>

<Then I will bite her arms off. Then she can't hurt you.>

<That would work, but I want you to stay back, away from her.>

<If she hurts you, I will hurt her more.>

<I need you to stay close to Monty. I promise, he will make you extra-large sausage.>

<How extra? The old bird man did not make the meat extra.>

<Monty will make it extra-extra, just for you, if you stay close to him. Even if it looks like she hurt me, you have to stay next to him. Understand?>

<I do not like it, but I will stay next to the angry man. Do you know what you are doing?>

I looked at my hellhound in puzzlement for a second.

<I do. Trust me.>

<I always trust you. You are my bondmate.>

"He's going to stay by you for the duration," I said. "You owe him extra-extra sausage."

"Of course, whatever that means."

"Marked of Kali," I heard Dira call out. "Show yourself."

"Showtime," I said and drank the vial of blood. The coppery tasting liquid burned my tongue, making me shudder in disgust. "That tastes horrible."

"You have five minutes," Monty said. "I will create some distractions once you 'die' to keep her occupied."

I reached out to the energy within me and formed the silver mist that would become Ebonsoul. It enveloped my arm, forming the dark blade in my hand. It shimmered, the red runes glowing as the silver band down its center pulsed with an inner light.

"Show yourself, coward," Dira called out. "I will put you out of your misery."

"That's new," Monty said, pointing at the silver band that ran the length of Ebonsoul. "What is that?"

"Half an elder rune."

"Half an—?" he started, then waved his hand. "We'll

discuss this at another time. Remember, keep her busy for five minutes and let the blood take effect."

"Four minutes thirty seconds."

Monty nodded.

"She needs to cross the threshold," Monty said. "Can you manage that?"

"I've been known to push a button or two in my time."

"Indeed," he said. "Ready to die?"

"Let's do this."

TWENTY-EIGHT

We moved back away from the entrance.

Depending on the angle, I could see the violet lattice shimmer every few seconds.

"Can anyone else see your wall of magic?"

"No, it's transparent to normals," Monty answered. "You can see it because, well, you're abnormal."

"I'm going to take that as a compliment."

"That is how it was meant," he said. "You may want to alert her to our location."

"I'm right here, successor," I called out. "Do you dare face me?"

"That should get her attention," Monty said as he gestured. "Make sure you stay in this room. Once she comes in, I'll harden the shield."

"Are you sure you'll be able to?" I asked with a smile. "You're only half the mage you used to be."

"Hilarious," Monty said. "Focus. Here she comes."

"Three and a half minutes," I said under my breath. "A lifetime when you're fighting to die."

"Remember," Monty said, stepping back and to the side. "Make it convincing."

Dira stepped into the hall.

The runes on her combat armor flared with orange energy as she crossed the threshold. She paused at the entrance and looked at Monty's lattice.

"I'm only here for him," she said, pointing at me. "This security measure is unnecessary."

"You'll forgive me if our previous encounter with a successor indicates otherwise," Monty said. "That ogre's collateral damage was quite extensive with no regard to the innocents on the street."

"I am not a mindless ogre."

"Doesn't matter," I said. "You're here for me and only me."

"You picked a peculiar place to die," she said looking around the empty hall. "A true warrior would have chosen a place of honor."

"I left my list of honorable death sites at home, sorry," I said with a mock bow. "This atrocious place will have to do. I think it fits. I can't stand the Tate and I have to say, you're right up there at the top of the people I don't like."

We were on the lowest level of the Turbine Hall, which housed an exhibit called Empty Space. It consisted of a single pedestal in the center of a vast open space.

The observer then had to step over to the pedestal to read a message which stated that you were now inside the Empty Space which was no longer empty—therefore, it was just space, and now we were a living part of the exhibit.

This was one of the reasons I disliked modern art.

Dira materialized her blade as she approached.

It was a sleek, dangerous-looking weapon. The blade was a dark silver, tinged with blue and covered in white runes. It was the same length as Ebonsoul, which surprised me, but made sense.

If they neutralized casts, the fighting would be up close and personal. That meant a shorter blade, capable of massive damage in close quarters. A long blade would only get in the way in close-quarters combat.

"A *Bas Magus*," Monty said, looking at her blade. "I've never seen a mage-killer wielded before."

"If you know what this is, then you know what it does, mage," she said. "That is my only warning."

I glared at Monty and gave him the *we are on a tight death schedule* look before he slipped into professor mode and began asking to examine the blade and discuss its various properties.

He nodded and stepped back.

"Duly noted."

Three minutes.

"You've finally decided to face your death," Dira said, closing the distance. "I will make it painless—mostly. Though you do not deserve it, I will give you an honorable death."

"I figured you were the 'share the agony' type," I said with a small smile as I circled around her. "I can only promise the same thing."

"Your mage will not interfere in this matter," she said, never taking her eyes off of me. "I only seek your life, but if he interferes, he dies with you."

"It's just you and me," I said. "Let's dance."

She nodded with a smile of her own.

She slid forward with a horizontal thrust. I parried her blade before it bisected my midsection. Immediately, I unleashed a fist to her face.

She slipped the punch, following up with a palm strike to my chest. I bladed my body, turning sideways, narrowly evading her strike. She forced me back as she slashed upward with her blade.

She was fast. Faster than I expected.

I thrust forward with Ebonsoul, aiming for her chest before changing direction mid-lunge, going for her stomach. She read my intention, rotated around my blade thrust to the inside, and drove a lightning-fast elbow into my face.

I staggered back, spots dancing in my eyes.

She saw the opening and attacked.

She slid to my left and sliced downward, cutting at my thigh. It caught some of my leg as I side-stepped away from her blade with a grunt of pain.

Too slow.

My focus on her attack caused me to miss her off hand as she drove a fist into my side, cracking some ribs. I backed off with a hiss, putting some distance between us, as the pain made it harder to breathe.

"You don't deserve Kali's attention," she said as she glared at me. "You are no warrior."

I could feel my body flush hot as it dealt with Piero's blood and the damage Dira was dealing. The healing was taking its time.

"Looks like someone is feeling a little neglected," I said, trying to buy some time to heal. Also, I just wanted to piss her off. The only people easier to trigger than mages were assassins with inflated egos. If her ego was any larger, she wouldn't fit into the Tate. "Did Kali ever pay any attention to you? I really doubt it."

We circled each other. I stayed just out of blade range. Her defense was exceptional and I wasn't in the mood to jump into a blender.

At least not before I was fully healed.

"You mock me as you face death," she said, her face

turning a nice shade of red. "You will beg for your life before you die."

"Not so big on the begging, sorry," I said. "Is that the new protocol? It's been a while since I've faced an assassin out to end me."

"Don't worry," she said with another smile. "There will be no more assassins after I'm done."

"So confident," I said, limping back to keep my distance. "Always good to see someone who takes pride in their work."

"You fool," she said, and dashed at me. "Die."

My body had healed the cut and rib damage, but I needed her to believe I was still injured to draw her in. She closed the distance, holding her blade in a reverse grip by her side.

One minute.

She inverted her grip and thrust forward, counting on my injuries to slow me down—except I wasn't injured. I spun around her attack to the outside. She switched hands as I cut through her side with Ebonsoul.

She cried out and buried her blade in my oblique before slicing horizontally in a classic *seppuku* cut. She was about to finish by going vertical into my chest with the *jumonji* finish, when I slammed a hammerfist into her temple, driving us apart.

I stumbled back and fell to the floor, holding my midsection and keeping my insides, inside. What surprised me, more than actually cutting her, was the absence of the siphon. Ebonsoul hadn't pulled power from Dira, or at least none that I had felt at the moment.

I heard Peaches growl behind me, but I knew he would stay next to Monty.

At least I hoped he would.

<Stay back, boy.>

<She cut you. I will bite her head off.>

<No...no biting. Stay with Monty.>

Dira closed the distance.

She wasn't leaving anything to chance. She was coming in for the final cut. A heart thrust followed by taking my head.

"He's dead," Monty said, stepping forward. "Take your victory and leave."

"Not before I take his head," Dira said. "It is my right as victor."

"Take it up with Kali, but his head stays attached," Monty said. "Unless you think you can defeat me?"

"I have destroyed mages with more power than you," she said as my vision started to tunnel in. "You will die with the Marked of—"

The world exploded as everything went black.

TWENTY-NINE

I opened my eyes to a world of concrete, tremors, and saliva.

Peaches slapped me a few times across the face with his tongue, then nuzzled me with his head. I groaned in response and he shoved me across the floor a few feet.

<I'm good, boy. Stop pushing.>

<My saliva saved you. I think that deserves meat. Don't you?>

<It sure does. Where's Monty?>

<He is over there trying to stop the building from falling. I think he needs more practice. The building is still falling.>

<He's what?>

I tried to sit up and the floor see-sawed forcing me to be still. I took a few breaths and waited for it to do the same. Monty came into my field of view with a concerned look on his face.

Whenever he wore that expression, I knew things were bad.

"How bad is it?" I asked as the pain in my midsection gripped my body. "You're wearing the face."

"What face?" he said, helping me to my feet. "We just have some complications."

I felt a tremor run through the building.

I lifted my shredded shirt and saw I had mostly healed, except for an angry red scar that was slowly fading. Monty grabbed my arm and propped me up as we walked through the barren concrete landscape.

"Where are we?" I said with a groan. "Is this still the Tate?"

"Not for much longer, I'm afraid," he said, walking through the empty areas. "We're underground. These are the Tanks. They're gallery spaces now, but they once used to hold oil for the power station."

"What do you mean, not for much longer?" I asked, grabbing my temples. "Ugh, my head. I feel like I'm having the hangover of the century."

"I may have miscalculated the deviation of the ley-line."

"That sounds like more than a complication. Break it down for me—in English, please," I said as we picked up the pace. "How much of a miscalculation?"

Another tremor shook the building.

"The ley-line I redirected fed too much power through my runes," he said. "They were supposed to act as power diverters I could use to bolster my own energy. Things didn't go exactly as planned."

"You mean you didn't plan a mini earthquake?" I asked. "Where's Dira?"

"I blasted her across the hardened lattice, right before the ceiling collapsed on her," Monty said. "That was the last I saw of her. After that, the structure of the building degraded considerably."

"Going underground was the solution?"

"The Tanks are the sturdiest part of this structure, at least for now," Monty explained. "The power diverted from the ley-line will rip through this foundation eventually. You may finally get your wish."

"My wish?"

"The utter destruction of the Tate."

He picked up the pace and I struggled to keep up. A few moments later, I stopped.

"Monty, the people," I said. "What about the people in the museum?"

"Evacuated after the first tremor," he said. "We've been down here for close to an hour. I've been shoring up the walls of the foundation to give them more time before the entire structure collapses in on itself. I sensed the last person leave shortly before I came to collect you."

"That's good," I said, relieved. "You didn't sense Dira after you launched her through the lattice?"

"My abilities are nowhere near their full strength," he said, shaking his head. "I had to focus on making sure we weren't trapped down here. I didn't have the energy to search for her."

"Is it possible she survived?"

"Anything is possible," he said. "If she survived, I'm certain she will find you, eventually."

"Where are we going now?" I asked, looking around at the blank concrete walls. "This all looks the same."

"There is an emergency exit on the other side of the last tank," he said, pointing down the wide corridor. "That should lead us outside where we can cross the Thames."

I was feeling better and we started moving again.

"You know, when I said I hated the Tate, I wasn't indicating you should level the place, especially not with us in it."

"That was not the intention," he said, stopping in front of a large steel door. "If the BPD gets wind of this—"

"We are so screwed. Well, you are."

"As are you. Guilt by association and all that," he said, opening the door. "Make haste. The support runes can only withstand so much weight before the walls give way."

We entered the tunnel which led to a service exit on Sumner Street, behind the Tate. We followed Sumner to Southwark Street and headed to the Hungerford Bridge.

We had reached Blackfriars Road when a massive *thwump* followed by the crashing of metal filled the air. We turned to see the Tate collapse in on itself as if the victim of a controlled demolition.

"It would be prudent to cross the Thames now," Monty said. "The farther away from the scene the better."

A huge debris cloud filled the air, obscuring the view of everything past where the Tate once stood.

"You think they'll reconstruct it again?" I asked as we walked away at a brisk pace. "I mean again, again."

"They have to," Monty said. "It's a strategic location."

"That we keep destroying."

"Unintentionally."

"Right, maybe we can make it a tradition?" I said. "We come here every few years and level the Tate?"

"Not remotely humorous," Monty said, looking around. "Keep your voice down."

"You think Adam will be upset about the Tate?"

"Even though it's visited often," Monty said, glancing back. "Or at least used to be. Most viewed it as an eyesore. Perhaps next time they will rebuild it in an aesthetically pleasing manner."

"Doubt it," I said. "They'll create the same ugly squat building and call it Ultra Modern or something pretentious like that. I'm really liking the idea of starting the Tate Neutralizing Tradition. We could call it the TNT."

"How about we focus on the matter at hand?" he said. "Verity is still out there and we have a mage to find. Let's change the subject."

I looked around at the panicked people running past us

and away from the site of the former Tate as sirens wailed in the distance.

"Good point," I said, lowering my voice. "Wouldn't want to raise any suspicion."

"Exactly," he said. "Let's get across the Thames. Things will be quieter on that side."

"I could use some coffee," I said. "I'm sure you could use a good cuppa of leaf water."

"I know just the place."

THIRTY

We crossed Blackfriars Bridge instead of the Hungerford to put the Thames between us and the Tate crater. Once across, we walked a short distance along the Victoria Embankment. Monty turned off at Carmelite Street and found a small shop named The Earl Grey.

I looked up at the ornate wooden sign: gold leaf on black-painted wood. A small plaque proudly stated that the shop had been in existence for five hundred years.

The small shop reminded me of some of the holdouts in Manhattan. Office buildings had been constructed around it, but it sat there defiantly, a throwback to a different era.

"This little shop is almost twice as old as the States," I said, admiring the black stone work and bright red door. "I hope they have coffee."

"Of course they have coffee," Monty scoffed and pushed open the door. "Even those with poor taste are allowed their freedom of expression here."

The Earl Grey was a small shop, filled with round tables around a center square bar. The lighting was dim, but not too dark. The natural light from the main window allowed plenty of light into the shop.

It looked like any other small tea house, except for the runes.

Some of the tables were occupied with patrons, but most of them were empty. In the center, behind the massive wooden bar, with his back to us, stood what I thought was an ogre.

At least he was large enough to be an ogre.

He wore a black skull cap and a black t-shirt that could easily double as a bed sheet for normal-sized humans, with dark jeans and a darker expression.

The bar itself pulsed with dark blue runes across its surface.

"Is this place a—"

"Null zone?" Monty finished. "Yes, probably the strongest in all of London. You can't even find this place unless you know how."

The bartender glanced at us as we entered and gave Monty a nod. He narrowed his eyes at me, scowled, and then glanced down at Peaches, cracking a smile.

It was the first time I had seen someone have that reaction when looking at my hellhound. Usually, it was fear with a dash of terror and sprinkled with the desire to leave the area —immediately.

"The bartender fits through the door?" I asked, keeping my voice low as I looked around. "Or does he use the window?"

"His name is Hont," Monty said, returning the nod. "From what I understand, he has been the only owner of this establishment since it opened its doors. Which means?"

"Hont has been around a long time," I said, looking up at the giant as we approached the bar. "How?"

"Clean living and staying out of trouble," Hont replied with a booming voice. He turned to Monty. "How's Dex?"

"Still alive," Monty said. "I'm sure he'll pay you a visit soon."

Hont nodded, before leaning close.

"I use the door, by the way," he said, looking at me. "Too expensive to replace the window every day."

"You heard me?" I asked, surprised. "No offense, it's just that—"

"I'm not your average-sized individual," he said. "I get that often. Save the giant jokes, I've heard them all and they're in poor taste."

"Understood," I said, looking up at him. "No giant jokes."

"Now that that's settled, what'll it be, gentlemen?"

"The usual for me," Monty said. "Coffee for my associate here."

Hont narrowed his eyes at me again, and put down the white towel he was holding. He cleared his throat before staring down at me and speaking.

"We don't do skinny mocha, splash of soy, sugar-free caramel, double blended with an extra shot of arrogance here," Hont said. "Here, you get coffee, as black as a Newgate knocker. That work for you?"

"I don't know what a Newgate knocker is, but if it's black, no sugar, and strong, it works for me," I said. "Thanks."

"And the hound?" Hont said, looking down at Peaches. "You plan on letting him starve?"

It was more of an accusation than a question.

"Do you have meat? Sausage?"

"We do," Hont said. "Figure a puppy like that needs a substantial amount. Five pounds should do, for now."

Hont left the bar and headed to the back room.

"Who exactly is Hont?" I asked. "He seems to know what kind of hound Peaches is just by looking at him."

"Hont is a giant."

"My eyes work perfectly fine," I said. "I can see he's a giant. It's a little hard to miss. He takes up most of the space back there."

"No, he's actually a giant—as in, descended from the race of giants," Monty said. "My uncle said he can trace his lineage back to the Nephilim."

"You mean a *real* giant?"

"As well as a proficient mage," Monty added. "I've never seen him cast, but I believe my uncle. Hont's energy signature is significant."

"Why does he keep giving me the stink-eye?"

"It may have something to do with your lack of an energy signature," Monty said. "The blood you drank is masking your presence. You read like the recently deceased. No energy signature."

"He's picking up on my lack of energy signature?"

"Yes."

"Is this going to be a problem?" I asked. "Because I really don't—"

"Only if you make it one," Hont said, materializing behind the bar. I jumped when he appeared. He placed a steaming teacup in front of Monty and a large mug of inky liquid in front of me. "One tea, one coffee."

"Thank you," Monty said as he took a sip and closed his eyes. "Still one of the best in the city. You outdo yourself, Hont."

"My pleasure," he said, reaching under the bar and pulling out a large iron bowl, filled with sausage. "Meat for the pup. Now, are you going to make a problem?"

"Not at all," I said when I could speak. "That was impressive."

"You are easily impressed, then," he said, placing the bowl on the bar. "Feed your hound."

I took the bowl off the bar and nearly dropped it. The weight of it caught me by surprise as I managed to place it in front of my ever-starving hellhound.

<The big man has good meat. Can I eat it now?>

<Please do. He wants you to be well-fed. He seems to like you.>

<I like him too. This is extra meat.>

<Make sure you say thank you.>

Peaches growled at Hont and then proceeded to inhale the meat in the iron bowl. Hont nodded and then turned to the side of the bar opposite us.

"We're closed for the day," he said in his booming voice. "You don't have to go home, but you can't stay here. Have a good night."

No one argued or raised an objection—not that I thought anyone was suicidal enough to complain to the giant. Everyone filed out quietly, some of the patrons raising their glasses in Hont's direction as they left.

The door locked after the last patron exited the shop.

"What are you?" he asked as the door locked. "You're supposed to be dead, yet here you are sitting in my shop drinking coffee."

"He's been cursed," Monty said before I could answer. "By Kali."

"That explains much," Hont said. "And the pup?"

"A gift from Hades," I answered, enjoying the aroma of the coffee filling the shop. "Unexpected but welcome."

"Some of the best gifts are," he said, eyeing my mug of coffee. "The coffee takes some getting used to. I suggest small doses."

I took a long pull of the ink Hont served me and groaned in pleasure. This was coffee on another level. The potency punched me in the brain, giving me an adrenaline rush mixed with a dangerous dopamine hit.

"What kind of coffee is this?" I said, pointing to the mug. "It's incredible."

"I call it my Elixir of Death," he said nodding approvingly in my direction. "Not many can drink that and remain upright. Now I'm the one that's impressed."

"So it's safe to say that anyone who drinks this has a—"

"Don't," Monty said. "Just don't."

"A Death Wish?"

"I suppose you could say that," Hont replied, rubbing his chin. "I don't get many requests for it, on account of it being too strong for anyone. I use it when some of the customers come in hammered. This clears them up straightaway."

"No kidding it clears them up," I said, taking another sip. "My brain is on fire. I think I can smell sounds."

"You may want to slow down," Hont warned. "It's strong. I also use it to wash the stones out front, keep them free of grime."

Monty stared at me, shook his head and took another sip of his tea.

"Thanks for the warning," I said, pushing the mug away, but not too far away. "That elixir should be illegal."

"It is," Hont said with a smile and then became serious. "Was that you earlier? At the Tate?"

"The Tate?" I said. "What do you mean?"

"Not you," he said, looking at me then turning to Monty. "Him."

Monty took another long sip from his cup.

"Yes," he said, placing the cup on the bar. "Is that going to be a problem?"

"Bah, never did like that eyesore of a building," Hont said. "Felt the backlash over here. Did you try to tap into the line?"

"No, I merely rerouted some of the energy."

"You merely rerouted? I had to bleed off the power headed to the Tate. That much energy would have taken out the bankside from the Blackfriars Bridge to the Southwark. What were you thinking?"

"I was... Thank you for intervening," Monty said quietly. "I didn't anticipate drawing that much power."

"Ley-lines are not to be trifled with," Hont admonished. "How did you manage to pull it off? You're not that strong and the island is being dampened."

"I don't know," Monty said, looking at his hands. "My intention was to create a reservoir of power to draw upon in case of an emergency."

"You nearly created a runic dead zone," Hont said. I barely followed what was being said, but judging from Monty's expression, it sounded bad. "Does Dexter know you wield this much energy?"

"I'm sure he knows by now," Monty said. "He's in the country."

"Bloody hell," Hont said. "He's going to be livid."

"Why?" I asked, confused. "Monty wasn't trying to blow up the Tate or the bankside. Even though, if you ask me, the Tate deserves it."

"He tampered with a ley-line," Hont explained. "Tristan, here, is not an Arch Mage. In fact, I don't know any Arch Mage mad enough to attempt what he did today."

"Why not?"

"Because ley-lines are mostly quintessence," Hont replied. "It would be the equivalent of stepping into an inferno to see if you could stay warm. Too much power to control and you end up turned to ash."

"That was not what I was trying to do," Monty said, his voice firm. "I know what runes I used. Control was never the point."

"If it's not the runes, then the issue lies with you," Hont said, pointing at Monty, then looking off in to the distance. "You can't stay long. If I felt that backlash, rest assured the

PC felt it too. Also, they may notice that one of their HQs is currently a burnt-out crater."

"Understood," Monty said. "The purpose of my visit—"

"You're looking for the mad mage, York."

"How did you know?" I asked. "We never mentioned—"

"You're in hiding," Hont said. "Verity has been activated. The only reason for them to go active are lost runes. Only one mage was insane enough to truck with those—York. Simple when you know the details."

"How do you know we're in hiding?"

"You're masked as a dead person, but bonded to a very live hellhound," Hont continued. "Tristan thought it was a good idea to draw power from a line because Mathers and the BPD dampened the entire island. Why would he need power if someone wasn't after him? Add a recently deconstructed Tate, the two of you sitting in my fine establishment—the strongest null zone in London, I might add—and the deduction is simple. You're in hiding."

"Now, *that's* impressive."

"Agreed," Hont said, looking at Monty. "York will be under surveillance. If I can put it together, so can the Consortium and Verity. They'll have Trafalgar under heavy surveillance."

"He hasn't moved from Trafalgar?"

"As far as I know, he's still down there. You need to be careful with him. He's a good mage, but manipulating those runes has damaged his mind."

"Do you know how many are around Trafalgar?"

"You have to figure the BPD is on high alert," Hont said. "The Consortium will have a presence and Verity will be in the shadows. Out of the three, Verity is the largest threat."

"Why?" I asked. "We've avoided them so far."

"You avoided The Eye," Hont said. "The Book is around

Trafalgar now. They present the greatest threat because they only have one focus."

"Monty?"

"No, the use or abuse of the lost runes," Hont replied, glancing at Monty. "For them, using a lost rune is the same as abusing it."

"They have a serious issue with these lost runes."

"They do, and with good reason. Those runes are too powerful to be used." He gave Monty a look. "Most mages understand this and refrain from trying to *find* the lost runes."

"I don't get it. How does this make them the greatest threat?"

"The BPD and Consortium are there to thwart an attempt to reach York," Monty said. "Verity's focus is singular —my elimination."

"Exactly. You can shift the other two groups, although it will be dicey," Hont said. "Nothing short of a national emergency will pull them off that detail."

"That still leaves Verity."

"Indeed it does," Hont answered. "Better to face them alone than all three groups at once."

"Then it seems we will have to create a national emergency," Monty said, standing. "Thank you Hont. The tea was extraordinary."

"Don't mention it," he said with a smile, then grew serious. "Actually, don't mention your visit here at all. Use the back room and watch your backs. The Book is prowling the streets."

Hont led the way to the back room.

"Thank you for the elixir," I said. "I hope to have some more someday."

"We'll see what the night brings," Hont said with a smile as he crouched down and rubbed Peaches behind the ears.

My ham of a hellhound stood still and enjoyed every second of it. "Trafalgar will be locked down tight. They'll place sleepers along every route for half a kilometer. Your best approach is Downing Street. Good luck."

We stepped out of The Earl Grey and into a small alley.

THIRTY-ONE

"Were you trying to get yourself killed?" I asked as I looked around the short alley. "There's a reason everyone stays away from those ley-lines, even Arch Mages."

"Yes," Monty said. "Fear...fear of the unknown. Fear of what they don't understand. It's why they ostracized York and stay clear of my uncle. They call them mad until, over time, they realize those they called mad were actually visionaries."

"I don't know," I said, shaking my head. "I've never met York, but Dex is definitely on the edge of madness. Sometimes, I think he steps over the edge. Way over."

"My uncle is not mad—unstable perhaps, given his history, but not mad," Monty said with an edge. "He's saner than most mages I know."

"Is that supposed to make me feel better? Because it doesn't," I said. "Did you know a side effect of using the lost runes is also losing your mind?"

"That remains to be seen."

Monty walked to the end of the short alley. I noticed the runes covering the ground and walls of the area behind The Earl Grey.

"This is still part of the null zone, isn't it?"

"Yes. Once we step out of this alley, Verity will know where I am," he replied, examining the runes. "You, being mostly dead, are safe from your successor. For now."

"Mostly dead means slightly alive," I said, following him. "Can Dira track Peaches?"

"I don't think so," he said. "As a successor, she's keyed to your signature, not your creature's. Once the effects of that blood wear off, though, she will be back and she will be angry."

"If she's alive," I said. "I hear having a building fall on you can be hazardous to your health."

"If she's alive, she will return and she will be upset."

"Upset is what happens when you spill your tea—"

"Spilling tea is unacceptable."

"She's not going to be upset," I continued. "She's going to be pissed beyond understanding."

"An apt description," he said. "Hont was right about one thing, though: Downing Street is our best bet."

"The Prime Minister is going to help us find York?"

Monty stared at me as we left the alley.

"Is that blood affecting your synapses?" he asked. "We use Downing Street to get the attention of the cordon around Trafalgar Square."

"Can you elaborate on the 'use Downing Street' part?" I asked. "You know, the part where, if something goes wrong and you blow up the Prime Minister, every mage in the country comes after us?"

"I will not be using ley-lines."

We walked down the block and ended up on Temple Street.

"Well, that's refreshing to hear," I said. "How are you going to get the attention of the cordon?"

"We're going to blow up the building across the street from the Prime Minister."

I stopped walking and stared at him.

"Are you serious? Did you not hear a word Hont said?"

"He didn't say anything we didn't know," Monty said. "This way"—he pointed ahead—"we can use the Temple Gardens to get to the Embankment. From there we can access Downing Street and the Ministry of Defense."

We crossed the street into a large park. Looking at the buildings, it felt like we had stepped back in time to the London of a few centuries ago.

"This must feel nostalgic," I said. "Is this what the city looked like when you were growing up?"

"I didn't visit the city often when I was a child," Monty said. "I was either with Nana or at the Golden Circle. There was little time for leisure pursuits."

"A shame," I said, admiring the buildings around the Temple Gardens. "I grew up on the streets of New York. I never had access to an amazing place like this."

"They made a concerted effort to preserve the property," Monty said, looking around. "I'd have to say they succeeded."

We kept walking for some time along the Embankment. I had some nagging questions, but mostly I was worried about Monty.

"How did you tap into the ley-line?"

"I didn't."

"The crater formerly known as the Tate would disagree," I said, keeping my voice even. "Are you sure you should be going for this Stormblood?"

"No," Monty said. "You want to know the truth?"

I nodded. "The truth will set you free."

"No, actually, it doesn't. It's been my experience that the truth can make you *less* free," he said. "Look around. What do you see?"

I looked around the Embankment as we walked. The Thames flowed by us on one side as people enjoyed the greenery, walking along the river.

"People out for a stroll enjoying the day?"

"Normal people enjoying a normal day by the river," he said. "Granted, they have their worries and concerns as all people do, but I doubt any of them are thinking about dealing with an old god out to kill them, or a group bent on expunging them."

"Or a successor trying to bisect them."

"Exactly," he said. "Would you like to tell them the truth? Pull back the veil and let them see what is happening in the shadows?"

"I don't think I'd get very far," I admitted. "At least not before they tried to lock me up."

"They'd call you mad first, then lock you up," he said. "The truth is this Stormblood frightens me. Not the ritual itself, but what I don't know."

"You mean, it can kill you?"

"I don't fear death, but there are worse things than death," he said. "I fear becoming something else, someone else, losing who I am to this power."

"I thought mages were trained to feel no fear?"

He shook his head.

"Mages, especially battle mages, are trained to fight, to cast, *despite* mind-numbing fear," he replied. "We're still human. We still feel."

"You have a choice," I said quietly. "We always have a choice."

"I do, but I also know the truth," he said. "If I choose to deny the Stormblood and walk away, Verity will still try to expunge me. Chaos won't have a change of heart because I opted to step away and, most importantly, I won't stop being the mage who refused to do all he could have done to stop evil."

"Sometimes the truth doesn't set you free, does it?"

"We must dwell in the shadows so others can enjoy the light," he said. "That is the price of knowing the truth and the cost of being a mage."

"Sometimes the choice isn't really a choice at all," I said, looking across the Thames to the city. "We know what we have to do. It's the doing that's hard."

"Which is why we have to get to York and complete this ritual," he said. "Despite my reservations, this is the path ahead."

By the time we reached Downing Street, the sun was setting.

"You aren't really going to blow up the"—I looked at the building opposite Downing—" the Ministry of Defense?"

"I'm not," Monty said, setting my mind at ease, "but I'm going to make it look like I have."

"This sounds like a terrible idea," I said, looking across the Thames at the Eye and recalling the destruction unleashed the last time we were here. "Why don't we try that shunt thing you did when you moved me from one Phantom to the other? That's not the same as teleporting, is it? We can reach York like that."

"Several reasons," he said, holding up a finger. "It's a form of teleporting, which I can't execute on this island because of the dampener." He held up another finger. "That method of teleporting only works well over very short distances; it's used for combat, not travel." One more finger. "The moment I try it, every mage in the vicinity will know my location."

"Won't that be the same as you unleashing destruction on the Ministry?"

"No, I'm actively masking my location and I intend on using what you would call pyrotechnics to give the impression of destruction," he said. "These casts can be set with a trigger and started remotely."

"Set a trigger and started remotely, like a bomb?" I asked, worried. "Why does this sound like a bomb?"

"No, not like a bomb—well, yes, like a bomb, but without an actual explosion," he said. "I'll set the runic pyrotechnics, then we backtrack to Northumberland Avenue. That will lead us straight into Trafalgar Square."

"Are you sure this won't blow up the Ministry building?" I asked warily. "You seemed certain about the runes outside of the Tate. Now the Tate is a memory, not that I'm complaining. I'm just pointing out your success rate for non-explosions today is 0 for 1."

"This is different. I'm not using ley-line energy," he assured me. "Once I set off the runic pyrotechnics, we make our way to Trafalgar Square and get that door open."

"If York hasn't changed the lock."

"If York hasn't changed the lock, yes."

"Now I feel much better," I said, feeling horrible. "What could possibly go wrong with this plan?"

"Plenty, but we will adapt as needed. The priority is getting to those bunkers, and then we find York."

"The priority is staying alive and not getting caught," I corrected. "The BPD and your pal Mathers will lose it if they see you on site."

"They will rush to the scene of the illusion, fearing another Tate incident, and he is not my pal."

"Leaving Verity around Trafalgar."

"They won't see us until the very last minute."

"I think we should rename your planning talks to anti-pep talks," I said. "Guaranteed to destroy morale in two seconds or less."

"The plan is sound," he replied. "What matters now is the

proper execution. Keep your eyes open for anything out of the ordinary."

"My entire life is out of the ordinary."

"You know what I mean," he said as he started gesturing and tracing runes. "Especially anyone that looks like a mage."

"You mean like those guys?" I said, pointing at some figures walking up the Embankment toward our location.

"Bloody hell," Monty said under his breath. "The Book."

THIRTY-TWO

"Walk away," Monty said quickly. "Step away from me."

"What are you talking about?"

"They are looking for a mage," he said. "To them, you're just out for a walk with your very large creature. You have no energy signature for them to read."

"Won't they find that strange?"

"They'll chalk it up to the dampening field interfering with their ability," he said, stepping away from me. "Now, walk away and wait for my signal."

The two figures kept approaching.

I moved away from Monty and stepped over the far side of the Embankment, keeping him in view, but far away enough that it looked like I was just out for a walk with my oversized hellhound.

I crouched down next to Peaches, making sure I had easy access to Grim Whisper, while keeping Monty and The Book mages in my sights. I could down the mages with Persuaders, if things went sideways.

As I looked at Monty, I saw him transform before my eyes. In the span of a few seconds he had turned into an old man, hunched over and walking slowly along the Embankment, enjoying the day.

His face had become wrinkled and his skin was covered in spots. He leaned on a cane as the two mages approached.

I let my hand drift to my side.

"Oi, you there," the mage on the right said. "It's getting late, you should be heading home."

"Eh?" Monty said, his voice thin and raspy as he held a hand up to an ear. "What was that? I should be eating bones?"

"You should go home," the mage on the left said, raising his voice while pointing away from the Embankment. "It's not safe."

"It's not Rafe?" Monty asked, stepping close to the left mage and looking into his face as he squinted. "My name isn't Rafe, young man. You must have me confused with someone else. Who's Rafe? Is that Rafe?"

Monty pointed in my direction.

The two mages turned to look at me, and Monty dropped the cane before placing a hand on each of the mages' necks. I saw a bright flash and they collapsed.

"What did you do?" I asked, looking around to make sure we were alone. I crouched down and checked on the mages. "They're out cold."

"Of course they are," Monty said, tracing some symbols on the ground near the Ministry building. "I merely overloaded their synapses, giving them too much information to process, causing them to shutdown."

"You short circuited them."

"An oversimplification, but yes, I short circuited them."

Mages. Ten words when three will do.

"We can't leave them here," I said, looking down at the mages. "I'm sure there will be other patrols."

"There's some thick underbrush over there on the promenade by the Royal Air Force Memorial." Monty pointed without looking up. "Hide them there. They will be out of commission for several hours."

"Are you going to be okay, old man?" I asked as I picked up one of the mages. "Careful not to throw out a hip while you're down there."

"Your wit never ceases to disappoint. Make haste," he said, waving me away. "I'll prepare the illusion."

"All of a sudden, I'm the muscle," I said with a grunt as I walked away. "This was not in the shield warrior job description, you know."

"I'd assist, but my frail bones are too delicate for such manual labor," he said as he moved to another location to trace runes into the ground. "You should respect your elders."

I hid the first mage and came back to transport the second.

"Actually," I said with a grunt as I lifted the second mage, "you *are* old enough to be my great-great-great-grandfather. Can't expect a senior citizen like you to exert himself like this. Sorry about that. This is a young man's job."

He gave me a glare and continued tracing symbols.

"It must be astonishing to be immortal and yet possess the mind of an infant," he said. "Your body is immortal, but I'm afraid your brain will never mature."

"That sounds like jealousy to me," I said, walking away. "I'll be right back. Peaches, keep Grandpa Monty safe until I get back."

Peaches chuffed and moved closer to Monty.

When I got back, Peaches was still guarding a glaring Monty.

"Tell your creature to leave me alone," he said. "I still have two more designs to draw and he keeps getting in my way."

"Peaches, let him go," I said. "Grandpa Monty still has more work to do. This going to take much longer?"

Peaches padded over to my side.

"Do you intend to keep calling me Grandpa?"

"As long as you look like that, yes."

"You know," he said as he moved to another location, "I've been working on a time-acceleration cast. Nothing major yet, but I'm sure I could age your appearance a few decades. Would you like me to try?"

"How about no?" I said. "That sounds like a bad idea."

"No worse than calling me Grandpa."

"Point made," I said with a smile. "No more Grandpa."

Mages and their fragile egos.

"I'm almost done, and then we will have to move with velocity to Northumberland," he said. "The trigger will prime in ten minutes. After that we'll only have five minutes to set it off remotely."

"Fifteen minutes to get from here to Trafalgar?" I said. "I can probably do it in ten. Can't speak for a certain senior citizen, though."

"We set off the illusion and make our way to York," Monty said, ignoring the jibe. "Once there, expect The Book to attack."

"Can I shoot them?" I asked. "I'm using Persuaders."

"Yes. At first they will ignore you," he said, still tracing. "Once they realize you're a threat they will use deadly force."

"Let me guess, you don't want me to respond in kind."

"If you can help it," he said. "Don't attempt to use your magic missile or your blade. We may need them later."

"Shoot to maim, got it," I said, looking at the symbols. "You're sure this won't tap into some ley-line and disintegrate us all?"

"There are no ley-lines present near here," he said. "This is to create a simulation of disaster, not an actual disaster."

"Just checking," I said. "Ready?"

"Almost," he said, before standing up, still looking ancient. "There, done."

"You plan on making this approach looking like that?"

"Yes," he said. "The best camouflage tries to blend in, not completely hide. You are signatureless, which means Verity won't expect you, at least not at first."

"Until I start shooting."

"Until you start shooting, yes," he said. "By that time, we should be at the lions."

We started moving fast toward Northumberland.

THIRTY-THREE

"Once we arrive at Northumberland Avenue I'll set off the illusion," Monty said. "Then we wait until the BPD and the Consortium response teams race to the Ministry building."

"Once that happens we approach Trafalgar?"

"Yes. Remember to keep your creature close," Monty said as we ran through Whitehall Gardens. "They won't expect a hellhound. We should keep every element of surprise in case of—"

"Blades?" I asked. "You think they may show?"

Monty nodded.

"Here," Monty said, coming to a stop. "We wait here."

We stopped at the corner of Northumberland and Whitehall Place. Monty raised an arm as he gestured with his other hand. White symbols floated into the air from his raised palm and raced away toward the Ministry building.

Nothing happened for a few minutes.

"Are you sure this illusion—?"

The night exploded with light as an enormous fireball billowed into the sky above the Ministry building. If Monty hadn't told me it was an illusion, I would've thought someone was carpet bombing the area.

"I'm sure," he said with a satisfied nod. "Response teams should be mobilizing as we speak."

The wail of sirens rose into the night as the streets became a hive of activity. Fire trucks and black response SUVs raced down Whitehall Street.

I noticed a group of runed vehicles without markings that could only be BPD and Consortium take off after the rest of the first-response vehicles.

"BPD?" I asked as the vehicles with darkened windows raced by. "Those runes tell me either BPD or Consortium."

"A combination of both," Monty said, peering at the vehicles. "Not our concern at the moment. Let's advance."

We moved down Northumberland and slowed our pace when we reached the equestrian statue of Charles the First. We stood in a wide open area and I felt extra vulnerable.

There were no cars in the streets and Trafalgar Square was empty of people. Still, I couldn't shake the impression we were being watched. Lord Nelson's column towered over us as the statue of Nelson stared down at us.

"Are you sure that's not Napoleon?" I said, glancing up at the figure at the top of the column. "Sure looks like him."

"Horatio Nelson, not Napoleon," Monty said, looking around as we moved forward. "Stay focused."

"I am focused," I said. "I was just wondering why Nelson is wearing Napoleon's hat."

"He is not—"

Several figures materialized around us. I counted five mages: two men, three women. The center mage was a woman who wore a scowl of extreme displeasure. Her expression was one of anger and disappointment, reminding me of every grade school teacher who informed me I had so much potential, if only I would only try harder.

The other mages all wore dark suits with dark shirts from the Zegna superstore. The center mage wore a dark suit with an off-white blouse. Her short hair was combed back and held in place with what I could only imagine was an entire tube of industrial-strength hair gel.

"I thought teleportation was off the table?" I asked as I looked at the assembled suits of mageness. "That looked like teleportation."

"They have fixed portals in place," Monty said. "It's not teleportation."

"You would destroy a protected site to achieve your ends?" the center mage said, glaring at Monty with disgust. "Surrender now and we will make your death swift."

"Is the Tate a landmark?" I said, under my breath. "If it was, we did them a favor."

"I think she's referring to the Ministry Building," Monty said, and stepped forward. "Who are you?"

"I am Mage Dolores of The Book," she said. "You, Tristan Montague, are guilty of using an elder rune—violating the tenets of Verity—and are hereby sentenced to death."

"Is it safe to say her power is affected the same way yours is?" I asked. "Is she at half strength?"

"Yes," Monty said. "She will resort to her weapon—a sword called a Soothsayer."

"I thought soothsayers were like fortune tellers?"

"Not in this context," Monty said. "Verity mages use them regularly, according to my uncle."

"Will you be able to use your wailers?"

"Sorrows," Monty corrected without taking his eyes off her. "Yes."

Another fireball bloomed into the sky behind us, casting her face in an eerie orange glow. She glanced up at the flames and hardened her expression further, before returning her gaze to Monty.

"I'm going to go out on a limb here and say diplomacy is not the way to go with them," I said, glancing at the other four mages who looked eager to unleash the agony. "Shoot first, ask questions never?"

"I will give them a chance to walk away," Monty said, smoothing out a sleeve. "It's the courteous thing to do."

"For once, could you stop being so English and blast them where they stand?" I said. "I don't see them offering you a chance to walk away."

"That's what makes us different," he said. "Get ready."

Monty took another step forward.

"Mage Dolores, this is the only opportunity I will offer you to cease and desist," Monty said. "Stop this and you can walk away with your lives."

A momentary expression of shock crossed her face.

"You dare threaten me?" she asked with barely controlled anger. "You dare to place conditions on your apprehension?"

"I do," Monty said calmly. "I do not wish to hurt you or your associates, but I will if I must."

I let my hand drift to my side.

<Get ready to bite them, boy.>

<Can I tear their hands off?>

<What's with the tearing of limbs all of a sudden?>

<Frank says I have to deal with problems by taking control of matters and ripping off hands. That way I can help you and get more meat.>

<It's taking matters into your own hands, which you can't do because you don't have hands.>

<No ripping?>

<None. Bite them, but no ripping off any body parts.>

<Will I still get meat if I leave their hands alone?>

<Yes.>

I was really going to have a conversation with that lizard.

"Hurt us?" Dolores scoffed. "You have an overinflated sense of importance."

"He really does," I said, stepping forward, hoping to diffuse the situation. "How about you let him off with a warning this time?"

Monty raised an eyebrow at me.

"A warning?" Dolores said, staring daggers at me. "He used an elder rune. There is no warning after a violation has occurred. Who are you?"

"Strong, Simon Strong," I said. "I'm Monty's friend and Aspis. If you're going to kill him, you'll need to go through me first."

She narrowed her eyes at me.

"Fine," she said. "Kill them both."

THIRTY-FOUR

"Not the answer I expected," I said as a red orb raced by my head. "Get them, boy!"

Peaches blinked out and reappeared next to one of the rear mages. He clamped down on his leg and began to shake his head. The mage didn't know what hit him as Peaches transformed him into a hellhound chew toy.

Even as I ran, I noticed Monty and Dolores hadn't moved. They were standing still, the eye of a hurricane of violence that swirled around them.

The other three mages converged on me as I ran forward to the lions, who observed the violence dispassionately. I shot another mage with Grim Whisper and ducked behind one of the bronze lions as an orb slammed into the pedestal, taking out a chunk of stone.

"There are going to be some pissed-off Brits if you destroy these lions," I called out. "You should give up now."

Another volley of orbs was the response. I counted down from ten, and waited. I could hear the groans of pain as the mage I shot was introduced to the effects of Persuader rounds. We were down to three mages including Dolores.

"You can't open the door," Dolores said. "We tried and we have the most accomplished mages on the planet. They all failed."

Another mage screamed in surprise as Peaches pounced on him. His screams were cut short as my hellhound bounced him on the stone. I peeked from my cover and saw Peaches' latest victim stir.

The last mage backed up and formed a lattice of golden energy. She threw it at Peaches, who blinked out, causing her to miss. I fired Grim Whisper and hit her in the leg as Peaches reappeared above her and landed on her chest. She was in for a bad night.

A moment later, the four mages were neutralized. Two were unconscious and two were having trouble controlling their bodily functions, their ability to cast nullified for the time being.

That left Dolores.

"Give it up," I said, aiming at her. "You *will* have a shitty experience if I hit you with one of these rounds. I mean that in every sense of the word."

Dolores reached behind her and drew a long blade.

A Soothsayer.

The silver steel of the blade was covered in black runes. The sword itself resembled a katana, and judging from the way she held it, she knew what she was doing.

I pulled the trigger and fired.

She stepped to the side and deflected the round with her blade.

She did know what she was doing.

"Don't waste your ammunition," Monty said, reaching behind him. "She will deflect them. We're running short on time. Find the plaque that depicts the death of Nelson at Trafalgar—Nelson's final battle."

I remembered Dex's words: *The entrance is where Nelson fell.*

Dolores laughed.

"You think you can succeed where we failed?" she mocked. "Your arrogance knows no bounds. First you think you can use an elder rune without consequence, and now you think you can open a door sealed for over a century?"

"I don't have another option," Monty said, drawing the Sorrows. They wailed as he brought them to his side. "There is no room for failure in this endeavor. Too many lives depend on us succeeding."

Dolores stared at the Sorrows for a few seconds as if determining to proceed with her current course of action. For a brief moment, she hesitated, and then the moment was gone. She slid into a defensive stance, her choice made.

She was going to kill Monty, or die trying.

She stepped forward with an upward slash that started low and raced up by her leg. It was a deceptive attack, but Monty was ready. He deftly deflected her blade with one of his, and slashed horizontally with the other.

She was outclassed and she knew it.

She ducked under his slash and backpedaled, unleashing a barrage of small orbs in his direction. He waved a hand, creating a violet shield to stop the orbs and sidestepped a thrust.

Her thrust had been a mistake.

Monty's evasion caused her to overextend. Monty brought one of the Sorrows down on her sword arm, shattering the bones in her wrist. Her sword clattered to the stone.

Monty, still moving, brought his other sword across her neck, freezing her in place. One subtle movement would remove her head from her neck.

"Do it," she said, defiantly. "Even if you kill me, Cain will hunt you down and end your existence."

"He will try," Monty said. "You should have accepted my offer."

He drew the Sorrows across her neck, barely breaking the skin. A thin cut appeared on her neck as droplets of blood formed along the wound.

Monty stepped back and absorbed the Sorrows.

"You should have killed me," she said with a sneer. "Now, I will end your miserable—"

The Soothsayer disappeared as she fell to her knees.

"My swords have distinct properties," Monty said, forming an orb of white energy. "Your abilities have been nullified."

"How?" she said, looking at her hands. "What did you do?"

"I spared your life," he said, releasing the orb. "I won't be so generous next time."

The orb slammed into Dolores and launched her across the Square. She landed about ten feet away and slid for another five.

"Ouch," I said with a wince as I saw her land. "What did you do?"

"The seraph properties of the Sorrows allow me to nullify energy, primarily demonic," he said. "I have been studying them. It appears I can affect other sources of energy as well."

"When did you learn this?"

"During my recent stay in Haven," he said. "I'll explain later." He looked off into the distance. "That illusion won't last much longer. We have to get this entrance open."

I pointed to the plaque on the south face of the column.

"I really hope you know the sequence," I said, looking at the plaque. "Because I'm not seeing any way of opening this supposed entrance."

The bronze plaque was an image of Nelson's men carrying him on a ship after he was wounded. I saw the image of a sail and a mast. There were men holding guns and everyone seemed worried Nelson was about to breathe his last.

The bottom of the plaque read that England expected every man to do his duty. I guess that meant making the ultimate sacrifice, in Nelson's case.

"Those things look heavy," I said, looking at the large plaque. "That has to be at least fifteen square feet of solid bronze."

"We aren't removing them," Monty said, examining the plaque. "This is supposed to be an entrance to the tunnels below."

"Monty," I said, pointing to the Ministry building. "You better find that key sequence quick. Your illusion is almost done."

Monty glanced over at the diminishing light and nodded.

"The rest of The Book will be here soon."

"Along with the BPD and the Consortium," I added. "Any clue on the key?"

"My uncle said I knew it," Monty said.

"But he also said it was lost," I answered. "That doesn't make sense."

Monty rubbed his chin and smiled—which concerned me, since his facial muscles weren't used to him smiling.

"If you keep doing that, your face is going to seize," I warned. "What is it?"

"How did Hont describe York?" Monty asked, climbing the lower portion of the column to get closer to the plaque. "Do you recall?"

"He called York insane."

"Not just insane," Monty said. "He said Mage York was the only one insane enough to truck with lost runes. If you were a mage who dealt with lost runes and wanted to secure an entrance, how would you guarantee you'd be left alone?"

"I'd use a set of runes no one can access, because the rune police would come after you and dust your ass?"

"Precisely," Monty said, snapping his fingers. "Verity's mages couldn't open this door, because?"

"They would never use elder runes," I finished. "Kind of goes against everything they stand for."

"No other mage would be able to open it, because the runes are lost," he said. "Not unless they knew a lost rune."

"The logic is sound," I said. "My question is: this rune you know, is it the right one?"

"Only one way to find out."

THIRTY-FIVE

Monty traced the lost rune on the plaque, violet energy emerging from his fingers and leaving an afterimage across the face of the plaque.

There was a low tremor, and for a few seconds, the entire column shook. I was about to blame him for destroying the column when the plaque swung inward, revealing a set of stairs leading down.

We stepped in, Monty swung the plaque closed, and we took the stairs. A beam of orange energy ran along the edge of the plaque, sealing it again. After about ten minutes, we reached the bottom of the stairs. We found ourselves in a cylindrical tunnel with sconces every few feet providing a dim light.

"This looks like a tube tunnel," I said, looking around at the smooth walls. "Is there a line that runs through here? Last thing I want to do is dodge trains as we wander around down here."

"This tunnel should lead to the bunkers," he said, pointing. "Over there."

At the end of the tunnel I saw a huge, circular steel door that would put bank vault doors to shame. It glowed with orange runes across its surface and definitely gave off a Gandalfian "you shall not pass" vibe.

"Same rune?" I asked, looking down at my holster and resting a hand on Grim Whisper. "I don't think we have the kind of firepower to get through this door without a runic nuke. Even then, I think the door would win."

"There's a panel over here," Monty said, pointing to a small glowing rectangular section of the door. "It's an inscription tablet; they're used as locks to secure locations."

"I would say this is about as secure as it gets," I said, looking up at the door. "Inscribe away."

Monty stepped close to the door and traced the lost rune on the tablet.

Nothing happened.

Monty scowled and examined the tablet.

"It should have worked," he said. "I traced it precisely."

"Maybe the tablet is out of energy," I said. "It has been a century since anyone has made it down here. Is there another way in?"

"No, not to my knowledge," Monty said, still looking at the panel. "These bunkers were designed to be impregnable. One way in, one way out."

"I call that bad planning," I said. "I mean what if—"

A section of the enormous vault door opened outward and a bald head peeked out. It was a short man, a little on the pudgy side. He wore thick glasses, which he pushed up on the bridge of his nose, a blue bathrobe, and a pair of fuzzy gray house slippers.

"Mage York?" Monty asked tentatively. "Is that you?"

"Of course it's me," he snapped. "I know who I am. Who are you?"

"My name is Tristan Montague, and this is—"

"Montague?" he asked. "Are you related to Dexter? Of course you are; look at that face. Come inside, come inside. Is that a hellhound?"

He waved us in after him and disappeared inside.

The door closed behind us with a hiss and I realized that while, we may have found the way in, that didn't guarantee we knew the way out.

"Monty," I said, under my breath. "I think he's been down here alone longer than is healthy."

I looked around the bunker.

York had everything he needed down here. Whoever designed the mage bunkers had been forward thinking. The open circular space was broken up into four quadrants with a dedicated purpose to each section.

One section contained a large library; another section held a small conference table with chairs. The other was a kitchen, and the last, sleeping quarters.

On either end of the circle I saw a tunnel leading away. I imagined there were several of these circular bunkers connected to one another through these tunnels.

"This way, this way," York called out. "I'm in here."

We traveled down one of the connecting tunnels and found ourselves in another open circular space. This one reminded me of Josephine's circle chamber.

I saw runes on the walls and floor, but no circle.

York stood in the center of the room and I felt an air of menace. It was coming from him, but I couldn't reconcile the image with the danger I felt.

He was standing there in a bathrobe and slippers, looking the opposite of menacing. Peaches whined and lowered himself into 'pounce and shred' mode.

"No, no," York said looking at Peaches. "We can't have any of that."

He waved a hand and a golden lattice surrounded my hellhound, freezing him in place. I let my hand fall to my holster only to find Grim Whisper gone.

"What the—?"

"Your weapon is secure in the armory," York said. "Now tell me, how did you open the door?"

"I didn't open the door," I said, looking at Peaches. "Is that hurting him?"

"He's in stasis, probably dreaming of large bowls of meat," he said, then looked at Monty. "I wasn't referring to you, Marked of Kali. Tell me, young Montague, how did you manage to open my door?"

"Your door?" Monty asked. "I thought this was the entrance to the Gallery bunkers?"

"Who do you think designed the Gallery bunkers?"

"You?" I asked. "You designed this place?"

"Much brighter than you appear," he said with a nod. "Kindly answer my question, young Montague."

"I used a lost—an elder rune," Monty said. "The rune of seals."

"The rune of seals?" York asked, narrowing his eyes at Monty. "Yes, yes, I can see the traces in your signature. Do you realize how dangerous this is? You are not strong enough to wield elder runes. You are too young and unskilled."

"That's why we're here," I said. "Monty needs access to Stormblood."

"Stormblood?" York asked. "What is this Stormblood?"

"Excuse me?" I said in mild shock. "You don't know what Stormblood is?"

"Never heard of it," York said. "I'm sorry you came all this way for nothing."

Monty narrowed his eyes at York.

"You're lying," Monty said. "You know exactly what Stormblood is."

York looked away and then back at us.

"What if I do?" he said. "You can't wield it. He will come for you. If the Stormblood doesn't kill you, he will."

"Who?" I asked. "Who will come for him?"

"Cain, the leader of Verity," York said, looking over his shoulder in fear. "If I help you, he'll know."

"Mage York, I need your help," Monty said. "I cannot do this alone and my uncle said you were the only one who could complete the ritual."

"Dexter, Dexter, Dexter," York said, shaking his head. "Why would you do this? He knows what this is, the danger it presents. That's why the elder runes were hidden. It's too dangerous. Too dangerous!"

"Mage York, I know you don't know us, but we're trying to stop some very nasty people from doing bad things," I said, keeping my voice low. "Verity is only one of several entities out there that we need to stop. They want to kill Monty."

"Narrow-minded fools," he hissed. "Always thinking short term. The elder runes should have been harnessed for good. Instead they criminalized them, hunted down mages. Our own kind!"

It was clear that York's mental train had left the station without him long ago. I gave Monty a glance that said, *Good luck, all yours.* Monty took a deep breath and let it out slow.

"Mage York, Cain needs to be stopped."

"Yes!" York said, raising his voice "We need to stop Cain, but you—you're too weak. You can't stop Cain. You used the elder rune, but you're too weak."

"I may be too weak, but what about the both of us?"

York focused on Monty and began muttering under his breath.

"What are you talking about?" I said, lowering my voice low to avoid triggering York. "The both of us? There is no both of us when it comes to this. Not a mage, remember?"

"Yes, yes, yes," York said, clapping his hands together. "It can work, but it has to be the *both* of you. Do you understand? The both of you?"

"No," I said. "I do not understand."

York narrowed his eyes at me.

"You," he said, pointing at me, then pointed at Monty, "and you, together, can be strong enough for the Stormblood. Yes—together, it can work. It can work! You can stop Cain. You can...kill Cain."

"Monty, this is a bad idea," I said. "I'm not a fan of this Cain character, but this sounds like suicide. Also, in case you haven't noticed, I'm getting serious mad-scientist vibes here from our resident mage."

"I'm not mad," York said, suddenly serious. "They called me crazy, they called me insane, called me dangerous, and locked me away. I escaped from them, then they created Verity to hunt me down. Called me a threat to society."

"Verity is after you?"

"They can't come here, though," York said with a short laugh. "Need an elder rune to open the door; I changed it one hundred years ago. The one thing they hate has stopped them. The fools. No one has come down here until now. Until you two. You will show them, yes. Show them I was right."

"How are we going to do that?" I asked slowly.

"Together, yes, together you will wield the Stormblood."

"Monty, do you want to explain to the nice mage why this may be a bad idea?" I asked. "You know that part about how it would kill us?"

"One of you, yes, but the two of you, the two of you," he said and looked up. "No, they're close. No time. Have to do this now before they stop me. You have the elder rune; this can work. It must work."

"Mage York," Monty said. "Perhaps we should reconsider—?"

"No time, no time!"
Mage York disappeared.

THIRTY-SIX

"We need to get the hell out of Dodge, Monty."

"I agree. If you could point me to the nearest exit, I'd be happy to evacuate the premises."

"What are you talking about? We came in right through—"

I turned toward the entrance we used, except that the entrance we'd used was gone. We were standing in an enclosed room with no exits.

The runes covering the walls and floor began to glow a deep violet.

"Where's Peaches?" I asked, whirling around. "He's gone."

"Your hellhound is safe," York said, his voice filling the room. "I would never harm such an exquisite animal."

"Mage York, listen to me. We need to discuss this. We need—"

"No," York said calmly, which creeped me out more than the mad-scientist babble. "I've waited for years to find a way. I can't face Cain; my mind, my mind isn't what it used to be."

No shit.

"We can find another way," Monty said. "My uncle Dexter can help us."

"No, we don't have time," York snapped. "Don't you understand? You used an elder rune to gain entrance. YOU USED AN ELDER RUNE. One hundred years that door has remained sealed. Until you. Cain is coming. I can't stop him. You can. I'm sorry, it has to be this way."

"Monty, it always gets worse when they apologize for wrecking you," I said, looking around. "How far underground are we?"

"Too far to teleport even if we could," Monty said, pointing at the runes. "Those are elder inhibiting runes and those"— he pointed to another set—"those are elder trans-mutation runes. Extremely rare. I don't know how I know that, but I do. I've only seen them partially drawn in books."

"The elder rune you used has increased your knowledge, yes," York said. "Both of you will share the Stormblood."

"Mage York, you need to stop this," Monty said. "There must be another way, another choice."

"Yes—*you* are the other choice," he said. "The ritual will commence shortly."

"What exactly is this ritual, Mage York?" I asked, trying to keep him engaged. "How are we going to get this Storm-blood? I don't know if you haven't noticed, I'm not a mage. This can't work."

"You have half the elder rune, there, inside you. The ritual will work."

"Shit, is he talking about—?"

"I believe he's referring to your blade, yes."

"How could he even know that?" I asked. "Mage York, that is part of a weapon. I repeat, I'm not a mage."

"The Stormblood isn't only for mages," York countered. "The weapon is part of you, inside of you. The ritual will add to the elder rune, enhance it, ascend you both to the Stormblood...or kill you. It really can go either way. I hope you survive."

"What the hell! Are you serious, York?"

"I will try to hold them until it's done. Your hellhound will wait for you at the exit. Goodbye. I hope we can meet again. If not, please understand: this was the only way."

The runes on the walls became more intense. They shifted from violet to orange, increasing in brightness until I had to avert my eyes. I reached inside to attempt my dawn-ward and came up empty.

"Shit, Monty, can you cast a shield?"

Monty gestured and nothing happened. He tried again with the same result. He tried one more time with no success.

"I can't cast anything, it seems," he said, looking down at his hands. "My ability is completely nulled. This is fascinating. Not even a null zone can equate this effect."

"Monty, we are in deep shit," I said, looking down to avert my eyes. "This is not the time to examine how amazing the null effects of this torture chamber are. We need an exit."

The runes on the floor began to get brighter. After a few seconds, they matched the intensity of the walls. Even with my eyes closed the light was blinding. It was like standing too close to the sun.

That was when it happened.

I felt a blast of energy rip through my body, lifting me off my feet. Behind me, I could sense Monty. The power intensified as I felt Ebonsoul being pulled from within. Even without opening my eyes, I could sense the presence of my weapon. I opened my eyes and saw the black blade hovering in front of me.

The silver band running down its length spread out, covering the entire blade. When the entire blade turned silver, it reverted to mist form. The mist stretched out into a long silver blade.

It hovered vertically in the air for a few seconds before lazily becoming horizontal, pointing directly at my chest. It remained in place, vibrating slowly.

"Monty," I said, knowing what was coming next. "I think this is where the pain starts."

The mist blade stopped vibrating and shot through my chest, punching through Monty, who hovered behind me.

We both screamed as the runes floated off the walls and cascaded into us, each rune burning into my skin as it impacted me. There was a pause in the onslaught, and I took a breath.

"Simon," Monty rasped and coughed. "I'm sorry I got you into this."

He coughed again and I knew he had spit up blood, because I had done the same.

We were dying.

I laughed.

And coughed again, spitting up more blood.

"I told...I told you that I was going to...going to remind you, that it was all your fault," I managed. "No fair, apologizing first."

He laughed.

"You are an incorrigible fool. It's been an honor fighting alongside you."

"Ditto."

He laughed again and we both gasped as the mist blade extended and wrapped us both in silver mist. The room filled with power and I started crying—only I knew it wasn't tears, it was blood.

That's when the lightning started.

I saw the small arcs race across the floor and the walls. The lightning arced along the wall higher and higher until it punched into my chest, setting the mist on fire.

I screamed until I couldn't scream any longer, and still I

tried, my voice gone, but the agony ever-present. The energy around us increased until all I could see was blue crackling lightning all around us.

I saw a large orb of lightning form in the air in front of me. It steadily grew and I tried to pull back, but I had no leverage. I twisted my head around and saw another orb of lightning in front of Monty.

"This is what I call going out in a blaze of—"

I never finished my sentence.

The last thing I remembered was the orb racing at me, punching me in the chest, and bathing me in a blast of energy and light.

THIRTY-SEVEN

I squinted up into the face of a worried-looking York.

"If I'm dead, and I'm stuck with you, this must be hell," I said, looking up into his face. "What happened?"

"You survived...you survived, yes, yes," York said. "The exit...must get you to the exit, now."

"Monty?"

"Right here," he said with a groan. "Are we dead?"

"No, not dead, but must get you out," York said, anxious. "No time to waste."

He waved a hand and an opening formed in the wall.

"This way," he said, pointing. "We must go. Cain is coming."

"Stop the world," I said, groaning as I got to my feet. "I want to get off."

"We need to go," Monty said. "If he gets too far ahead we'll lose him down here. These bunkers are a maze of modules."

"Right," I said, stumbling to the exit. I looked ahead and saw York moving fast. "He's over here."

We followed York through winding tunnels. After a few

minutes I was completely lost. I'm sure some of it was due to the lightning therapy I had just gone through; the rest of it was Monty's accurate description of the bunkers.

The place was a maze.

When we started heading to the surface, I noticed York became calmer, and that made no sense. He was a bundle of nerves when we were underground, and now he had ice in his veins?

"You notice anything different about our guide?" I asked Monty as he drew up next to me. "From Nervous Nelly to Calm Cucumber?"

"He's made his peace," Monty said, moving ahead. "Mage York, where does this tunnel lead?"

"Sainsbury Wing of the National Gallery," York said. "You did it. It's up to you, now."

York led us to a door and into a small room. My hellhound lay on a small bed still covered in the golden lattice and frozen. On a small table beside him I saw Grim Whisper. York handed me my weapon and removed the lattice from my hellhound, who stood and shook himself.

I crouched down and hugged him before rubbing behind his ears. He smacked me in the face with a deft tongue fu move, which I didn't mind.

<I was dreaming of meat.>

<Do you dream of anything else?>

<The guardian.>

<I'm not surprised. No dreams of your favorite bondmate?>

<You're my only bondmate. You have grown stronger, much stronger. What did you do? Did you eat meat?>

<I'll explain later; right now, we have to get out of here.>

<There is a bad man coming. He smells bad.>

"We have incoming," I said, pointing at Peaches. "Hell-hound detector of badness."

York nodded and looked around.

"You can't face him, not yet," York said. "You're not strong enough. I will keep him busy. Get to the Square. I have a friend there who can protect you."

"York, even though you almost barbecued us to death, you don't have to do this. We can—"

"He will *kill* you," York hissed, gripping the door handle. "I will slow him down, but you must get to the Square, back to Nelson's Column. She will be there. You'll be safe with her."

"She?" I said. "Who?"

"No time," York said, shaking his head. "It was an honor knowing you both, even for a brief moment. Promise me you will stop Cain."

"I promise," I said.

He looked at Monty, who nodded.

"I promise," Monty said.

York opened the door into the empty museum.

We had covered half the wing when I felt the presence.

"What have you done, York?" a voice said from our left. "How could you? I showed you mercy. I let you live, and this is how you repay me? You aid criminals? Increase their power?"

Cain.

"You are the criminal," York said, his voice even and calm. "You are the one with the blood of innocents on your hands."

"No one is innocent, York," Cain said. "You taught me that."

I turned to face Cain.

He was wearing a heavily runed, dark blue bespoke Zegna mageiform. His black hair was cut short, almost military style. Put him anywhere else, and the first impression was CEO or banker. His gray eyes bore into us as he stood at the end of a short corridor.

"Keep moving," York said under his breath. "You must get outside."

"Leaving so soon?" Cain asked almost casually. "You aren't going to introduce me to your new friends?"

"No," York said, hanging back and covering our rear. "We have nothing to discuss."

"You used High elder runes, York," Cain said. "I wouldn't be here if you hadn't. What did you do?"

"What I should've done years ago," York said. "I've ended you."

Cain shook his head.

"I didn't want to do this, but you forced my hand, old friend."

"I'm no friend of yours," York spat. "Never was."

"Your mind is addled," Cain said. "You've been in that bunker too long. Now you've done something irreparable, something that will cost you your life."

"Run," York hissed. "Run, now."

He threw up a golden shield of power as a beam of blue energy slammed into it and bounced off, punching holes in exhibits and the walls behind them.

"Can you cast, Monty?" I said, drawing Grim Whisper and switching out the magazine for entropy rounds. "I think I can hit him, as soon as I stop seeing double."

"No!" York screamed. "Run!"

He gestured and blasted us with a kinetic blast that launched all three of us away. We landed near the exit. I turned to see York fall to one knee as Cain hit the shield with another blast.

This one cut through the shield and York. He looked at me and closed his eyes, his face tranquil.

"Go," he mouthed and gestured. *Please.*

"We need to go now," Monty said, shoving me out the door. "Run!"

We ran out of the Sainsbury Wing and onto the empty street.

"Don't stop," Monty said, pushing me as we stumbled away. "Keep going!"

We were halfway to Nelson's Column when the Sainsbury Wing disintegrated. I would say exploded, but that would be inaccurate. One moment, there was a Sainsbury Wing, the next moment it was debris, unrecognizable as the building it was seconds earlier.

We'd nearly reached the Column when I heard him, his voice carrying clearly through the Square. He stepped out of the debris unscathed.

"Dramatic, but ultimately a futile gesture."

Cain had survived the blast.

I turned to Monty.

"How are we doing on the casting front? Anything?"

Monty shook his head.

"Shit," I said, looking around. "Why did York want us to come here? To die under fake Napoleon's watchful gaze?"

"I have a better question," Cain said as he approached. "Why did York sacrifice himself for you?"

"Some sacrifices are worth making," I said. "Maybe he saw something you can't."

"I'll tell you what I see," he said, standing still. "I see a rogue mage who dared to use elder runes. Tristan Montague, by the authority vested in me by Verity and the High Tribunal, I sentence you to death. Do you have any final words?"

"Fuck you," Monty said defiantly. "We will not die easily."

"That's my line," I said, looking at Monty in mild shock, before turning to Cain and drawing Grim Whisper. "We won't be doing the dying tonight."

"Oh, I rather think you will," Cain said, approaching

again. "I know Tristan can't cast and your abilities are practically nonexistent. This is your end."

The sound of slow clapping filled the Square.

"You really enjoy the sound of your own voice," a woman said from the darkness. "You were never one to take in your surroundings, Cain."

Cain stopped walking and I saw fear flit across his face.

"This doesn't concern you, Anastasia," Cain said. "This is a Verity matter. I am here in my function as leader of The Blades."

"And I," the woman said, stepping out of the shadows, "am here in my function as his kin. Walk away or die here tonight."

"You know I can't do that," Cain said, regaining some of his composure. "The tenet has been broken and the price must be paid."

"You will find that exacting this price will prove costly," she said. "Final warning: walk away."

Her voice sounded familiar.

"Are you siding with these two scum?" Cain demanded. "Against Verity? Against the High Tribunal?"

"Yes."

That one simple word reverberated with power, sending waves of energy throughout the Square.

"Very well," Cain said with a nod. "For aiding and abetting these criminals you, too, shall perish tonight."

"Oh, child," the woman said with a hint of mirth. "I was old when you were still swimming your father's nether regions."

"Nana?" Monty said. "Is that you?"

"Aye, it's her," another voice said. "Pain in my arse as usual."

"Dex?" I said. "That you?"

"Aye, boy," he said and appeared on one of the lions.

"Seems like you found York." He looked around the Square. "Where is the old nutter?"

I shook my head.

"He didn't make it," I said, turning to look at Cain. "Mostly because of him."

I didn't feel bad at all painting a huge target on Cain's forehead. Dex's expression darkened as he slid off the lion.

"Anastasia, York was a fellow mage and my friend," Dex said. "Deal with this upstart, or I will."

A short, older, heavyset woman stepped out from behind the pedestal that supported the lion Dexter sat on. Nana, the only reason Dex wasn't in shred mode this very second, looked the same as I remembered her. She was the quintessential grandmother. Her gray hair was pulled up into a bun that rested on top of her head, and was wearing a black rune-covered gown that flowed around her.

"I will show you mercy, but I will not ask for it," she said, her voice slicing through the night filled with the promise of death. "Tonight you offered death to me and mine. I will leave you with your life, but you *will* desire death."

Cain formed a red orb of energy.

"Your words are meaningless," Cain said. "Verity is my strength."

He unleashed the orb as Nana started walking toward him. She caught his orb and crushed it in her hand. He unleashed another, which she batted away.

Cain stepped back and formed a black orb the size of a basketball. It crackled with dark energy and Nana stopped walking.

"What have you done, child?" Nana asked. "This is not the work of Verity."

"If I must uphold the tenet of Verity, no spell is forbidden," Cain declared smugly. "Now you realize my true power."

He released the black orb. Even I felt the power coming off of it as it raced at Nana.

Nana caught the orb.

She wrapped both hands around the black energy and whispered a word under her breath. The orb transformed from black to golden to a deep violet.

She tossed the orb back at a shocked Cain.

Cain backpedaled as he threw up shield after shield. The orb tore through every shield as if it didn't exist, picking up speed each time. By the fourth shield, Cain had run out of space and time.

The orb enveloped him, slamming him to the ground with an audible *thump*. Nana walked over to where he lay, gasping for breath. She gently placed a finger on his forehead.

"Tell Verity I'll be paying them a visit soon," she said walking away. "Now, off you go."

Cain jumped to his feet and gestured.

Nothing happened.

He traced runes in the air, creating angry red symbols which fizzled out as soon as he made them.

"What have you done to me?" Cain demanded. "You dare interfere with my power?"

"I dare," Nana said turning around. "You want your power?"

She formed a small violet orb.

"I demand it."

"Of course you do," she said, looking at the small orb. "This is your power. Are you certain you desire it?"

Cain glared at her. He was either suicidal or monumentally stupid. I was leaning toward both.

Nana waved her hand and the small violet orb raced at Cain, hitting him at speed. His body absorbed the orb and glowed with violet energy.

Cain laughed and began gesturing.

He screamed and fell to his knees.

"What have you done?" he asked. "This is not my power."

"It is," Nana said. "I merely added a little something. Every time your intention is to do harm, your power will punish you. When you no longer wish to cause harm, you will no longer feel pain. Dex? He needs to get back before the Tribunal misses him."

Dex nodded.

"No," Cain said. "You can't do this. How can I lead The Blades like this?"

"I'd suggest kindness and compassion," Nana said, turning away. "But the choice is yours. If you threaten my kin again, I will not be merciful. Goodbye, Cain."

A green circle formed under him and rose into the air, disappearing Cain from sight.

"I thought you couldn't teleport?" I asked as Cain vanished. "That was a teleport."

"Wrong," Dex said. "That was me sending him back to his fixed portal. The High Tribunal is going to have some words for him, I think."

I turned to Nana who headed over to where Monty stood.

"Why didn't you kill him?" I asked. "He threatened to kill us all. He's the reason York is dead."

"No," she said sharply. "York made a choice. The moment he decided to perform the ritual on you both, his fate was sealed. He chose how he wanted to die. We should all be so fortunate."

"But you could have ended Cain."

"Yes, I could have," she said. "I didn't kill him. Because I could, I chose to spare him. You may choose differently if he rises against you again, but it was my choice to make tonight."

I shook my head.

"The learning curve in this world is steep."

"It is, but you're coming along nicely," she said. "A few more centuries and we can start training you properly."

She gestured and materialized a long bench with a cushion for Monty, who sat wearily. I looked around and saw no other benches. I headed over to Nelson's Column where Dex rested against a lion.

"He's her favorite," Dex said with a chuckle. "Don't mind her."

"I'm sorry about York," I said. "We went through the Stormblood ritual and he saved us."

"We?" Dex asked. "What do you mean *we*?"

"They share the elder runes between them," Nana said. "How are you feeling, Trissy?"

"Please don't call me that," Monty complained. "I'm over two centuries old."

"Oh? Look who's the grown man?" Nana answered. "You will always be Trissy to me. Accept it now, and make your life easier."

"Yes, Nana."

"What do you mean they share the elder runes between them?" Dex asked, throwing his hands in the air. "The whole point of this bloody trip was to get Tristan the Stormblood."

"And he has it, with his shield warrior, Simon, as a catalyst," Nana replied. "It's not complicated, Dexter. If York were to send Trissy through the ritual alone, it would have killed him. With the bond he shares with Simon, together they were able to survive the ritual."

"Do you know what this means?" Dex asked, shaking his head. "This is a world of pain."

"I'm afraid so," Nana said. "Cain was only the beginning of your troubles, boys. Verity will seek to expunge the both of you now."

"We still don't know how this is going to work," Dex said. "I've never heard of a shared Stormblood."

"I'm sure Tempest can shed some light on their situation, now that York is no longer with us."

"Aye," Dex said. "I'm going to miss him."

"He never wanted to leave that bunker," Nana said, looking at Monty and me. "Yet he did, for you two. He must have seen something great in each of you."

"I hope we can live up to what he saw," I said. "He sacrificed everything to make sure we had this Stormblood."

"He did," Nana said, getting to her feet. "Make sure you honor that sacrifice. I'm going home. I've had enough excitement for one night."

"Good night, Nana," I said. "Thank you for...everything."

"You're welcome, child," she said and looked at Monty. "Were you responsible for the Tate?"

"I—yes," Monty said. "It was unintentional."

Nana patted him on the shoulder.

"I thought as much," she said. "You may want to leave before the BPD catches wind of your involvement. That Mathers is quite excitable. Dex, you'll make sure they leave the country?"

"Aye. Right after we see the witch, we're gone."

"What about the Consortium? Won't they get involved?"

"I'll deal with the Consortium," Nana said, making it sound like a threat. "Maybe I'll visit you in the States when I'm done. I'm due for an extended vacation."

"So many other places to visit, woman," Dex said. "Your vacations always end up in disasters."

"I'll consider it," she said, walking away. "I'll see you soon, Trissy."

Nana disappeared a second later.

"Don't tell me that wasn't a teleport," I said, pointing at where Nana stood seconds earlier. "That was a teleport."

"Aye, but that's Nana," Dex said with a grin. "A little dampening field isn't going to stop her."

I looked over at the destruction of the Sainsbury Wing and a pang of sadness hit me. York may have been batshit insane, but he was Dex's friend.

Dex had one less friend in the world.

"Let's go see Josephine at first light," I said. "We have a few things to set right before we leave."

"Aye," Dex said, looking at the debris. "A good plan."

THIRTY-EIGHT

"Are you sure you want to do this?" I asked. "He's definitely going to lose his mind and then call in for reinforcements."

"We won't be there long enough for him to react," Monty said. "Besides, this needs to be settled."

"If this goes sideways, he's the Director of the BPD."

"I will retain my composure," Monty said. "I am not a child."

"This whole thing seems petty to me."

Monty walked up to the house and knocked on the door. It was six in the morning and I was certain he was waking everyone up.

"Who is it at this ungodly hour?" Mathers asked groggily through the door. "Who's there?"

"Tristan," Monty said as the door flew open to a now wide-awake Mathers. "Hello, Matthew."

"I should have known you were in the country. The Tate is a complete disaster," Mathers said. "Was that your work?"

"I want you to know that I know," Monty said calmly. "I know what you did."

"What did I do?" Mathers said, stepping outside and closing the door behind him. "What are you accusing me of, Montague?"

"I know about the mages who died under mysterious circumstances," Monty said. "How a certain BPD Officer Mathers was lead investigator. I also know how the evidence was tainted and deemed inadmissible."

"You know nothing," Mathers scoffed, but it wasn't convincing. "Where's your proof?"

"I don't have any," Monty said. "I wanted to let you know that one day, I will be coming for you, Inspector Mathers."

Monty formed a white hot orb in his hand.

Mathers opened his eyes wide in shock.

"Get away from me," he sputtered. "I'll have you arrested."

Peaches growled and Mathers stepped back, stumbling up the steps.

"Good boy," I said, heading back to the Urus. "That deserves extra meat, I think."

Peaches growled again and then jumped into the SUV.

"That was satisfying," Monty said. "Let's go."

"For a second there I thought you were going to barbecue him," I said. "He didn't know you're a mage?"

"He knows, but some people are blind even when the truth is staring them in the face."

"And some just can't handle the truth," I said in my best Nicholson. "Where to? Do you have anyone else you need to terrorize?"

"Josephine's," he said. "Are you going to be able to drive this vehicle, or should I?"

"Cecil was nice enough to get me a proper left-handed car," I said. "I think I can handle driving on the wrong side of the street."

"I'm going to rest my eyes," he said, closing his eyes. "I'd greatly appreciate you avoiding any collisions."

I sped off, leaving a glaring Mathers on his doorstep.

A few hours later we entered the New Forest. I took my time getting there because I wanted to enjoy the scenery. Seeing this much green was a nice change from the concrete and steel of the city.

I parked close to her mound and we got out.

She was waiting for us outside with Dex.

"Let me look at you both," she said when we got close. She narrowed her eyes at Monty and then at me. "It's there, but I don't know how he did it. That crazy mage was a mad genius. Are you sure he's dead?"

"He blew up the Sainsbury Wing while he was still in it," I said. "That sounds pretty lethal."

"I heard there were a couple of individuals who brought down the Tate while they were still inside," Josephine said, cocking her head to one side. "I wonder what happened to them?"

"Are you saying there's still a chance he's alive?"

"Aye," Dex said with a grin. "York isn't that easy to kill. He always was a tad overdramatic, though."

"I saw Cain hit him with a blue bolt of death."

"Did you see him die?"

"Well, no."

"Did you see a body? One devoid of life?"

"No, the Sainsbury Wing was rubble," I said. "You wanted me to go searching through that?"

"If he's alive, he'll turn up sooner or later," Dex said with a nod. "Now, what do we do with these two? They have Storm-blood but don't know how to activate or use it."

"I've never seen this. My only suggestion is take them to the training grounds," she said. "I'm sure TK and LD can coax it out of them—or kill them. Either way, it will be a good experience."

"Aye, that's an excellent idea," Dex said with a smile. "Thank you for everything, Jo. My apologies for any misunderstandings."

"Apology accepted," she said. "Are you leaving the way you arrived?"

Dex nodded.

"The Shrike is waiting for us close by," he said. "We'll be out of your domain inside the hour."

"Thank you," she said. "I appreciate you not destroying my land."

"I'm curious. The storm we ran away from," I said. "Did that destroy the land?"

"Good question," she said. "No, the land is insulated from the storms. The energy always finds ground and redirects itself into the land."

"Uncle Dex?" Monty said. "Do you have it?"

"Aye," Dex said, reaching into a pocket and handing something to Monty. "Are you sure you want to try this?"

"Yes," Monty said, his voice firm as he stepped away. When he was a dozen feet away he crouched down and put something into the ground. "This needs to be done."

He focused and pressed his hand to the ground while whispering some words under his breath. I saw lightning crackle around his hands and Dex looked at Josephine, who nodded approvingly.

A few seconds later a small tree pushed its way up out of the soil.

"Please accept this sapling as my apology for my earlier behavior," Monty said and bowed. "I've been taught to use my power for destruction. Standing in your domain, I realize there is a choice. I can use my power for creation instead."

Dex beamed as he tapped the sapling.

"This is a solid tree. I say we dub it the Dexter."

"Nonsense," Josephine said, giving Dex a look. "It will be named the Montague. I will make sure it grows tall and strong, powerful enough to withstand the greatest of storms, yet pliable enough to know when to bend."

"Thank you," Monty said. "I hope to visit again in the future."

"You are always welcome in my home," she said, touching the sapling. "Go, learn to harness the Stormblood, and prepare. There is still much darkness in your paths."

I bowed.

"Thank you, Witch Josephine," I said. "I'm all for visiting you again as long as we don't have to dodge another of your storms."

She laughed.

"I would hope by your next visit you won't need to."

We got into the Urus and drove off.

Once we were in the Shrike, Captain Daniel took off in under ten minutes, getting us airborne and at a cruising altitude of sixty thousand feet in minutes.

We still had much work to do. The blood mask I had drunk was gone. Hopefully Dira would stay in London for a few years before hunting me again. I knew that was wishful thinking.

I didn't look forward to the tort—training with TK and LD. I didn't understand this Stormblood or how it could be part of me and Monty. I also hadn't tried to form Ebonsoul since the ritual. I felt it there, just under the surface, but it was different, stronger. It felt almost alive, and that concerned me. The last thing I needed was some psychoblade out for blood.

I put those thoughts out of my mind as I stepped into the

living module and crashed on the bed. I had four hours to let these problems go. I'd pick them up again when we landed, but for now, all I wanted to do was sleep.

I laid my head against the pillow and drifted off.

THE END

AUTHOR NOTES

Thank you for reading this story and jumping into the world of Monty & Strong with me.

Disclaimer: The Author Notes are written at the very end of the writing process. This section is not seen by the ART or my amazing Jeditor—Audrey. Any typos or errors following this disclaimer are mine and mine alone.

London once again.

This time, the Destructive Duo kept the damage to a minimum. The last they were in London it was a storm of destruction. This time, the damage was very focused to one particular building. I want to express that it's nothing personal. I truly do enjoy London as a city (one of my favorites after New York City) and intensely dislike the Tate as a museum, which is demonstrated in its repeated destruction.

That's not to say I dislike every building or landmark that gets renovated in my stories. It just seems to be a side effect of Monty and Simon visiting certain areas. I'll have a *conversation* with them about the destruction, but no promises.

So here we are, Book 15 and this part of the story is just beginning to ramp up. I initially projected that STORM BLOOD would be around 50k (what's that definition of insanity again?), but there was too much story to tell and too many seeds to plant. Those seeds will grow into trees that will bear fruit in later books. Some of those fruits will be sweet, others, extremely bitter, and deadly.

Another member of the Ten has made an appearance. I wanted to break the stereotypes and truly make witches powerful...and scary. This concept was a difficult one to pull off (Thanks Jo) and I hope any witches reading this story, feel properly represented and refrain from flinging any hexes my way.

This year promises to be a busy one.

Initially STORM BLOOD was being written simultaneously with SEPIA BLUE-DEMON and WAY OF BUG. What I found was that writing three stories at the same time is a good way to stress yourself sleepless.

Not the best recipe for writing.

I paused SEPIA and focused on STORM BLOOD and WAY OF BUG. Easier, but Monty & Simon started giving me stink eyes, then I paused WAY OF BUG, and dove into STORM BLOOD. That story then exploded into the story you have read. There is something to be said for undivided attention on one story.

Now I work my way backwards.

This story is done, I go back and finish BUG which is nearly done (lol did I just type that out?) provided she doesn't go feral. After BUG, I dive back into SEPIA which is more than halfway done.

I also paused SEPIA because it's her last book. I didn't want her story rushed, which I felt was happening because of the pace I was maintaining. Live and learn.

Simon and Monty are growing stronger. I was hesitant to write this story at first because the antagonist almost feels ephemeral, but this story kicks everything up several levels and is important. After getting into the story, I realized the antagonists are very real. Dira is a present threat (did she die?), and Verity poses a serious danger to Monty and Simon.

There are other situations just simmering and brewing (can you tell I've made my Deathwish?) with brief reveals that will become important in later books. I'm really amazed and humbled that you have stuck with Monty & Simon through all these books and destruction.

As always, I have several ideas for the upcoming stories I can't reveal...yet. Michiko is preparing the Dark Council for something. Something that involves Simon, whether he wants to be involved or not. The Storm Blood ritual they experienced will also have consequences. You don't use elder runes and expect everything to be right with the world.

Very often when you close one door, you open another. What walks through that open door is usually something frightening and dangerous, at least that's the case when your name is Monty & Simon.

I want to express my deepest thanks to you, my most amazing reader. It's an honor to be able to write these stories, and an even deeper honor to hear your stories regarding how these stories impact your life. If that's not a Sid sentence, I don't know what is.

I had less asteroid flinging days on this story, mostly because I was caught up in the story itself. Even though their future is still uncertain, and they now have to make a trip to Fordey Boutique to deal with the Stormblood (I foresee pain. Large doses of pain), there are a few things I'm certain of. Simon will always try to do his best, even if his best makes things worse. Monty, in his own way, will look out for Simon as buildings crumble around them, and Peaches (the official unofficial star of the series) will always want more meat.

Thank you so much for going on this adventure with me. As always, as long as you keep reading, I'll keep writing.

Thank you again for jumping into this story with me!

SPECIAL MENTIONS

To Dolly: My rock, anchor, and inspiration. Thank you...always.

Larry & Tammy—The WOUF: Because even when you aren't there...you're there.

Larry Tushman: Have you gotten the new album of Misaligned Buttcheeks yet? It totally ROCKS!!

Tammy Tushman: Some of us have walked through oceans of pain. The journey only makes us stronger.

Paul Clarkson: Yes, Monty would call it by its proper name...the Tower of London.

Jim Ziller: For magic-disrupting chaff...Get. Out. Of. My. Head. LOL.

Jo Dungey: For all things related to Tempest. Thank you so much, Jo!

Orlando A. Sanchez
www.orlandoasanchez.com

Orlando has been writing ever since his teens when he was immersed in creating scenarios for playing Dungeons and Dragons with his friends every weekend.

The worlds of his books are urban settings with a twist of the paranormal lurking just behind the scenes and with generous doses of magic, martial arts, and mayhem.

He currently resides in Queens, NY with his wife and children.

BITTEN PEACHES PUBLISHING

Thanks for Reading

If you enjoyed this book, would you please **leave a review** at the site you purchased it from? It doesn't have to be long... just a line or two would be fantastic and it would really help me out.

Bitten Peaches Publishing offers more books by this author. From science fiction & fantasy to adventure & mystery, we bring the best stories for adults and kids alike.

www.BittenPeachesPublishing.com

More books by Orlando A. Sanchez

The Warriors of the Way

The Karashihan*•The Spiritual Warriors•The Ascendants•The Fallen Warrior•The Warrior Ascendant•The Master Warrior

John Kane

The Deepest Cut*•Blur

Sepia Blue
The Last Dance*•Rise of the
Night•Sisters•Nightmare•Nameless

Chronicles of the Modern Mystics
The Dark Flame•A Dream of Ashes

Montague & Strong Detective Agency Novels
Tombyards & Butterflies•Full Moon Howl•Blood is
Thicker•Silver Clouds Dirty Sky•Homecoming•Dragons &
Demigods•Bullets & Blades•Hell Hath No Fury•Reaping
Wind•The Golem•Dark Glass•Walking the
Razor•Requiem•Divine Intervention•Storm Blood

**For those of you that prefer to listen to your books,
you can find the entire M&S Series on Audiobooks.**

Montague & Strong Detective Agency Audiobooks
The War Mage•No God is Safe•Tombyards & Butterflies•Full
Moon Howl•Blood is Thicker•Silver Clouds Dirty
Sky•Homecoming•Dragons & Demigods•Bullets &
Blades•Hell Hath No Fury•Reaping Wind•The Golem•Dark
Glass•Walking the Razor•Requiem•Divine Intervention

Montague & Strong Detective Agency Stories
No God is Safe•The Date•The War Mage•A Proper
Hellhound•The Perfect Cup•Saving Mr. K

Brew & Chew Adventures
Hellhound Blues

Night Warden Novels

Wander•ShadowStrut

Division 13
The Operative•The Magekiller

Blackjack Chronicles
The Dread Warlock

The Assassin's Apprentice
The Birth of Death

Gideon Shepherd Thrillers
Sheepdog

DAMNED
Aftermath

RULE OF THE COUNCIL
Blood Ascension•Blood Betrayal•Blood Rule

NYXIA WHITE
They Bite•They Rend•They Kill

IKER THE CLEANER
Iker the Unseen

Tales of the Gatekeepers
A Bullet Ballet

*Books denoted with an asterisk are **FREE** via my website
—www.orlandoasanchez.com

ART SHREDDERS

I want to take a moment to extend a special thanks to the ART SHREDDERS.

No book is the work of one person. I am fortunate enough to have an amazing team of advance readers and shredders.

Thank you for giving of your time and keen eyes to provide notes, insights, answers to the questions, and corrections (dealing wonderfully with my extreme dreaded comma allergy). You help make every book and story go from good to great. Each and every one of you helped make this book fantastic, and I couldn't do this without each of you.

THANK YOU

ART SHREDDERS

Amber, Anne Morando, Audrey Cienki
Beverly Collie
Cam Skaggs, Cat, Chris Christman II, Colleen Taylor
Davina Noble, Dawn McQueen Mortimer, Denise King,

Desmond, Diana Gray, Diane Craig, Dolly Sanchez, Donna Young Hatridge

Hal Bass, Helen

Jasmine Breeden, Jasmine Davis, Jeanette Auer, Jen Cooper, John Fauver, Joy Kiili, Joy Ollier, Julie Peckett

Karen Hollyhead

Larry Diaz Tushman, Laura Tallman I

Malcolm Robertson, Marcia Campbell, Maryelaine Eckerle-Foster, Melissa Miller

Paige Guido, Penny Campbell-Myhill

RC Battels, Rene Corrie

Sara Mason Branson, Sean Trout, Stacey Stein, Susie Johnson

Tami Cowles, Tanya Anderson, Ted Camer, Terri Adkisson

Vikki Brannagan

Wanda Corder-Jones, Wendy Schindler

ACKNOWLEDGEMENTS

With each book, I realize that every time I learn something about this craft, it highlights so many things I still have to learn. Each book, each creative expression, has a large group of people behind it.

This book is no different.

Even though you see one name on the cover, it is with the knowledge that I am standing on the shoulders of the literary giants that informed my youth, and am supported by my generous readers who give of their time to jump into the adventures of my overactive imagination.

I would like to take a moment to express my most sincere thanks:

To Dolly: My wife and greatest support. You make all this possible each and every day. You keep me grounded when I get lost in the forest of ideas. Thank you for asking the right questions when needed, and listening intently when I go off on tangents. Thank you for who you are and the space you create—I love you.

To my Tribe: You are the reason I have stories to tell. You cannot possibly fathom how much and how deeply I love you all.

To Lee: Because you were the first reader I ever had. I love you, sis.

To the Logsdon Family: The words *thank you* are insufficient to describe the gratitude in my heart for each of you. JL, your support always demands I bring my best, my A-game, and produce the best story I can. Both you and Lorelei (my Uber Jeditor) and now, Audrey, are the reason I am where I am today. My thank you for the notes, challenges, corrections, advice, and laughter. Your patience is truly infinite. *Arigato-gozaimasu.*

To The Montague & Strong Case Files Group—AKA The MoB (Mages of Badassery): When I wrote T&B there were fifty-five members in The MoB. As of this release, there are over one thousand four hundred members in the MoB. I am honored to be able to call you my MoB Family. Thank you for being part of this group and M&S.

You make this possible. **THANK YOU.**

To the ever-vigilant PACK: You help make the MoB...the MoB. Keeping it a safe place for us to share and just...be. Thank you for your selfless vigilance. You truly are the Sentries of Sanity.

Chris Christman II: A real-life technomancer who makes the **MoBTV LIVEvents +Kaffeeklatsch** on YouTube amazing. Thank you for your tireless work and wisdom. Everything is connected...you totally rock!

To the WTA—The Incorrigibles: JL, Ben Z. Eric QK., S.S., and Noah.

They sound like a bunch of badass misfits, because they are. My exposure to the deranged and deviant brain trust you all represent helped me be the author I am today. I have officially gone to the *dark side* thanks to all of you. I humbly give you my thanks, and...it's all your fault.

To my fellow Indie Authors, specifically the tribe at 20books to 50k: Thank you for creating a space where authors can feel listened to, and encouraged to continue on this path. A rising tide lifts all the ships indeed.

To The English Advisory: Aaron, Penny, Carrie, Davina, and all of the UK MoB. For all things English...thank you.

To DEATH WISH COFFEE: This book (and every book I write) has been fueled by generous amounts of the only coffee on the planet (and in space) strong enough to power my very twisted imagination. Is there any other coffee that can compare? I think not. DEATHWISH—thank you!

To Deranged Doctor Design: Kim, Darja, Tanja, Jovana, and Milo (Designer Extraordinaire).

If you've seen the covers of my books and been amazed, you can thank the very talented and gifted creative team at DDD. They take the rough ideas I give them, and produce incredible covers that continue to surprise and amaze me. Each time, I find myself striving to write a story worthy of the covers they produce. DDD, you embody professionalism and creativity. Thank you for the great service and spectacular covers. **YOU GUYS RULE!**

To you, the reader: I was always taught to save the best for last. I write these stories for **you**. Thank you for jumping down the rabbit holes of *what if?* with me. You are the reason I write the stories I do.

You keep reading...I'll keep writing.

Thank you for your support and encouragement.

CONTACT ME

I really do appreciate your feedback. You can let me know what you thought of the story by emailing me at:
orlando@orlandoasanchez.com

To get **FREE** stories please visit my page at:
www.orlandoasanchez.com

For more information on the M&S World...come join the MoB Family on Facebook!
You can find us at:
Montague & Strong Case Files

Visit our online M&S World Swag Store located at:
Emandes

If you enjoyed the book, **please leave a review**. Reviews help the book, and also help other readers find good stories to read.
THANK YOU!

Thanks for Reading
If you enjoyed this book, would you **please leave a review**
at the site you purchased it from? It doesn't have to be a book
report... just a line or two would be fantastic and it would
really help us out!